Wives, Fiancées, and Side-Chicks of Hotlanta

Wives, Fiancées, and Side-Chicks of Hotlanta

SHEREÉ WHITFIELD

Dafina
BOOKS

KENSINGTON PUBLISHING CORP.
www.kensingtonbooks.com

DAFINA BOOKS are published by

Kensington Publishing Corp.
119 West 40th Street
New York, NY 10018

ISBN-13: 978-1-4967-1833-4
ISBN-10: 1-4967-1833-X
First Kensington Trade Edition: February 2017
First Kensington Mass Market Edition: July 2018

eISBN-13: 978-1-4967-0988-2
eISBN-10: 1-4967-0988-8

10 9 8 7 6 5 4 3 2 1

Printed in the United States of America

To my children, Tierra, Kairo, and Kaleigh. You're the reason I continue to push, strive for the best, and stay strong.

To my mom, Thelma, who is an excellent example of what it means to be a strong woman.

To all of those who knowingly or unknowingly inspired this novel—the good, the bad, and the ugly . . . I thank you!

And to my family and friends who truly have been supportive, loyal, and just wonderful. Know that it's not in vain. I see you and I love you!

Prologue

"Atlanta is the Hollywood of the south, baby, what did you expect?" Norman said as he sipped his peach margarita. "Your hubby is gone half the week for practice. Did you really think he'd spend his time sitting in the hotel room pining away for you? Child, bye!" Norman waved his hand and wrapped his lips around his straw, fluttering his eyelids while sucking in the fruity, frozen alcoholic beverage. "Ahhh!" he said, then looked over at his friend.

Sasha Wellington pursed her lips as she stared down at the large plate of loaded nachos she'd been smashing. She suddenly lost her appetite. She frowned and pushed the plate away from her.

"Ooooh, you did think that, didn't you?" Norman let out a harrumph and then shook his head with dismay. "You acting more naïve than the ugly, fat girl in high school who thinks the captain of the football team really just wanted to take her out for ice cream. And you ain't no more a virgin than this margarita I'm drinking with an extra shot of tequila. So quit playing with me." Norman rolled his eyes, perturbed at how gullible his friend was turning out to be.

Sasha was even more pissed off at herself. Her husband hadn't come home last night. They'd been married for half a minute and he was already out chasing ATL hoes, just like her ex-coworker, Casey's husband. Sasha had stood by watching Casey accept all the crap her husband piled on her, all the while vowing to herself that she'd never be *that* woman. Sasha had been warned by Casey, though, about this kind of behavior; the typical behavior professional male athletes are known for. But Sasha hadn't thought it would happen to her, and damn sure not this soon! She expected her husband to come home to his new wife.

"You can stop sitting over there looking like the victim," Norman said. "You know I give it to you straight with no chaser. I have a saying that sometimes people don't get what they deserve in life, but some of them sure do get what they ask for."

"I thought you asked me out to make me feel better," Sasha said. "I feel ten times worse than I did when I left my house."

"Norman is not one to butter the roll, honey." Norman spoke in the third person, which meant he was really about to go in. "I tear it apart and devour it bite by bite. If you wanted to get all buttered up and sweetened with a sugary coating, then you should have called ya mama up. Chick, you knew the deal when you got with Terrance. Now take the hand you were dealt and play it." Norman downed the rest of his margarita. "Or get played by the hand." He motioned to the bartender for another drink.

"Make it two," Sasha called to the bartender. Norman frowned but Sasha shook her head. "It's for you. Since I'm eating for two, you have to drink for two." Sasha nodded down at her stomach.

Bringing up the fact that there was a baby growing inside Sasha's womb changed the mood. There was silence as a melancholy feel took over both Sasha and Norman.

"What am I supposed to do about all of this?" Sasha felt the tears coming. She couldn't believe that she'd been married for two days and she already wanted out. Maybe those other wives of pro athletes had something she didn't. Or were more tolerant of marital infidelity. Sasha knew she was the best that Terrance would ever have, so how dare he step out on her, and on their wedding night no less?

Norman put his hand on top of Sasha's. "You know what you're supposed to do, girl. You do what every other last one of them wives does."

"Look the other way and be miserable?" Sasha said with attitude. "Oh, no. Not this born to be a boss chick! I will not sit around and allow my husband to have side-chicks posting pics of themselves and my man on Instagram. Seriously? Where they do that at?"

"In the NBA, in the NFL, in the—" Norman started counting on his fingers until Sasha cut him off.

"It was a rhetorical question, Norman, geesh." Sasha placed her elbows on the bar, crossed her arms, then looked down defeated.

She had no concrete proof that Terrance had spent the night with another woman, but she wasn't stupid. No man stayed out all night unless he was cheating. If Sasha's grandmother had told her once, she'd told her twice; the only things open all night long are 7-Eleven and legs! Sasha got sick to her stomach imagining some groupie's legs wrapped around her husband.

"You can look the other way, but that doesn't mean you have to be miserable while doing it," Norman said as the bartender placed two margaritas down in front of him. "Atlanta's golden boy, Terrance McKinley, has the money. As the new Mrs. Terrance McKinley, live the lifestyle you want, queen."

Sasha's eyes lit up at Norman's words. "You're right!" Sasha said, her lips spreading into a grin. "While Terrance is out doing Terrance, I can be out doing me . . . with his money!"

"Now you're talking," Norman said proudly, sipping on one of the two drinks.

"I could use Terrance's money to help with opening my boutique, which is what I came to Atlanta to do in the first place." Sasha's mind went wild thinking about all the gorgeous and expensive fabrics she could buy now that she had practically unlimited funds thanks to the United Bank of Terrance Clark McKinley.

Norman raised his glass. "Yas, girl! Now dry those eyes and stop with the tears. Turn that frown upside down and laugh all the way to the bank."

Norman was right. Norman was always right it seemed, which is why Sasha called on him whenever she was at her bottom lowest. He might stomp her down further to the curb than she started out, but in the end, his words always lifted her back up. She picked up a napkin and dabbed under her eyes. "Let's get out of here. I'm in the mood to go out and buy an entire new wardrobe . . . for each month of my pregnancy. Ha! How about that?" Sasha popped one last nacho into her mouth.

"But my drinks." Norman looked from one delicious-looking margarita to the other. "This is like me leaving money on the table."

"I'll pay." Sasha stood while going in her purse. She pulled out three twenty dollar bills and laid them on the counter. "There, now it's like me leaving money on the table."

Norman sucked his teeth and stood. He stared at the drinks one last time as if he was a little boy who got two new puppies and had to leave them home while he ran off to school. The next thing Sasha knew, Norman had pulled both drinks together, placing a straw in each corner of his mouth, and began to suck those drinks down quicker than she'd ever seen it done before.

"My God!" Sasha said once Norman came up for air.

Looking as if he was in pain, he threw his hand over his forehead. "Brain freeze," he whined.

"You think?" Sasha said. "You sucked those drinks down as if your life depended on it. Where did you learn to do that?"

Norman removed his hand from his forehead and stared at Sasha with a raised eyebrow. "Trust me, darling, you don't even want to know."

Sasha thought for a minute as to what Norman may have been alluding to. "You know what? I think you're right. Come on, let's get out of here."

Sasha flipped her hair, linked arms with Norman and then put her hand on her belly. She would have to be strong for her baby. Even though the baby bump was barely there, Sasha felt strength coming from her child. In that moment she made up her mind that in the midst of the lies and deceit, she would carve out a piece of heaven for her and her baby, even if it meant she had to go through hell first.

Chapter 1

Six months earlier . . .

"What in God's green creation have I gotten myself into?"

Sasha stood in the living room of her new apartment located in what looked to be a fairly decent neighborhood in Atlanta, Georgia. It wasn't the best. It wasn't the worst. But then again, she had never been to Atlanta a day in her life before this afternoon, so how would she know? She'd have to feel the area out and then determine if it met not only her needs, but her standards, which were by all means anything but below average. Keeping it one hundred, they were actually higher than the normal person's. And Sasha had no qualms nor made apologies about having above average criteria when it came to all things in life. What some people were willing to settle for, she wouldn't think twice to. That didn't mean she felt she was better than everybody else, but try telling that to some of the so-called friends she'd come across.

"Stuck-up bitch!"

"Always acting like some white girl."

"Sasha thinks she's better than everybody else."

"She lives one block from the hood, not in one of Trump's towers."

"She thinks her shit don't stank 'cause her nose too far up in the air to smell it."

It was nothing unusual for Sasha to hear these comments made about her—not only from the mean girls back when she was in high school, but now she even heard them from grown women. Sasha shook it off as pure jealousy. She'd always had an attitude that exuded confidence. It wasn't her fault hating-ass hoes mistook it for conceit.

Sasha was poised and well spoken. Every other word out of her mouth was *not* a cuss word or ghetto slang. She chose college over the club, and chose independence over becoming the baby momma of a dope boy like some people she knew.

So what if her playlist was smooth jazz instead of rap or R & B songs about screwing and getting butts eaten like groceries. People needed to get over themselves, or better yet, get over the fact that Sasha was living her life how she wanted: a life with no regrets. A life she didn't need to take a vacation from. It would do folks good not to concern themselves at all with her business and start fostering their own game plan for their personal come-up and success the same way she had done. That way they wouldn't be hatin', but participatin'. That way everybody could be celebratin'.

The funny thing was, because Sasha carried herself with such class and grace, hood chicks thought that gave them a pass to try her. Little did they know, Sasha had a tank full of ratchetness that she kept on reserve. She could go toe to toe and tongue to tongue with the best of them, if taken there. Thank God, though, that she'd never had to embarrass herself or her mother by going there. But you best believe she'd pack her bags and take the trip if need be. But again, her momma hadn't raised her like that, to be a messy instigator. But she hadn't raised her to be no punk either.

An only child, Sasha had been spoiled by her mother, who raised her singlehandedly. Not Kardashian spoiled, but what she got, even if it was a little, seemed like a lot, considering she didn't have any siblings to divvy it up with. So it was safe to say that Sasha wasn't really into sharing, which was typical of an only child.

One good thing about not having any brothers or sisters was that Sasha didn't have to worry about hand-me-down clothing from older siblings, or being forced to give away her favorite article to a younger sibling. As much as Sasha was into clothing and fashion—she had been playing dress-up in her mother's closet ever since she could crawl to it—that would have been cruel and unnecessary punishment.

When most teenagers' bedroom walls were covered with the latest star in film and music or the "it" teen idol, Sasha's were always covered with poster boards of outfits she'd cut out from magazines, sometimes mixing a shirt one model might have had on and placing it over a skirt another model was donning. Her eye for coordinating outfits was impeccable and unique.

Sasha's mother took note of her daughter's interest in clothes, and when the latest fashions came out, she couldn't always afford to get them for her child immediately, but she always managed to make a way eventually, as soon as they went on sale. By then other girls at school would have already shown theirs off, so Sasha would put a little extra spin on hers by either removing this or sewing on that . . . anything to make it unique. Pretty soon when the kids would see her sporting one of her creations, they'd say, "Wow, another Sasha Original, huh?" At least the ones who didn't mind giving props where props were due.

Some girls who'd had a beef with her since elementary even humbled themselves, asking Sasha to hook up their wardrobe with her skills. This was definitely where Sasha's interest in fashion was piqued. She breathed, drank, and ate fashion, even choosing fashion and design as her major in college. And now here she was in Hotlanta, hell bent on building the empire to reach her ultimate goal of becoming a fashion mogul.

Just six months ago, the day she'd graduated college in Cleveland, Ohio, Sasha had basically opened up a map of the United States, closed her eyes, and pointed. Wherever her finger landed once she opened her eyes was where she'd decided she'd go live. No ifs, ands, or buts. Not even her dear and very persuasive mother could talk her out of the move.

"Are you sure that's where God wants you to go?" her mother had asked her.

Sasha and her mother attended Sasha's grandmother's church on occasion. They didn't have a church they called home that they attended regularly, but that still didn't keep Sasha's mother from always bringing God into things whenever she could.

"At least it's Atlanta," Sasha had said when she'd opened her eyes to find her manicured nail resting smack dead on the city of Atlanta. "And not some place like Alaska or Utah." It didn't matter where Sasha's finger landed, if it wasn't in Cleveland, Ohio, her mother wasn't going to be happy. She wanted her baby girl near her, no matter what God said.

Sasha looked around the apartment in awe. Not in awe of how grand or sophisticated it was, but how totally opposite it looked compared to the pictures she'd seen of it on the Internet. She'd watched enough court TV shows that she should have known better than to pay a deposit on a place she hadn't physically inspected. Folks sued one another for this type of scam all of the time. But this wasn't some vacation spot she could check out of if it wasn't to her satisfaction. This was where she had to live for at least a year, according to the lease she'd signed less than five minutes ago.

Sasha was already using her life's savings to move from Ohio to Atlanta. Spending extra money to take a trip just to come see the place with her own two eyes would have put a major dent into her finances. She needed to hold onto every last dime she had for as long as she could. She had big dreams in moving to Atlanta. Dreams cost time and money. She had neither to waste.

Most people had a five-year plan. Sasha had a one-year plan. Five-year plans were for people who planned on taking a break to sleep. For Sasha, sleep was overrated. She'd sleep at her vacation home in the Hamptons, which was part of her dream. No matter where on the map she decided would be her permanent residence, she'd planned on having a vacation home in the Hamptons. After seeing a reality show where the group of girl-friends vacationed in the Hamptons every summer, Sasha added that to the vision board she kept stored in her head. But for now, it looked like Atlanta was home year 'round.

"I can't believe you're going there without even having a job in line," Sasha's mother had said in an effort to talk her out of going to the city that was being branded the Black Hollywood.

"I've signed up with a temp service. They have my résumé. They assured me they'd have no problem placing me," Sasha said. "I'll start with something temporary until I can find something permanent in my field. I'll be fine, Ma. Everything is going to work out, trust me. I wouldn't be doing it if I wasn't sure."

Looking around at mistake number one, AKA her apartment, Sasha didn't even know if she could trust herself, let alone get her mother to trust her. She made a mental note to exaggerate the beauty and size of the apartment once she called her mother to check in.

"A thousand dollars a month for this little ole piece of place?" Sasha questioned, standing there with her suitcase at her feet, purse swinging from her arm and a cardboard box in her other arm.

She walked over to the tiny kitchen where, if two people wanted to share cooking duties, they'd be all on top of each other trying to maneuver. Perhaps Sasha could overlook that, considering she was one person and didn't plan on having any roommates. It was a one-bedroom apartment and nobody was sleeping on her couch—that is, once she purchased one.

Taking in the smell that permeated the place of

the new beige carpet, Sasha walked back through the living room to the first door on the right. It was a half bath, toilet and sink. Nothing really to complain about there. Had she been the one to design it, she would have chosen a sturdier cabinet base for the sink. "Did they find the cheapest cabinet Home Depot stocks?" She opened the cabinet door and then let it slam shut. She looked down and refused to voice her concerns about the cheap floor tile that was bubbling up and had glue capped up around some of the edges.

"I should have kept my black tail in Ohio," Sasha mumbled to herself. She quickly rebuked her own words. That's probably exactly what all the nay-sayers would want her to do, fail. Yeah, people smiled in her face, complimented her on her fashion sense, and some probably genuinely wanted her to do well . . . just not better than them. Well, Sasha would do better.

"You'll be back. You're too stuck up for the A," one of Sasha's so-called friends had told her after Sasha shared the news about her pending move to Atlanta. "Besides, you all bougie and you going down there where there ain't nothing but black folks." She shook her head adamantly and shooed her hand. "You'll never make it there. You'll be running back home to be with all your friends, because I don't see you making any new ones down there. You'll never fit in."

Sasha pushed her reserve button two seconds before she reached for ol' girl's cheap red-and-blond weave and pulled her close to her face. She'd wanted her to be able to at least read her lips just in case she didn't hear her clearly when she gave her the read of her life. But instead, she ran on the remaining fumes of dignity she had in her system and simply smiled, batted her eyes, and said sarcastically, "Thank you so much for the vote of confidence." Needless to say, that heifer didn't get an invite to the going away party.

Although her friend's words were meant to discourage Sasha, they had only encouraged her that much more. If only her critics knew that they were the fuel motivating Sasha. Failing in Atlanta and going back to Ohio was not going to happen. It was not an option. She was Sasha Renea Wellington, a woman with a plan to make it in the ATL, so that is exactly what she was going to do, no matter what it took. Once Sasha made her mind up and put the period at the end of the sentence, that was it. Nothing else needed to be said. She could show a person she was about her business better than she could tell them.

Sasha had been saving up every dime she'd earned since graduating high school to make this kind of move. She'd worked as a waitress at every restaurant she could while at the same time attending college. She'd even worked in a bookstore and at a call center. She got a headache every time she thought about how much money she owed in student loans for her four years of higher education. But those were all deferred for now. By the time Sasha would have to start making payments, she planned on being the owner of one of the hottest boutiques in Atlanta. That meant she had one year to achieve such, or get an extension on her deferral.

Closing the bathroom door behind her, Sasha walked into the room right across the hall from the bathroom, which was the only other room left in the apartment. As she looked around the bed-room, all she could do was shake her head. "This isn't any bigger than the bathroom." She allowed her head to fall back. Her spirits were darkening by the second, but trying to stay positive, she lifted her head, thankful that at least she had a private attached bathroom. She walked over to one of two doors in the room and opened it. It was a closet. It could only be considered a walk-in closet if a bur-glar broke into her apartment and she had to walk in it to hide.

She took a deep breath. *Stay positive, Sasha.* She opened the other door that led to her private bath. A toilet, a sink, and a shower. Not even a linen closet, but a floor-to-ceiling shelf instead to store her things. It was small. She felt like Snow White invading the seven dwarves' spot. But she could take the small space. Again, it was just her, but what she couldn't take was the fact that there was no bathtub. That had always been Sasha's thing, her way of winding down. A bubble bath and, on rare occasions, a bottle of bubbly. No yoga. No Whoosah. No meditation. She'd tried it all and only one thing put her in a good place after a bad day. "No tub!" This was the deal breaker. "Oh, hell to the no!"

"I can't do this," Sasha told herself. Realizing that *can't* was not supposed to be a part of her vo-cabulary, she took her own words back. "You can and you will." She paused. "But how?" she asked herself, trying to hold in her tears. How in the world was she going to make this work? She didn't know, but she knew someone who might. Her one true friend and confidante who had been her biggest cheerleader from day one.

Sasha pulled out her phone and dialed. She placed the phone to her ear while the phone rang. It barely rang once before the person on the other end picked up.

"Didn't I tell you to call me as soon as you got there? What took you so long? You had me scared to death! It wasn't nothing but a, what, nine-hour drive or so? It's been ten hours? You know I'm an ID Channel addict."

"Ma, please just relax," Sasha said, now wondering if calling her mother had been such a good idea after all. She wanted her mother to help calm her down and give her some advice on her current situation. Instead, it looked as though her mother was the one who needed calming down. "Why didn't you just call me if you were that worried?"

"I dialed your number so much I broke a nail," her mother admitted.

"I didn't hear my phone ringing."

"That's because I always hung up once I got to the last number." Her mother exhaled. "You're my baby and you always will be, but you're not that little girl who I always had to guide. You're a grown woman now, Sasha, and with you being halfway across the world now, it's fine time I start treating you like one."

"Ma, I'm not halfway across the world. I'm still right here in the United States of America." Sasha shook her head at her mother's exaggeration.

"You know what I meant," her mother said in a scolding tone. "Anyway, I raised you to be strong and independent. I have to trust my job as a mother and believe that you've got this. You don't need me always telling you what to do. I've taught you well. You can figure things out on your own." Her mother exhaled. "And I sure am glad that you figured out how to get to Atlanta on your own. And that you are safe and sound." Her mother paused and then said in a worried tone, "You are safe and sound, aren't you?"

"Yes, Ma," Sasha said. A smile spread across her lips. Her mother was something else. She always had a way of soothing Sasha, even when she didn't know that was exactly what she was doing.

Sasha felt that her mother was right; she was on her own now. She couldn't call her mother up every time she had a problem or had a situation. Well, she could, but she didn't want to. It was fine time she started handling everything in her life herself, especially the little things. She'd start with handling the tub situation.

"I am safe and sound," Sasha told her mother. "And that's all I was calling to let you know." Sasha smiled, happy with her decision not to burden her mother with the first thing gone wrong. "I'm going to call you later, once I'm settled and everything."

"Okay, baby. I love you!" Sasha's mother exclaimed. "And I'm so proud of you. I know I gave you hell about moving away, but that was for my own selfish reasons. It's been me and you since I can remember."

Sasha heard her mother's voice break. She then heard her take a deep swallow and clear her throat before she spoke again.

"But like I said, you got this."

Sasha nodded while wiping away a tear that had formed in her eye. The confidence her mother had in her was so moving. "Yeah, Ma, I know. I got this. I love you. Good-bye." Sasha ended the call.

She had to take a deep breath and gain her composure. She stared ahead replaying her mother's words in her head. "Yeah, I got this."

Sasha exited the bathroom, stormed out of the bedroom and back into the living room. She snatched up her purse and walked right out of the door intent on heading over to the rental office she'd just left ten minutes ago after signing the lease. The only reason the manager hadn't come to let Sasha into the place himself was because a prospective resident was there wanting to be shown an available apartment. It was a mother with three kids. She had one in a stroller, one on her hip, and one running around the office getting on both Sasha's and the manager's nerves.

For fear the manager might ask the woman and her children to tag along to the walk-through, Sasha did the nice thing by showing herself to her own place while the manager took care of the woman. Besides, she'd taken a virtual tour of the place back when she first found it online. She knew what to expect and assured the manager if she found any issues and things that might need tending to, she would take pictures and let him know. Nothing needed fixing, but she had an issue that definitely needed tending to: no bathtub.

After Sasha locked up the apartment door, she abruptly turned around.

"Uhhgg!" Sasha said as she smashed against the chest of a gentleman who was walking up near her.

She pulled away to see the print of her lipstick on his crisp, white tee shirt. The groceries in the two brown paper bags he'd been carrying had fallen to the ground, canned goods and a spaghetti jar just rolling around.

"Oh, I'm so sorry," Sasha apologized. She covered her mouth, licking her lips to make sure she didn't taste blood. She'd slammed into him pretty hard. Fortunately, though, she hadn't cut her lip or anything.

"It's okay," the tall, well-built gentleman said. He wasn't a bad looking guy by far. He had smooth, golden, clear skin, a nice shaven goatee, and he smelled damn good.

All of this hunk of man didn't make Sasha pause at all, though. She was on a mission. Her mission never had and didn't now include a man. The only thing she was interested in was apologizing, hopefully him accepting, and then going to do what she'd set out to do before the bodily collision.

"It's all good," the nice looking brotha said. He looked down at his groceries. "It doesn't look like anything broke or busted open."

"Sorry about your shirt." Sasha pointed to her lipstick print on his tee shirt.

Sasha saw him look down and pull at his shirt.

"Oh, damn." A look of terror appeared on his face. "Fuck!"

Why he was tripping so hard over some lipstick, Sasha had no idea. But she figured it must have been pretty major when she saw sweat beads start to form on his head. Was it really that serious? Sasha carried some *Shout* wipes in her purse she could use to get rid of the stain almost instantly if it was that big of a deal.

She gave him the once-over and thought, *This big negro better not try to hustle me out of some dry-cleaning money.* She was the new girl in a new city, but she was no fool. No one was about to take advantage of her.

Just then Sasha saw the door across the hall fling open.

"What the hell is going on out here?"

Sasha observed the woman who stood in the doorway with hands on hips and foot tapping. She wore a pink wife-beater with denim cut-off shorts. Had it not been for all the fringe at the bottom of her shorts, her coochie hairs might have been showing. She had a tropical look to her, like she might have been mixed with something. Her skin was not a natural bronze. Sasha figured the woman's complexion was aided by either weekly suntan sessions or a tan in a bottle.

Her dark hair was in two high ponytails. Her extra-long fake eyelashes fluttered so much, Sasha wondered if the girl had something in her eyes she was trying to blink out. The pink lip gloss on her lips matched the color of her shirt. As far as Sasha was concerned, all she was missing was big hoop earrings and a lollypop. Stereotypical 'round the way girl.

"Oh, babe, this is . . ." the man had started, fear prevalent in the way he began to stutter at just the sight of this chick. He looked to Sasha, urging her—no, pleading with her—to help him out.

Sasha obliged. Seeing a big dude like himself act like he was Tina and his girl was Ike was embarrassing even for Sasha. She hated to see a man emasculated. "I'm Sasha." She extended her hand to the woman. "I'm your new neigh—"

"Well, Sasha, I'm his woman." The girl pointed to her man, completely cutting Sasha off. That's when the girl's eyes bulged. "What the fuck?" She yoked the dude up by his shirt. "What's this shit?" She pointed to the lipstick.

"It's, uh—"

Before the poor fella could even get the words out of his mouth, Sasha flinched as she watched his girl slap him in the mouth.

"I knew your ass didn't really need to go to no goddamn store," the 'round the way girl spat. "Who was it this time? Shelia? Wait, let me guess, it was that freak Monique who works at the store, wasn't it?"

"Kels, you tripping," he spoke up. "I told you there is nobody else."

Sasha figured this was not his first time at the rodeo based on how exasperated he sounded in making his claim.

Sasha had heard that in Atlanta there were ten women for every one guy. It looked as though Kels was constantly accusing him of cheating with the other nine allotted to him.

"Nigga, you take me for a fool or something?" Kels spat.

It was at that moment Sasha determined that whatever Kels was mixed with, it must have been black. Only black folks were allowed to say the N-word . . . right?

Sasha couldn't stand there and watch the poor guy get beat up, literally, for something that she was to blame for. She had to speak up and tell Kels what had actually happened. It wasn't Shelia's or Monique's lipstick. It was hers.

Sasha flinched once again when she heard a loud whopping sound.

Once again, Kels slapped her dude, this time on his arm. It sounded like it stung. Sasha grabbed her cheek just thinking how it might feel to have Kels's hand connect with her face. That's when she decided now was not the time to confess that it was her lipstick on his shirt. Something told Sasha that Kels was not one to reason with, which could make things go left really quickly, causing Sasha to have to show her butt. But was there ever really a time to act out of pocket? All a person ever ended up doing was embarrassing herself. Sasha wore a lot of things well, but embarrassment was not one of them. Self-control was a characteristic Sasha was glad she possessed. Besides, if Kels could whoop her dude, she might break Sasha's size-six self in half.

Sasha knew when she might end up getting the short end of the stick in a fight. Her momma ain't raised no fool. The last thing she needed was to show up at the temp service looking like she'd been initiated into a gang. So Sasha used wisdom. While Kels continued going off on her man, mugging him in the forehead with her index finger and him trying to get a word in edgewise to continue trying to convince her that he was faithful to her, Sasha tiptoed out of the building and marched over to the rental office.

If this is how they got down in the ATL and that is what she had to look forward to as far as neighbors, Sasha wanted no part of this place, whether it had a tub or not. Of course her apartment not having the tub that was advertised would be her only legitimate grounds at this point to get out of the lease. She racked her brain trying to recall whether or not in the virtual tour it showed a bathtub. It had to have, which meant they had falsely advertised the apartment. That alone gave her legal grounds to break that lease without even spending one night in the place.

Sasha approached the rental office and went to open the door. Unlike the first time she'd turned the knob, entered the office, and introduced herself to the manager, this time the door was locked. She cupped her hands around her face, pressed them against the glass door and looked inside. It was dark. She pulled away. That's when she noticed the sign that read, "WILL RETURN IN 15 MINUTES."

"Ugghh," Sasha groaned. "This is some bull . . ." Her words trailed off as she tried to get herself together. She rubbed her throbbing temples. She'd stomped so hard over to the rental office that the arches of her feet were throbbing as well. Ironically, she could really use a nice, hot bubble bath right about now.

Sasha allowed her arms to drop weightlessly down to her sides. She leaned against the rental office door and sighed. Realizing the manager was more than likely still showing the woman and her children around the property, she went and sat on one of the three plastic chairs on the rental office's mini awning-covered patio. She pulled out her phone. She wanted to have proof positive about the false advertisement when the manager returned, so she decided to pull up the website for the apartment. It was stored as a favorite link, so she was able to go right to it. She clicked through the pictures. After getting to picture nine of eleven, she squirmed a little in her seat. She hadn't yet come across the picture showing that the one-bedroom apartment had a bathtub.

"That can't be right," she said to herself. "I would have never even considered this place if it didn't have a bathtub." Sasha had looked at so many apartments online, was it possible she'd gotten mixed up?

She then clicked on the virtual tour. It showed the apartment at such an elongated angle that she could now see why it appeared to be much bigger than it actually was. She sucked her teeth at the trickery. It was like airbrushing a fat chick for the cover of the *Sports Illustrated* swimsuit issue. She waited until the camera entered the bedroom and the attached bathroom. Sasha got excited with anticipation. A few seconds later a frown covered her face. "What the . . ." Neither the photos nor the virtual tour showed a bathroom with a tub.

Sasha flopped back, legs spread and arms dropped between her legs with phone in hand. "How did I miss that?" It was her own oversight. She took one of her hands, washed it down her face, and moaned. She hadn't even been in Atlanta an hour and already things weren't looking good.

She exhaled and then stood. "Guess I'll have to take up yoga," she said out loud, sounding defeated.

Since she was outside, she walked over to her four-year-old Honda SUV and grabbed a couple more things to take into the apartment. She'd stuffed everything she owned in that car. As she walked back to the apartment, she recalled nine hours ago driving away from the only home she'd ever known. It was the one she'd shared with her mother. A proud smile spread across her lips when she thought about her mother, a strong black woman. Sasha thought of all the struggles her mother had gone through to raise her. Being a single mother was no joke. Sasha was reminded of that as in the distance she saw the manager escorting the woman and her children back toward the rental office.

"Dante, if you don't get your tail over here," the mother snapped at the toddler who was trying to wander off in the opposite direction.

Being a single mother, in Sasha's eyes, had always looked as though it was the hardest job in the world. She watched so many of her friends either become teenage mothers during high school, or end up as single mothers sometime between graduating high school and college. Her best friend had even ultimately become a single mother, which ruled out the dreams she and Sasha used to share about being roommates in a college dorm. Because her best friend had to dedicate so much of her time to mothering her child alone, the two eventually drifted apart.

Just thinking about how much both her best friend and her mother had on their plates as single mothers made Sasha shake her head. She'd rather follow behind dogs and scoop up their poop for a living before becoming a single mother. Financially, the hardest job in the universe had no monetary payment. Sure there was the joy of motherhood in itself. Nonetheless, Sasha declared that she would be and could be, just as Chaka Khan had declared, every woman. But she would not be a single mother. That was something she'd promised herself.

After three hours of lugging in all her belongings, which included her sewing machine, unpacking and putting away things, Sasha didn't even want to be a single woman. Where was the shirtless hunk of a neighbor who showed up to help a sister move like the ones that appeared in all the romance movies? All that hoopla about Atlanta and its fine black men. Well, where is just one of them right about now?

"Oh yeah, that's right," Sasha said to herself. "He's getting his butt beat by Kels."

Sasha lay with her arms spread-eagled on the oversize chair she'd lucked upon at an estate tag sale. The apartment manager had seen her struggling with the piece of furniture she now rested on and had the decency to help her remove it from the back of her SUV and carry it inside. Her body was so stiff, it hurt to move a muscle. After a five-minute breather she managed to peel her body off of the chair and drag herself to her bedroom. Although someday, after the phenomenal success of her fashion boutique, she would own at least a five-thousand-square-foot home with a spiral staircase, at the moment she appreciated the short trek from the living room to her bedroom. A spiral staircase would have kicked her butt.

With nothing but a blow-up mattress, nightstand, lamp, and television in her bedroom, there was no dresser drawer for her to go retrieve her pajamas from. Nope, just a laundry basket and some boxes. She rummaged around until she found her blue-and-white-striped with red trim Ralph Lauren pajama short set. She'd been a college student on a budget, but thank God for the boutiques and consignment shops she loved spending hours in. She'd been able to treat herself to a designer brand item here and there on a budget, thanks to those classy shops that most of her friends weren't up on. They had no idea how financially smart it was to let someone else pay full price for a garment, but end up enjoying the comfort and perfect fit of a designer classic . . . for less than half the price. And Sasha always considered it a good thing when every item she lucked upon still had the original tags on it.

She went into the bathroom and set her pajamas down on the closed toilet lid. She then removed her sweaty, dirty clothes and placed them on the floor. She slid the frosted shower door back and turned on the water. She grabbed her shower cap off the hook on the back of the door, where she'd placed it, and looked into the mirror. Her soft brown hair, which usually cupped her neck in a bob haircut, today was in a ponytail. She figured she would have sweat it out with all the unloading and unpacking she had to do today. She made sure she tucked all of her hair into the shower cap, especially the loose strands that had fallen out of the ponytail holder over the hours.

Sasha walked back over to the shelf and out of habit picked out a bubble bath scent. After a day like today, a bubble bath would have definitely been in order. Once she realized what she'd done, she shook her head and set the bubble bath back on the shelf along with four of her other favorite scents. She picked up a bottle of skin cleanser instead. Before walking away, she looked down at all the bubble bath scents that she now had no use for. In one swoop, she scooped them off the shelf and into the trash can she'd placed beside the shelf. There was no use in keeping things around that she didn't need. All they would do was take up space.

So as Sasha stepped into the shower, she made a mental note that as long as something didn't have a place in her life or she didn't have a need for it, she'd discard it. That went for people, too. Everything in life was replaceable. That's why Sasha vowed she'd never find herself in Kels's position. If a man had proven to her that she couldn't trust him, she would not make a fool of herself over him. She'd kick him out of her life just as quickly as she'd let him in. Eventually Sasha would learn that it was easier said than done.

Chapter 2

Sasha held the hanger that safeguarded the long multicolored maxi sundress from making its home on the floor among all of the other secondhand garments. In pursuit of a couple new outfits for her new position through the temp agency, Sasha had stumbled upon this particular piece. Considering that she was shopping in one of the upscale Atlanta consignment shops she'd searched and found on Google, she wasn't on a shopping spree for spanking brand new clothes. But anything she purchased and brought home today would be new to her closet.

The particular dress she was eyeing was low cut with a plunging back. It would complement Sasha's figure in all the right places. Not too much of her 36Cs would be on display. Just enough of her back muscles and all of her arms would show, displaying how those fitness training classes she'd managed to squeeze into her busy schedule had paid off. There was no doubt—she had a sexy figure.

She ran her hand down the silky dress with her

free hand. Next she brought the dress to meet her nostrils and inhaled. The corners of her mouth lifted as her lips formed a smile. She exhaled and let out an almost orgasmic breath. Only someone who breathed, slept, ate, and thought fashion got this kind of high from the scent of clothing. This was also part of Sasha's test. It was a requirement that underneath it all, she had to be able to smell just a hint of the new clothes scent before she took a secondhand garment home. This meant that the item still had a story to tell. This dress definitely passed the test.

Like a good smelling man, this dress wanted Sasha to take it back to her place. She wouldn't mind having it wrapped all around her. Looking down at the tag, she saw the price was right. Sasha draped the dress across her arm without another thought and then went to walk away. Buyer's remorse hit her before she could even get away from the clothing rack for good. She stopped in her tracks and looked down at the dress. It was definitely not what Sasha had set out to purchase. "Work clothes, Sasha. Stay on point," she scolded herself and then reluctantly put the dress back on the rack. She had a one-year plan that required her to adhere to a particular budget. How would she be able to invest in her own business if she was steadily feeding her pennies to fund everyone else's business?

"Hunty, that dress is calling your name. It was made for you."

Sasha initially didn't realize she was being spoken to until the voice continued and she turned around to see that the owner of the voice was making eye contact with her.

"That's why it's in this secondhand boutique. The first bitch knew she didn't have no business buying it in the first place. She probably wore it out and her real girlfriends told her the truth: that she looked like a fat prostitute on her last ho stroll before Jenny Craig gets a hold of her. So she had the decency to do the right thing and bring the dress here in hopes of its rightful owner finding it. And you, dear, are the rightful owner. So please don't fuck up a divine moment by being disobedient and not accepting your blessing."

Sasha was truly taken aback. She had to ask herself, had she really just been read by a complete stranger. She had to have been, because she didn't know a single soul in Atlanta well enough that they would approach her like that. She looked up and stared at the stranger who'd just said a mouthful. In her quick but discreet once-over, Sasha's eyes caught the red patent leather pumps. Next there were the skinny jeans, which didn't need to be that skinny on all that extra meat, but they were hot. The vintage red, royal blue, black, and gold Versace shirt, tied at the belly button, screamed that this person knew fashion. It was all so well coordinated. Sasha would have done a couple things differently as far as makeup. She would have trimmed the fake eyelashes down just a tad and used matte instead of gloss lipstick. The shiny gloss of the lips was fighting for attention with the shiny shoes. But that wasn't a biggie. After all, they were in a neighborhood consignment shop, not somebody's red carpet event.

Sasha looked down at the extended hand of her unauthorized fashion consultant.

"Hi, I'm Norman," he said, "but my friends call me Norma."

Sasha shook his hand while admiring his manicured gel nails, which looked better than her own. She prayed her surprise at the man's amazing fashion choices didn't show on her face.

She couldn't help her immediate reaction. Back in her little town in Ohio, Sasha had never run into someone as . . . let's say as flashy and open as Norman or anyone with such divine taste in shoes. She was a little beside herself, but would try to not snatch that gorgeous bag away from him. "Hi, I'm uh . . ." Sasha stammered as she pulled her hand away.

"A fool if you don't snatch that dress right back up off that rack." He laughed, doing the stereotypical hand flip that some people imitate gay men doing.

"You think so?" Sasha asked with uncertainty. She slowly lifted the dress back off the rack again.

"I know so. This is what I do for a living," Norman said. "I dress the stars, hunty. The ones with some real movies under their belts as well as the ones with nothing more than a so-called leaked sex tape."

Sasha chuckled when he winked at her, his long eyelashes beating against his eyebrows. "So you know fashion, huh?" she asked, although it was obvious.

"Chile, asking me if I know fashion is like asking Precious does she know all thirty-one flavors of Baskin Robbins' ice cream."

Sasha laughed. She hadn't chuckled and laughed this much since she could remember. She'd always been so serious. She'd always had a one-year plan for something or other. This meant she was always focused on meeting her goals. There was never time to be laughing and joking and carrying on. The time for her to let out a great big, hearty laugh would be when she was laughing all the way to the bank after reaching the level of success she'd imagined.

"You think I'm joking," Norman said. "But you gon' be kicking yourself for not buying that dress. The next time your boo wants to take you out for date night and you all up in your closet looking for something to wear, you gon' wish that baby was a part of your wardrobe." He folded his arms and nodded his head up and down.

Sasha looked back at the dress again. She then looked up at Norman, whose facial expression showed that he was dead serious. Once again, she flung the dress over her arm. "You're right. I'd be a fool not to buy this dress. And a double fool not to take advice from a professional like yourself."

"Umm hmmm, Miss Thang. And I gave you that for free."

"And I'll take that freebie," Sasha said. "A sistah is on a budget."

"All the more reason for you to cop that dress. Your boo is going to appreciate it even more that you look damn good and you didn't break the bank."

This was the second time Norman had mentioned Sasha having a boo. She decided to correct him so that there wouldn't be a third. "Well, there is no boo, but I'm still getting this dress . . . for me."

"Ohhh, independent woman. I see you, girlfriend," Norman said. "One of those 'I don't need a man' kind of chicks."

"I don't!" Sasha declared. "But sometimes I want one." She scrunched her nose and smiled. Every now and then, after watching an episode of *Rosewood* with Morris Chestnut's fine self, Sasha had urges and desires that only a man could fulfill. But she'd quickly get her mind off of that by watching an episode of *Project Runway*.

"Then as fine as you are, why don't you have a man?" Norman put his hand up. "Oh, chile, I almost forgot. You are in Atlanta. Unless you like sharing, they are hard to come by."

"I don't know about all that. I've only been in Atlanta a week."

"Oh, so you just a nectarine. You ain't quite a Georgia peach yet. Gotta get a little fuzz on ya."

"Fuzz?"

"Boo, yeah. You gotta get out here and learn the city. Learn how the city operates. Hunty, the city of Atlanta itself is like a person. It's set in its ways. You can never change it, but it can change you."

A look of fear shadowed her face, which didn't go unnoticed by Norman.

"Have no fear, your official teacher is here," Norman said, throwing his fists on his hips, spreading his legs, and going into his Superman stance. "I'm here to school you on the ins and outs of this town. You look to be too nice of a girl for me to just let you out in the jungle on your own."

"Jungle? No one has ever referred to Atlanta as a jungle."

He leaned in and whispered to Sasha, "That's because they never made it out alive." He pulled back, nodding like he was telling the truth and his word was bond.

Sasha swallowed hard.

"But, honey, God must really be watching over you today. You got a new dress and a new BFF." Norman looped his arm through Sasha's arm that held the dress. "Now let's go ring up this dress and get started on lesson number one, which is simply an introduction to Atlanta over a drink over at Marty's Bar, right across the street." He pointed out the store window.

Sasha stopped in her tracks. She would have loved to go over and shoot the breeze with Norman. He was so refreshing, plus she'd been cooped up in her place Googling and researching the town the entire week she'd been in Atlanta. A new scene wouldn't have been so bad. But she was already splurging on the dress, which wasn't on her list. She refused to throw caution to the wind and pay for one glass of wine what she could pay for an entire bottle if she'd go back to her place to have a drink. She decided to keep it real with her new friend. After all, lies were no way to start off a new friendship. "Well, I'm kind of on a budget and—" Sasha started.

"It's on me," Norman said, pulling Sasha over to the cash register.

"Well . . ."

"And I won't take no for an answer. Girl, get that dress and let's go. Like I said, it's on me."

Sasha gave in and agreed, placing the dress on the counter.

"Hi, did you find everything you were looking for?" the clerk asked Sasha.

Sasha nodded.

The clerk rang up the dress and bagged it. "That will be twenty-seven dollars and thirty-three cents with tax."

Sasha looked to Norman.

"Bitch, please," Norman said to Sasha. "I meant the drink was on me, not the dress. I don't know you like that." Again, Norman was over-the-top serious with his neck snapped back, eyeballing Sasha, then giving her the side-eye.

Sasha paid the clerk and then she and Norman exited the shop. They jaywalked across the street over to Marty's Bar, where in a couple hours Sasha would not only get to know Norman like that, but the city of Atlanta as well.

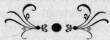

"A zombie," Norman told the bartender after he and Sasha took two seats at the bar. He looked to Sasha. "And you?"

"A wine spritzer for me please," Sasha said to the bartender. "Made with Moscato, thank you."

"A wine spritzer?" Norman turned his nose up. "It's bad enough wine by itself is only a step up from Kool-Aid. And you want to water it down. Tuh!" He looked to the bartender. "Just a glass of Moscato wine for the lady, please. Minus the Spritzer."

The bartender nodded. "Coming right up."

Sasha watched the bartender walk away and begin preparing their drinks, leaving the two, ten minutes short of being practical strangers, alone to get to know one another.

"A wine spritzer," Norman said, rolling his eyes and sucking his teeth.

"I'm not a big drinker," Sasha informed him. "I need my mind alert and functioning to the best of its ability as much as possible. Otherwise I'll end up exactly like the name of the thing you ordered," she said. "What is a zombie, anyway?"

"It's a tricky drink. Kind of like me." Norman wriggled in his seat, crossing his legs. "It's full of all different kinds of vodka."

"Sounds hard," Sasha said, frowning.

Norman made googly eyes. "But it has orange juice, pineapple juice—"

"Oh, so it's fruity, too."

"Girl, did you not hear me say it was just like me. Hard and fruity. Yes, Gawd!" Norman raised his hand to high-five Sasha.

Sasha laughed and slapped Norman a five.

A couple minutes later the bartender returned. He placed Sasha's glass of wine in front of her and Norman's zombie in front of him.

"Thank you," they each said upon receipt of their drink.

"Umm, I needed this," Sasha said after taking a sip of her drink.

"Girl, we all need to unwind. Atlanta will do that to you." Norman drank some of his zombie. "Damn, these shitz are good." He looked to Sasha. "You want to try it?" He pushed his glass toward her.

Sasha put her hand up. "Oh, no, thank you. Moscato is hard enough for me."

"For now. But just give it a month. You'll be downing these babies like bottled water after a five-K run." He took another sip and then placed his glass back down on the bar. "So, what brings you to the ATL anyway?"

"Chance, really," Sasha said. "I mean, I always knew that as soon as I graduated college I was leaving Ohio. It's not artsy enough for what I want to do."

"Which is?"

Sasha's eyes lit up. "Be a fashion designer. Be the owner and operator of a boutique with vintage designs as well as my own originals. Have some of the best up-and-coming designers working for me, you know, to give them a chance at making it big. Maybe ultimately have a chain, then open up boutiques in France and—"

"Whoa, slow down, Dorothy. You're still in Kansas," Norman said. "Take a breath."

Sasha inhaled and then exhaled.

"Now take a drink."

She guzzled down several swallows of Moscato.

"Another one for the lady," Norman told the bartender, who nodded. Norman turned in his chair to face Sasha. "You all right?" He sipped his drink as he waited on her reply.

Sasha nodded, using a napkin to wipe the corners of her mouth.

"So that's what gets your panties wet, huh?"

Sasha scrunched her face and twisted her nose up at Norman.

"Fashion, clothes, design," Norman clarified. "That's what gets you all riled up, huh?"

Sasha relaxed her shoulders and sighed. "Yeah. Pardon me for going on and on, but it's been my dream ever since I can remember."

"Well, you've come to the right place. Atlanta is just the spot for you to get your foot in the door or to just start up a business period. These divas down here are always getting dolled up for this event or the other, even getting dressed up to go to the mall. They are always trying to outdo one another with these parties they be throwing. Then you have all these theater stage plays, Tyler Perry's studio.

The gigs for costume and fashion are endless. Honey, this might as well be the black capital for fashion and designs. They can take Manhattan, honey, leave Hotlanta for *moi*!" Norman fanned himself with his hand and fluttered his eyes.

The bartender placed Sasha's second glass of wine in front of her. She nodded her thanks and he walked away.

"For you and *moi*," Sasha corrected Norman. "But watch out, because I didn't come here for sloppy seconds."

"Oooh, is she trying to read me after I just bought her two drinks? Rude." Norman rolled his eyes and turned his chair away from Sasha.

"You are too much."

"So I've been told," Norman said. "That's why I left Alabama. Chile, talk about being too much for a place that I couldn't be myself there even if I tried. Everything and everybody is so country there."

"Yeah." Sasha sounded sympathetic. "I'm sure it was difficult coming out and trying to live the life of a gay man there."

"Gay?" He had the most shocked looked on his face. "I'm married with a wife and two kids. What made you think I was gay?"

Norman's words gave Sasha pause. She sat there with the glass of Moscato to her lips. Her mouth was wide open and the horrified look on her face was definitely a Kodak moment.

Norman gave her the evil eye a few seconds more but then, unable to keep a straight face, he burst out laughing. "I'm just playing with you. Chile, bye." Norman shooed his hand at Sasha and continued laughing. "Did you really think for one second I wasn't gay?"

Sasha tightened her lips and shook her head. "You play too much." She allowed a smile to spread across her lips.

"And you don't play enough," Norman shot back, taking a sip of his vodka concoction.

"How do you know?" Sasha asked. Norman had only known her all of five minutes.

"I had to twist your arm to buy that fun maxi dress, to get you to come over here and have a drink. Honey, you got the word 'intense' engraved on your forehead. Next to me folks are going to think you are deadpan, 'cause, honey, I'm a live one." He snapped his fingers in a circle.

Up until now, Sasha hadn't minded the fact that people felt she was straitlaced or even uptight. But Norman made it sound like she was the walking dead. "You act like I'm Bernie or something."

"Bernie?" Norman questioned.

"Yeah, from that movie *Weekend at Bernie's*. You act like I don't even have a pulse. Like you're going to be dragging me around Atlanta trying to resuscitate me."

"Ah, ha, ha, ha, ha," Norman laughed, pointing at Sasha. "You made a funny. You're getting the hang of this thing already."

Sasha sucked her teeth and rolled her eyes.

"Oh, don't worry," Norman said, playfully nudging her. "By the time I get through with you, you'll want to go back and repeat kindergarten, you're gonna wanna play so much."

"I don't know about that," Sasha said in disagreement. "I'm on a mission. I came here for a reason. I have some goals to achieve and I'm not leaving here until I do. I'm going to focus more on business than playing."

"I hear you. Well, should I say Norman hears you? But once Norma—my alter ego—gets a hold of you, you'll be able to find that happy medium between business and pleasure. You have to get some play time in. All work and no play makes Sasha—"

Sasha cut Norman off and finished his sentence. "A very dull girl."

"No. All work and no play makes Sasha too serious for Norman or Norma to rock with. And trust me, I can show you some thangs in this town, sweetie." Norman let out a harrumph.

"Hmm, now you got me scared."

"And you probably should be. They don't call it Hotlanta for nothing. Chile, you can get burned. But just roll with me and I'll be your fire extinguisher."

"And why should I trust you to put all the fires out?" Sasha asked.

Norman turned and gave Sasha a serious diva look. "Because, hunty, nine times out of ten I started them. Now let's turn up." Norman raised his glass to toast with Sasha.

Sasha hesitantly raised her glass. She wasn't a turn-up kind of girl, so she didn't know exactly what to make of her connection with Norman. But what the hell? Perhaps Norman was right. Maybe she didn't have to be so serious all the time. There had to be a balance between working hard and enjoying life. But Sasha's mother had always taught her to work hard and play later.

As Sasha raised her glass to toast with Norman, she couldn't help but wonder if for the first time ever, her mother could be wrong.

Chapter 3

Sasha was grateful that the temporary agency had been able to place her on a job. There was really never any doubt in her mind that they would be able to. When she filled out the five-page online application it asked her about higher education and what she'd majored in. There were inquiries about her skills, goals, and hobbies. Every last one of her replies, in one way or another, had something to do with fashion. She figured they'd place her in a department store, clothing company corporate office, or something of that nature. She didn't mind if it was clothing retail. She just wanted to be near clothes. The look of it. The touch of it. The smell of it. The feel of it. The sound it made when sliding on one's body; buttons snapping and zippers zipping. She'd use all five senses and taste it if she could. There was so much to learn about the fashion industry on any and every level. Sasha didn't care exactly where she started. She just wanted to start somewhere.

To find herself sitting behind a desk in a stuffy

law firm was not a start as far as Sasha was concerned. Maybe it was a start for a wannabe lawyer or paralegal. But not for Sasha. This was definitely not what she'd imagined. She couldn't help but wonder why they'd even bothered asking her all those questions if they weren't going to take the answers into consideration when placing her at a job. Nonetheless, two days earlier when she was offered the assignment, she accepted it. She was picky, but not stupid.

"I've got you down for your appointment next Thursday at ten a.m.," Sasha said into the phone receiver. "Thank you and you have a great day as well." Sasha ended the call and hit the enter button after having logged the appointment into the firm's appointment app.

The job was easy; both easy to do and easy money. It consisted of basically being the living datebook for the five attorneys she was assigned to. She routed phone calls, scheduled appointments, and signed for deliveries. In between all that, she drew design sketches and blueprints for her dream boutique. She tweaked her business plan and researched various areas with commercial properties for lease. By the time she was ready to open her first boutique, none of those properties would be available. At least she'd have some idea of how much money she'd need to bring to the table. Sasha kept everything she did pertaining to her dreams in a set of black three-ring notebooks. When things fell into place she wanted to be ready.

After about a week on the job, Sasha's entire opinion of working in the firm had changed. This particular job had actually allowed her to learn quite a bit about setting up shop in the fashion industry. She had a tremendous amount of time to do research and sketch. In her down time at the job, she accomplished a great deal of things, things that she perhaps wouldn't have been able to accomplish at any other nine-to-five. The things she was doing on her down time at the job she would have spent her entire evenings at home accomplishing. Thanks to her receptionist job, of which she only spent about four of the eight hours doing actual receptionist duties, her evenings could be spent doing other things. And those things could ultimately put her on the road to a successful career in the fashion business, if she was careful and kept her eyes focused on her path. Otherwise, if she didn't keep her eyes on the road, she could possibly find herself veering off course and stranded in a ditch.

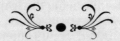

"Are you sure it's okay that you invited me?" Sasha asked as she and Norman headed up the long circular driveway, on foot, of what looked like a castle to her eyes. The driveway was packed with everything from Mercedes-Benzes and Range Rovers—new money—to BMWs and Jaguars—old money. Sasha was thanking her lucky stars that Norman had opted to pick her up and drive his Cadillac to the affair. Her Honda just didn't seem like it would fit in . . . with old money or new. And for the first time since she could remember, Sasha was starting to wonder whether she would fit in as well.

"I'm on the list plus one. You, my friend, are my plus one," Norman replied. "You sound like you're the one who is not sure whether you should be here," he added.

"Oh no, I want to be here. I definitely want to be here," Sasha said, now removing all thoughts of doubt that she might not fit in or belong.

When Norman first mentioned the affair, it was actually Sasha who hinted around about wishing she could attend. With her mind always focused on her career in fashion, she felt that shadowing Norman whenever possible would allow her to make some really great connections.

As they walked, Sasha looked down at the maxi dress Norman had encouraged her to buy from the consignment shop. She gave her Gucci shoes a glance as well. She wasn't quite sure how they did it in Atlanta. Even though this party was in honor of a charity, to help raise money for the SHE Foundation, which stood for Self-esteem, Health & Fitness, and Education, Sasha hoped she wasn't underdressed. She fingered the necklace, which had a matching bracelet. The brushed bronze flowers made the pieces look antique, classy, and expensive. They weren't big and gawky, but enough to catch one's eye and generate a compliment or two. It had been custom made, not by some big-name designer in Italy, but by her cousin, Chelsea, back in Cleveland. Don't knock Cousin Chelsea back in Ohio, though. Home girl was on her way to the big league. Her online custom jewelry business was booming thanks to the power of social media and word of mouth. Who cared if she made everything in a work area in her basement? Dreams had to start somewhere. And if Sasha had her way, Chelsea's dreams would be starting right here in Atlanta.

Sasha, so busy checking herself out, stumbled. Norman had to grab her elbow to help her balance.

"If you stop worrying about what you have on and pay attention to where you are going, you'll have a better chance of not landing on your face and losing a front tooth," Norman said. "Stop messin'. You look fine. You think I would let you come somewhere with me looking cray? I know we've only known each other two weeks, but haven't you realized by now that I tells the truth and shames the devil?"

Norman's words gave Sasha more confidence. When she had first opened the door and walked out, he would have given her the stank face if she wasn't on point. That much she knew. So she lifted her head and continued the trek.

"See, that's more like it," Norman said. "Walk like you own this motherfuckin' town. You are looking snatched in that dress." Norman pretended as though he had yanked something up out of thin air. "You better work it! If you don't, I will. You don't want me to take you in the bathroom, mug you for your gown and come out screaming, 'Who wore it best,' 'cause I'll do it. You know I'll do it." Norman began doing the crack head dance Samuel L. Jackson did in the movie *Jungle Fever*.

The more Norman praised, coaxed, and egged Sasha on, the more she strutted.

"That's right, *chica*," Norman cheered as he pranced right alongside of her.

By the time they made it to the door, they both had to catch their breath and sooth their aching calves.

"Cheap bastards," Norman huffed. "How they gon' rent a mansion but not hire a valet?" Norman asked, hunched over, breathing heavily. He looked up and noticed more guests coming up the drive, so he immediately stood up straight. He brushed his iridescent wine-colored capri suit off and rang the bell.

The huge door opened to a gentleman in a tux wearing white gloves. "Welcome," he greeted.

Norman stepped in, Sasha on his heels. "Good evening," Norman returned the greeting. He then looked to the two ladies at his immediate left who were sitting behind a table. "Norman Bradshaw," he said to them as he approached the table. "Not only am I on the list, but I should be on the top of the list." He let out a chuckle and the women duplicated it as they scanned the list.

"Here you are," one of the women said, crossing his name off. She looked over his shoulder at Sasha, who stood in the foyer admiring the beautiful home.

Norman followed the woman's eyes. "And that's my guest." Norman confirmed what the woman's eyes were questioning. "That's *the* Sasha Wellington."

Upon hearing her name, Sasha's eyes went from scanning the home to the registration table.

Norman continued. "Sasha Wellington of Wellington Vogue Boutiques."

At first Sasha frowned, but then Norman pressed her to play along. Sasha nodded and smiled at the woman.

"It's an honor, Ms. Wellington." The woman's eyes lit up as she greeted Sasha. She then turned her attention back to Norman.

Sasha continued admiring the home as Norman continued with registration.

"Thank you, Mr. Bradshaw. You and your guest enjoy yourselves."

"Absolutely, doll." Norman winked and then walked over to Sasha.

"Bradshaw?" Sasha questioned. She might have been drooling over the expensive and lavishly decorated home as she stood on the cream-and-gold marbled floor, but she hadn't been so distracted that she missed Norman telling his second little white lie for the night. "I thought you said your last name was Jenkins."

"It is. But do you think the stuck-up ruddy poos in this town are going to let someone named Norman Jenkins dress them? Besides, I love me some Carrie Bradshaw from *Sex and the City*. Thanks to her, the name Bradshaw just screams unique, original, quirky fashion." He pulled at the shoulders of his suit. "That's me." He wriggled his head as if he was slinging long blond hair from out of his face.

"Wellington Boutiques?" Sasha wasn't going to let Norman slide on that, either.

"Wellington Vogue Boutiques," Norman corrected. "If you're going to lie, memorize it at least."

"That's the thing, you lied . . . and then put me in the middle of it."

"Chile, you better speak your life how you see it into existence," Norman said. "You can't come up in places like this talking about what you're gonna be and what you're gonna have. People only care about who you are now. What you have now."

Norman had a point. "I hear you," Sasha said, even though she still wasn't completely comfortable with having cosigned his lie. But if all went well, a year from now it wouldn't be a lie. And in two years from now, a home like this would be where she could be resting her head every night.

Sasha continued to look around. She admired the crystal chandeliers hanging above her head. She was discreet in eyeing the expensive artwork, vases, and statues. She didn't want to look like she'd never been anywhere this sophisticated before, even though she hadn't. There was a set of spiral staircases to both the left and the right that met at the top of the second floor. All Sasha could do was imagine what was up there. Probably a master suite fit for Obama and Michelle. The more she saw, the more she realized that this was the sort of lifestyle that she wanted. She wondered what she'd have to do to get it.

Sasha was so engaged in the home's décor that she never even noticed the tall, brown mass of a man who had been eyeballing her from just a few feet away. On top of that, she didn't realize how rude she'd been to him, unknowingly of course. He'd raised his hand and waved at Sasha, but she didn't return the gesture. She didn't even crack a smile of acknowledgment his way. Although it appeared she'd been staring right at the man, she'd actually been staring at the framed artwork directly behind him.

"Well, nectarine, you ready to start earning your fuzz?" Norman looped his arm through Sasha's, tearing her attention away from the artwork.

Sasha took in a deep breath and then exhaled. "I guess so."

"Then let the fun begin." Norman escorted Sasha into the main room where the party was taking place.

Sasha had been to a house party before, but nothing of this caliber. It wasn't a party, it was a damn fashion extravaganza. There were hostesses and waiters walking around with trays of Champagne and hors d'oeuvres. There was a live band playing and a makeshift dance floor on the patio. Dress wise, Norman was right. Sasha fit right in. In fact, she was one of the best dressed women in the room. But despite the fancy setting, there were some real trashy bitches up in the party. Only the host of the affair was wearing a gown. Sasha had yet to meet the fair-skinned woman sporting a short Toni Braxton do. Every time Norman was on his way across the room to introduce Sasha to her, someone he knew stopped him. He seemed to know every single person at that party. That suited Sasha just fine. The more people Norman knew, the more people she could eventually get to know. It was quickly becoming clear that in the ATL, it was all about who you knew. And who knew about you. Some of the people Norman introduced her to were just friends, others clients, others friends of clients who had summoned his business card or who had given him theirs. All Sasha could do was thank God for connecting her to Norman. He most definitely was the exact tour guide she needed to navigate the new city she now called home. The fact that he was in the fashion business as well was a true bonus. Sasha's smooth talking charmed business cards right out of Hugo Boss pants pockets and tiny little Prada bags. Norman stayed by her side to introduce her to all the right people.

"Oh, here comes Gabrielle," Norman said to Sasha, slightly elbowing her as he took a sip of his fourth glass of Champagne in the hour and a half they'd been there.

Gabrielle was the host. She came gliding over toward Norman and Sasha in her long, red gown, accented with crystals, like she was floating in a Spike Lee joint.

"Norman, darling," she said upon approaching him.

Sasha took note of the sense of urgency in Gabrielle's voice.

"I need you. I think I might have had one too many shrimp quiches. This zipper isn't catching under my arm." She discreetly lifted her arm to show Norman the problem area that was right under her armpit. "I need you to come put a clasp on it or something. I don't know what happened."

"Oh, no, we can't have that now, can we?" Norman said.

Gabrielle shook her head with a pout on her face.

He looked to Sasha for confirmation. "Can we?"

Catching on that she should play along with the fashion tantrum, Sasha began shaking her head frantically as well.

"By the way," Norman turned to Gabrielle and said, "this is my friend, Sasha. Sasha, this is the one and only Gabrielle. She's responsible for this magnificent charity event."

"Nice to meet you," Gabrielle said, not even looking at Sasha, therefore she didn't see Sasha extending her hand.

Sasha could see that Gabrielle was totally uninterested in meeting Norman's plus one and totally distraught by her minor wardrobe malfunction.

Sasha let her hand drop, unoffended. She could see ole girl was completely wired.

"Don't you worry," Norman said, pushing his Champagne glass toward Sasha. "Norman will have you all fixed up in under a minute."

Once Sasha relieved Norman of his half-empty Champagne glass, Norman grabbed the host by her size two waist and began ushering her off. He looked at Sasha over his shoulder, rolled his eyes, and mouthed, "Drama queen." He then quickly turned and began pacifying Gabrielle's garment boo-boo.

Sasha shook her head and laughed. She looked down at Norman's glass of Champagne. She'd already had her limit of one glass for the night, but she figured finishing Norman's glass wouldn't hurt. After all, if she was going to play in the ATL, she had to learn to make sure expensive champagne didn't go to waste. She downed the drink and placed the empty glass on a tray one of the waiters was carrying past her.

Not wanting to stand in the middle of the great room, which was more like a huge ballroom, Sasha decided to go out to the balcony/patio area where the band was playing to enjoy the evening breeze. She made her way through the guests, smiling, nodding, and giving a hello here and there. She even ignored the ogling eyes of a couple of the fellas.

She stepped onto the balcony and walked over to the railing. It overlooked the beautifully landscaped backyard. Even in the dark with just a few lit areas here and there, the colorful flowers planted in the flowerbeds glowed in the night. Sasha closed her eyes and inhaled, hoping to become intoxicated by the scent of the flower gardens.

Standing there with her eyes closed, Sasha did truly feel as though she was living a dream. The smooth sound of the band playing, the night breeze, and the sweet smell of the flowers below her, all things she'd never experienced back in Ohio, but had definitely known would be the life she lived someday. And on a regular basis and not just as a guest in someone else's home. As long as she continued to do everything she was supposed to, it looked as though that someday was going to happen sooner rather than later. She'd ended up in the right place and seemed to be meeting the right people so far. She couldn't do anything but stand there and be thankful.

"Oh, stop it! Boy, you so crazy!"

Sasha's serene moment was interrupted by a loud voice followed by a cackling laugh. She followed the irritating shriek over to the dance floor where she saw some tall, short-haired woman in a turquoise sequined dress that rose just above her knees. Her hair was dyed bright pink. In Sasha's opinion, she had on way too much makeup, from the caked-on foundation to the mascara on her fake fluttering eyelashes.

Did she really need those five-inch stilettoes on, since she was already an Amazon? She was a nice looking woman. She would have definitely generated some attention, without purposely and overtly drawing it to herself. But as it was, the girl looked as fake as her hair color.

Surprisingly enough, Sasha was able to take her interest away from the woman to the man she was cackling it up with. She recognized him as the hus-

band of one of the girls she worked with at the law
firm. Sasha had been introduced to him when
he'd come to take his wife out to lunch. Sasha was
glad to see someone she knew, so she decided to
walk over and say hi to him.

"Eric," Sasha said, as she walked up behind him.

He turned, still laughing at whatever the tall
woman was saying that was so funny. "Hey, how are
you?" He hugged Sasha. He pulled away and then
looked at her. "You work with my girl Casey."

"That's right." Sasha was relieved he remembered her. She would have been too embarrassed
if he hadn't. "Yes, I'm Sasha."

He snapped his finger. "Sasha. That's it." He
turned and faced the woman he'd been talking to.
"Sasha, this is an old friend of mine from college,
Paris."

"Yes, honey," Paris said loudly to Sasha. "We go
wayyyyy back." Her nostrils flared as she did this little laugh that seeped between her closed lips. She
then extended her hand to Sasha. "Nice to meet
you, girl." She allowed her index finger to trace
Sasha from head to toe. "Love the dress."

"Thank you," Sasha said.

"You gon' have to let me borrow that one right
there."

Sasha smiled, although Paris appeared to be serious.

"Hey, you're new in town, right?" Eric said to
Sasha.

"Yes," Sasha confirmed.

He looked to his old college friend. "Paris, you
should hook up with Sasha and show her around.
You two can do lunch or something," Eric suggested. He then looked to Sasha. "Paris's not from

here, either. We went to school together back in Augusta. But she's been here in Atlanta a couple years. She knows her way around." He playfully elbowed her.

"Do I ever," Paris said, slapping him on the shoulder and roaring out in laughter.

Her laughter was indeed contagious. Sasha couldn't help but smile. Her smile then turned into a laugh of its own. With a smile on his face as well, Eric looked to Sasha and pointed at Paris. "You're going to love this girl. You won't have a dull moment in the ATL as long as you stick with her, that's for sure."

"Yes, girl, 'cause I likes to have me some fun," Paris said to Sasha. "Life is too short." She began snapping and dancing to the upbeat song the band was playing.

"I see," Sasha said. If she'd been wearing pearls, God knows she would have clutched them. She tucked her lips in and bowed her head just slightly. She could feel the eyes gazing in the trio's direction, thanks to how loud and over-the-top Paris was, not to mention the shaking of all her assets. With her eyeballs lifting and shifting back and forth from Eric to Paris, neither of them seemed the least bit embarrassed. Perhaps Sasha was being what Norman had accused her of being, which was too serious. Maybe if she loosened up some, she wouldn't feel so tense about Paris's personality. Didn't seem to bother Eric any.

Sasha had to admit that back at home if she'd encountered someone the likes of Paris, she'd have run in the opposite direction. The only thing the two had in common, from what Sasha could see so far, was that they were both black women. So even though this Paris character was Sasha's polar opposite, so was Norman, and that appeared to be working out well for Sasha. Besides, Norman himself had said that Sasha needed to live a little. Have fun. What could be more fun than living vicariously through Paris? Besides, one could never have too many friends. Even if some of them turned out to be frenemies.

"I know they ain't playing my song!" Paris shouted.

Sasha stood back and watched Paris groove to the beat of the song the live band was playing. Her body rolled like a wave in the ocean. It would hit the shore, and then the tide would roll back out. The way Paris moved was like magic. But when she bent over, touched her toes, and then twerked a little bit, Sasha admired the confidence Paris had to do that right in front of someone else's man. She would be worried about getting slapped.

Eric was only about a foot away from Paris. He was all smiles while watching her drop it like it was hot, then pick it back up like it had cooled off just enough to be handled. Clearly he wasn't the least bit offended. Sasha wasn't certain she would have been able to say the same for Casey had she been on the scene. Nonetheless, Paris did her thing as she dipped it low and then brought it back up.

"Go on, girl," someone cheered her on.

Sasha looked in the direction the voice had just come from. She wanted to see who in the world would be egging on such actions. That's when she saw two females wearing mischievous grins, hee-hawing in each other's face. It didn't take a genius to realize they were laughing at Paris and not with her.

As far as Sasha was concerned, ole girl did not need any cheering on, genuine or fake. Paris was her own biggest cheerleader indeed. Self-proclaimed number one fan.

Sasha watched as, without a care in the world, Paris made a complete spectacle of herself. Only she didn't realize she was doing just that. She was having fun, oblivious to the snickering, finger pointing, and turned up noses. Sasha had to admit that Paris took self-confidence to a new level. Paris was all into herself. She was looking down at her boobs, twisting her head around to watch her own behind as she bounced it in the air. There was no shame in her game and she was the epitome of carefree. And just when Sasha thought she couldn't possibly meet anyone more over the top than Norman in this town, along came Paris.

Sasha tried her best to keep a permanent smile etched on her face as she watched Paris dance. She remained aware of her expression, and even though she believed in keeping it real, she felt a mask was in order for this situation. She didn't want to come across as a prude. Perhaps she wasn't as lively as some, but she didn't want to be a killjoy and rain on anyone else's parade.

Eric clapped and others watched the one-woman act. Sasha looked around and noticed the disdain and disbelief that could be seen on the faces of the guests who were witnessing the act.

"This is a charity event, not Magic City," an older woman snapped, then walked away shaking her head.

The two women who meant no good continued

to cheer on Paris while others turned up their noses, some women grabbing their men and running as far away from the dance floor as they could. Some men grabbed their women and took off, just in case it was contagious. The last thing some of those broads wanted was a big-booty down-south girl stealing their man. And the last thing some of those men wanted was everybody stealing a peek at their down-south girl's big booty! They didn't want their chicks getting any idea that what they had under their dress wasn't just for their man's eyes only.

Sasha had to admit that ordinarily she wouldn't be caught dead rolling with someone like Paris, but this was Atlanta. It wasn't nearly as conservative as Ohio. It might as well have been an anything-goes type of town . . . pretty much like Vegas. Because there was a showgirl right there in the middle of the dance floor. Ordinarily, another place and another time, Paris's actions might not have stood out so much, but like the older woman had pointed out, it was a charity function.

"Go, Paris, go, Paris," Eric chanted like he was at a ball game.

His wife had told Sasha he was a popular basketball player back in college. His skills ended up landing him in the first round draft of the NBA. He was currently a starter on Atlanta's professional basketball team; this was probably how fans cheered for him on game night. Sasha wouldn't know personally because she wasn't a basketball fan and couldn't think of the last time her television channel rested on ESPN.

Sasha shook her head at Eric. The same way Sasha knew, he had to know that he was wrong for pumping Paris up. The sly grin on his face told Sasha that he knew exactly what he was doing. The more he cheered, the harder Paris popped . . . as did a few onlooking eyeballs.

Finally the song ended and Paris began to fan herself and huff and puff. Eric summoned a server over, who delivered a glass of Champagne.

As far as Sasha was concerned, that song couldn't have ended fast enough.

"Here you go, girl, you deserve it," Eric said, handing the glass of Champagne to Paris. "You showed out!"

"Oh, you know I know how to get down," Paris said, taking the glass.

"That you do," Sasha said. "Girl, you were doing things with your body parts that if I dreamed about doing I would wake up in pain."

The three laughed.

"Do you dance or something?" Sasha asked.

"You mean like for the Falcons or something?" Paris asked, twisting up her nose.

"No, I mean like for Magic City," Sasha said with a straight face. She hadn't been in Atlanta a good month, but she'd been there long enough to have heard about the hottest strip club in the city.

"Are you asking me am I a stripper?" She didn't even wait for Sasha to answer. "Girl, bye," Paris said, shooing her hand and gulping down her drink.

"Do you need another one?" Eric asked Paris as he turned to try to get the server's attention.

"Oh, no, I'm fine," Paris said. "But I do need to sit my ass down somewhere."

Sasha recalled the bench that was over by where she had been standing. "There's one right there." She pointed.

"Ooh, yes, child, that's perfect," Paris said.

Eric led the way. He then fell back, extending his hand for the women to go before him.

"Where's Casey?" Sasha decided to ask Eric the whereabouts of his wife as they walked over to the bench.

"She had a meeting to attend for some board she sits on," Eric replied.

"Well, she don't know what she's missing," Paris said, as she sat on the bench. "According to Sasha here, a sneak peek of what goes on at Magic." Paris winked at Eric.

Sasha wasn't sure if that was an inside joke or if Paris felt as if Sasha was throwing shade back when she suggested she was a stripper.

"I hope I didn't offend you," Sasha said, standing in front of Paris. "You know, by suggesting you were a dancer at a strip club. It's just that, girl, you were working it." Sasha had a genuinely complimentary tone, but at the same time she wanted to clean up any mess she'd made.

"I do not offend easily," Paris said, the only one sitting down.

Eric extended his hand for Sasha to sit.

"Oh, no, I'm fine," Sasha said, choosing to remain standing.

Eric decided to sit down in the space he'd offered Sasha.

"So how long you been in Atlanta?" Paris asked Sasha.

"Around a couple weeks," Sasha replied.

"Do you have family here?" Paris asked.

Sasha shook her head. "Nope. I just graduated college this year. Since I have a gazillion dollars in student loans to pay off, the least I can do is work in the field I majored in and make enough money to pay it back. Atlanta, so far, seems like the right place."

"Girl, you ain't said nothing about college debt. I'm still paying off student loans myself, and I only went one semester," Paris said. "And them student loan people is like God. All omnipresent and stuff."

The three laughed.

"I'm serious," Paris continued. "It don't matter where you go. Where you move to, they are right there where you at, all on your phone. Calling your job. Hell, I was in the grocery store shopping one day and them bastards paged me on the loud intercom."

Once again they all laughed.

Eric looked at Sasha and pointed to Paris. "I told you she's a trip."

"For real," Paris said. "Y'all think I'm playing." Paris laughed at her own nonsense. "I tell you, I got on the phone with the student loan people one day and they were like, 'Ma'am, so do you plan on paying off this college debt or not?' I was like 'not.' I mean why the hell should I pay off a college student loan? A bitch ain't graduate." And that was the truth. Paris had only completed a single semester of college before realizing it just wasn't her cup of tea. She never looked back, nor paid the money back she owed in loans.

Eric and Sasha hollered. Not even Norman had made Sasha laugh this much and this hard. Sasha couldn't help it; Paris was funny. It was almost impossible to separate laughing with her from laughing at her. Sasha meant no harm, though.

Sasha was laughing so hard that tears began running from her eyes. "I need a napkin to wipe my tears," Sasha said. No one had a napkin on hand. She had to use her hands to carefully wipe the tears away so as not to smudge up her makeup too badly.

"You think I'm crazy like Eric does, huh?" Paris said to Sasha.

All Sasha could do was nod as she wiped her tears away.

"I must say I had you pegged wrong at first," Paris said to Sasha. "I thought you were going to be one of those stuck-up chicks who turned their nose up and had a stick in their butt. Just boring."

"Well, dang, tell me how you really feel," Sasha said, putting her hands on her hips. "I know I may not be the loudest Rice Krispie in the bowl, but cut me some slack." Sasha was immune to folks thinking she was just some boring dud just because she chose to be quiet and laid back at times. That was because her mother had once told her that the loudest person in the room isn't always the smartest or most successful. It was usually that laid back person who was about their business. That person who did more listening than talking. That person doing the observing, taking it all in. That was Sasha and that was who she was going to remain. Life wasn't some high school where she spent her time fighting to fit in with the cool kids. She'd be that boring nerd for now if it meant she'd be that chick with the coins later.

"I'm just keeping it real," Paris said. "But you cool people. I could see me having fun, laughing and carrying on with you."

"That's why you two need to exchange numbers and connect," Eric reiterated.

"Absolutely," Paris said before Sasha could express how she felt about it one way or the other. She took her cell phone out of her Chanel clutch. "What's your number? I am definitely going to lock you in."

Sasha, being put on the spot, spit out her phone number to Paris.

"Take my number," Paris said and waited for Sasha to take out her cell phone in order to add her to her contacts.

Sasha pulled out her phone.

"I'ma make sure I call you," Paris said to Sasha.

"Oh, most definitely," Sasha said. Paris was not someone Sasha would have normally connected with. But on the bright side, between Paris and Norman, Sasha figured she was never going to have a dull moment.

"And you call me, too," Paris added.

"Of course." Sasha smiled.

Just then Sasha heard her name being called.

"Diva, I've been looking all over for you."

Sasha looked to see Norman sashaying her way. "I was just thinking about you. Speak of the devil," she said as Norman approached, his eyes not leaving her since spotting her from across the room.

"And the devil appears."

Everyone looked to see Paris rolling her eyes.

"Oh, Paris. I had no idea you were on the guest list," Norman said with his nose turned up at Paris.

"And why should you? You ain't the one throwing this shindig," Paris shot back. "I know you're a jack of all trades, so what are you now? The guest list police?"

Norman shook and shimmied as if he'd caught the chills and was trying to shake them off. "Ooooh, stay in your face, Norma," Norman coached himself. "Do not come out of your face at this troll," he said under his breath.

"What did you say?" Sasha asked. "Norman, are you okay?"

"I was . . ." He looked over at Paris and then rolled his eyes. "Until two seconds ago."

Paris poked her lips out, twisted them, and snapped her neck. "Let me go on and mingle around this place." She stood and smoothed her dress.

"Yeah, I think I saw your meal ticket at the balcony," Norman said to Paris, nodding his head back toward a group of men standing around congregating.

"So what you trying to say?" Paris said, getting extra loud.

Eric stood. "Come on, Paris. I think I need another drink. Come to the bar with me." Before Paris could decline, Eric took her by her hand and escorted her away. "It was nice seeing you, Sasha," he said over his shoulder.

"You too, Eric," Sasha said. "Tell Casey I said hello."

Norman stared Paris down, snapping his neck until she was no longer in sight. He then turned abruptly to Sasha. "I leave you alone for five minutes and you find a pig to play in the pigpen with."

"Me play in the pigpen," Sasha said. "You were the one who came over here slinging mud. And we were having a good ole time."

"I bet. There's never a dull moment with goodtime Paris."

"I take it you know Miss Paris."

"I know Paris and Delicious," Norman spat.

Sasha had a confused look on her face.

"Chile, Paris and Delicious are one and the same," Norman explained. "Miss Thing is Delicious after dark when she's sliding down the pole over at The Gentleman's Club."

Sasha chuckled. "You crazy. You must have seen her dancing on the dance floor, too, huh?"

"Uh, no, I've seen her sliding down the pole in the titty bar she works at."

Sasha twisted up her lips. "For one, you're gay. You like men. What would you be doing at a titty bar? And for two? I asked her if she was a stripper. She said no."

"Umm, hmm, just like her to start off a conversation with a lie, but if you must know, a lot of business is handled in titty bars, thank you very much. White men handle business on the golf course, black men do it in strip clubs." He held up his index finger. "That's for one." He raised a second finger. "For two, I am a man. Yes, I like men, but gay, straight, bisexual, no matter who you are, there is something wrong with you if you don't admire the female body. It's just capable of doing so much. Human beings grow and are nurtured inside the female body. I mean, it's like a garden for life."

Norman quickly snapped out of adoration as he heard the guttural sound of laughter that he knew to belong to Paris.

"Spite what she told you, Miss Paris is a dancer." He jerked his head in her direction. He watched with disdain as Paris sat over at the bar hee-hawing and cackling in some older white man's face who looked to be on the other side of sixty. She was seductively rubbing her hand up and down his back. "When she's not working overtime with Atlanta's elite at social gatherings. If you know what I mean. Girl is a gold digger."

Sasha followed Norman's gaze over to the bar. "So she really is a stripper?"

"Chile, yes . . . slash whore. And you over here all up in her face." Norman looked to Sasha. "Stay clear of that one. You don't want anybody thinking you're cut from the same cloth, honey, trust me."

Sasha looked down with a guilty-as-charged look on her face.

"What?" Norman said, giving her the side-eye.

"Nothing, it's just that . . . I kind of told her I would call her. She gave me her phone number."

"Oh, hellllll no," Norman spat. "Those bitches will give you a bad name and once you're on that list, good luck getting off."

"Eric, the guy she was with, he's the husband of a girl I work with. He connected us." Sasha was trying to defuse the situation. Sasha listened to the words she'd just spoken. Eric was the husband of a girl she worked with. So why in the world would he be with a stripper?

"Well, you lose her number, 1-800-666, right now and forget you ever met her." He began sniffing. "Chile, I can smell the scent of sulfur she left behind. Just the devil," Norman said.

Once again, Sasha looked down with a guilty expression on her face.

"Don't tell me," Norman said. "You gave her your number."

Sasha shrugged. She shook Norman's actions off as being his usual over-the-top, dramatic self. Add the fact that there might have been a little friendship jealousy to that, and she completely wrote off Norman's warning about Paris altogether. He was up in his feelings. Clearly his thing with Paris was personal. That was between him and Paris. Sasha would never want anyone having misconceptions about her based on someone else's perception. So she wasn't going to be guilty of the very act she'd have an issue with herself.

"Ump, ump, ump," Norman said, shaking his head. "You just signed your ticket to hell in a hand-bag." He glared back over at Paris.

"Well," Sasha said, watching Paris walk off with the man she'd just been entertaining. "At least it will be Chanel."

"You mean more like Nine West," Norman said. "And that's all I have to say about that. Now let's go mingle. Introduce you to some real players out here in the ATL."

And with that, Norman and Sasha went back inside to mingle with the so-called real players. Let the games begin, Hotlanta!

Chapter 4

"I heard you turnt up this weekend," Casey said to Sasha.

Sasha had just entered the break room to get her Monday morning cup of coffee before her workday got started. Working in a law office, be it as an attorney, paralegal, secretary, receptionist, even a mail room clerk, was serious business to most. These attorneys always seemed to be tense; they were constantly running around like chickens with their heads cut off in order to meet filing deadlines. Therefore, all those working in connection with them were usually chasing behind the suits on ten as well. If Sasha were into the type of things some of the other folks at the office were into, she might opt to start her mornings off with something a little stronger and *recreational* to get her through her days at the office. But for her, caffeine sufficed. Besides, Sasha was a master at time management. In her first week alone she'd figured out how to stay on top of her attorneys' business as well as her own business. It reminded her of a tip she'd read in the book *Rich Dad, Poor Dad*. She was minding their business while minding her own.

Casey was the assigned receptionist for three of the fifteen total attorneys who worked at the firm. Her attorneys specialized in international law and were rarely in the country, so Casey only worked part-time. That was long enough for her to do what she needed to do . . . for both the firm and herself. Sasha wasn't the only one who used the time on the job to benefit her outside endeavors. Right before Sasha had entered the room, Casey had had her cup to her lips, about to take a sip. But she couldn't help but throw that little teasing greeting in her coworker's direction before taking a swig. After having made the comment, Casey's lips spread into a mischievous smirk. Noticing the questioning look on Sasha's face, she could tell she had gotten to her. Mission accomplished; therefore she could now indulge in her coffee as she raised it to her creamy pink lipstick–covered lips and took a drink.

"You heard wrong," Sasha said, making her way over to the coffeepot. "The only turn-up I know is the turnip I used to help my grandmother plant in her garden."

Casey swallowed her coffee and then chuckled. "Oh, really now?" she said in a knowing tone. "Eric told me he ran into you and Paris at that party this past Saturday."

"It was more like I ran into Eric and Paris," Sasha corrected as she poured herself a cup. The law office didn't have just your regular old coffeepot station. It was a Starbucks set-up with a few different varieties of coffee flavors to choose from. "And let me tell you just in case you don't know, that Ms. Paris is something else." Sasha shook her head. She looked off almost as if she were reliving the moments of watching Paris at the party doing her thing.

Casey let out a laugh. "Trust me, I know. Eric knows her from back in the day. She dated his best friend before so we all went on a couple double dates. She and the guy didn't work out, but she and I got pretty cool," Casey said. "Paris may be a difficult pill to swallow; you might choke the first couple of tries. But eventually she goes down as smooth as brandy. The more doses you take of her, the higher your tolerance level." Casey twisted her lips and then said, "Or maybe you just get immune." She shrugged.

"As smooth as brandy, huh?" Sasha cleared her throat. "You mean tequila." Sasha began to add the desired amounts of sweetener and creamer to her cup.

Casey laughed again. She flipped her long, black hair over her shoulders. Standing five feet tall even, Casey was a shadow up under Sasha.

Petite and pretty with fair skin, Casey was what the stereotypical ball player's wife was expected to look like. Kind of like Kobe Bryant's wife.

"Paris is good people once you get to know her," Casey said, sipping her coffee. "Just don't tell her your personal business or it will be all over Atlanta in five minutes flat," she rambled into her mug, making the words she'd said almost inaudible to Sasha. "Ahh," she said after swallowing her coffee. "But Paris is a real good time."

"So I hear." Sasha made that last comment partially under her breath as she hurried to sip her coffee to keep from saying something else that might come out the wrong way. She wasn't sure just how close Casey was with Paris. She didn't know if Casey would go back and make mention of her little comment to Paris. The last thing Sasha wanted to do was offend someone's friend, especially since she really didn't have anything against Paris, even though Norman apparently did. And on top of that, Sasha didn't do messy, not intentionally anyway. She was not trying to be in the middle of anybody's he said–she said.

"What was that?" Casey said, hinting for Sasha to repeat her last comment.

"Oh, nothing." Sasha quietly exhaled, grateful her words had traveled under the radar of Casey's ears. "I was just saying that I hear Paris is really fun." To confirm to Casey that she truly had nothing against Paris she added, "I even gave her my phone number. It was your husband who suggested the two of us connect."

"Oh, cool," Casey said, excited. "Perhaps we can make it a threesome one of these evenings. I have been out with Paris and it's a riot," Casey said. "She's one of Eric's old school buddies from Augusta, which is his hometown."

Sasha nodded, already having been privy to this information. "So Eric moved to Atlanta to play professional basketball?" Sasha said, repeating what Casey had mentioned to her before.

"Yes, and that's how I met him. I used to cheer for his team."

Sasha thought for a moment. "Isn't there some rule about you guys not being able to fraternize with the players?"

"Yeah, so I threw in my pom-poms when I decided to take up with one of the Atlanta Hawks' guards." Casey then said in a whisper, "After he sucked on 'em, of course." She jiggled her double Ds and then laughed.

Sasha shook her head and smiled. She could definitely see how Casey could get along with Paris, not to suggest that Casey was as off the chain as Paris. At least Casey had the decency to jiggle her breasts in privacy and not for the whole world to see.

"Seriously, though," Casey continued, once again flipping her hair, "Eric and I didn't meet on the court, at a game, by the locker rooms or anything like that. I actually bumped into him one day at the mall. He had no idea I even cheered for his team, considering I was a rookie and hadn't been cheering too long. I didn't tell him, either. We went on about three dates before he actually found out."

"Good thing you told him. It's never good to start a relationship out keeping secrets." Sasha took another sip of her coffee; her chest rose and then dropped in relaxation. No wonder they'd put a patent on that brand. It was the only cup of coffee in the world Sasha, while out and about, would pay as much for one cup as she would a whole bag to brew in her own kitchen.

"Girl, I didn't tell him," Casey said. "The big jumbo cam thingy did. The cameraman zoomed in and focused on me while I was just a-kicking and a-smiling. Eric happened to be benched at the time and looked up and saw me." Casey laughed. "He said one of the players was like, 'Yo, Eric, man, ain't that ya girl?' " She laughed again. "He was humiliated. Didn't talk to me for two weeks. Even took one of the other cheerleaders out on a date to make me jealous."

Sasha paused from drinking her coffee and looked at Casey over the rim. "Okay, now that's taking it a little too far. He actually hooked up with one of your friends?"

"She wasn't really one of my friends. We didn't hang out or anything like that," Casey said. Sasha could tell she was downplaying it. It had to have pissed Casey off.

"I'm sorry, but I don't care if you two were tight or not. I'm not going to get with a man someone I know has already been with." Sasha recalled a similar situation with two girls she went to college with. One dated a guy first. They knew they weren't right for each other after the first couple dates, so they went their separate ways. The other girl, who ran in the same circle as the first girl, ended up hooking up with the same guy, and not only that, but ultimately married him. "I don't know if I'd be able to stop picturing my dude with that girl. And then have to still be in the girl's face." Sasha shook her head.

"He felt played. He wanted to hurt me the same way I hurt him."

Sasha could already tell Casey was the type of woman who made excuses for her man's wrongdoing. Sasha laughed inside, thinking that perhaps she should introduce Casey to Kels. Not that Sasha condoned domestic violence, be it man against woman or woman against man, but she bet if Casey made Eric wear his balls as earrings the same way Kels did with her man, Casey would be telling a different kind of story right now.

"Eric had really started to like me and had talked about me and introduced me to a couple of his teammates. So after learning that I'd kept something from him, he thought I was some trick trying to stick him for his paper . . . trying to snag a baller like most of the skanks in Atlanta."

"I guess I can see him thinking that about you since you weren't up front from the jump." But in Sasha's mind, that still didn't justify him getting with another cheerleader on the team just to spite Casey. He sounded like a jerk.

"That's the way it works with ballers." She shrugged and continued, "It's just that I'd never met a man like Eric before. He was so well put together, nothing like the guys in the trailer park I grew up in."

"Trailer park?" Sasha said a silent prayer that her face hadn't been scrunched up when she said that. Either way, she was sure her tone reflected what her face would have read anyway. "I'm sorry," she immediately apologized. "I didn't mean to say it like that. It's just that, girl, you look far from . . ." Sasha paused to choose her words carefully.

"I look far from trailer park trash." Casey let out a snort. "Yeah, I know. And trust me, it took a lot of work trying to look like I belonged, trying to act like I belonged. The last thing I wanted was for people to look at me and be able to tell that I'd once lived with my mom and alcoholic stepdad along with two siblings in a trailer the size of a Johnny on the Spot outhouse."

"Wow, that many people lived in one trailer?" If that was the case, Sasha at least hoped it was a double-wide.

"Yep," Casey said. "And sometimes even more . . . if one of my stepdad's other much younger women decided to spend the night." She shook her head. "My stepdad was abusive to both us kids and my mom. So in order to keep him off our ass, if he asked us to make up excuses about who these side-chicks were, we did." Casey shrugged.

Sasha knew right then and there where Casey had learned to make up excuses for men. Sasha had to take a breath. She was getting an earful. Casey was spilling the tea and wasn't adding a lick of sugar. It was a bitter truth, but she appreciated the fact that Casey was choosing to share this with her. She just wondered if she'd shared this with Eric off the bat.

"So let me guess, you didn't tell Eric about your background at the start of your relationship, either?"

Casey shook her head.

"Then surely you can understand why Eric might have thought you were a gold-digger. You kept things from him, so he was probably leery that you had something more to hide." Sasha had to admit that Casey did look like the kind of chick who had something to hide. Although she'd never done anything sneaky or manipulative in the little time Sasha had known her, there was still something about her that Sasha couldn't put her finger on. Perhaps it was the fact that she'd admitted she'd kept things hidden from her own husband at the start of their relationship. So why wouldn't she do it in any other relationship?

"And I understood that," Casey agreed. "The cheerleaders are like the enemies to the wives, fiancées, and girlfriends. Heck, believe it or not, some of the players see us that way, too; the enemy with a capital 'T.'"

Sasha looked a tad bit confused.

Casey explained. "Temptation."

"Oooh," Sasha said, then drank her coffee.

"Most of those ball players are really some good guys that are just there to play a game. But then you have chicks, yes, some of the cheerleaders, whose sole mission is to land in one of their beds, get pregnant, trap him with a baby, and get a paycheck for the next eighteen years. That is exactly why I'd told myself I would absolutely not get with a professional ball player. I don't even care if it was a golf ball he played with. Look at Tiger."

Both women laughed.

"I'm serious," Casey said. Her laughter ceased and the look on her face expressed just how serious she was. "I saw more wives and fiancées embarrass and humiliate themselves by checking those side-chicks than I care to recall." Casey shook her head. "I vowed I'd never allow the actions of a man to make that my reaction. Plus, I figured if they were treating their wives that badly, then imagine how they'd treat the side-chick or trap hoe."

Sasha sipped her coffee as she continued to listen.

"I didn't want Eric to think I was the latter chick, which is exactly why I didn't let him know who I was at first," Casey admitted. "I didn't want him to think that I was just some cheerleader trying to trap one of the players. In addition to that, here he was some millionaire and I was making minimum wage, if that, bouncing around on a basketball court. I didn't finish college. It wasn't even like I had a vocation to fall back on. I was just some dumb cheerleader."

Sasha witnessed sadness covering Casey's face.

Sasha put her hand on Casey's shoulder to console her. "You are a beautiful and *smart* girl, Casey." Sasha had no idea how Casey could ever think otherwise. A woman didn't need a college degree to be smart. Sasha had noticed the way Casey interacted with these attorneys and their top-notch, Harvard-grad-type clientele. She could converse with the best of them. Sasha thought that once she'd even overheard a client telling Casey that his wife couldn't wait to get together with her again. These prestigious clients were particular about who their wives were seen with, so that alone should have told Casey something.

"Thank you, Sasha, so are you. But you went to college. You are beautiful and have a degree proving you're smart. When people see me, they just see a cute face." She looked down at her breasts. "With pom-poms." She laughed.

It didn't go unnoticed by Sasha that Casey did a lot of laughing. Sasha suspected that she often laughed to keep from crying. "You're just as smart as I am. Look around." Sasha looked around the break room. "We are both working for one of the most successful law firms in Atlanta."

"It's different, though. You have a piece of paper that confirms and justifies your status and bank account. I have a piece of paper, too, a marriage license." Casey sighed. "I married a baller. All people see me as is just one of Eric's many trophies scattered about the mansion."

Sasha saw the hurt in Casey's eyes. "Bothers you a lot what people think, huh?"

Casey shrugged. "I know and Eric knows that what we have is real love. After he got over the fact that I really wasn't a gold-digger after his riches, we grew closer than ever. We became inseparable, and within months we were married. People didn't think it would last. But our marriage has lasted three years thus far."

"Good for you," Sasha cheered. "Now you're beautiful, smart, and rich!" The two women high-fived.

"Yes, I must admit the perks of wealth are endless." Casey laughed again. "I have a shoe closet bigger than the trailer I grew up in. Girl moved up!"

Casey's last comment had her thinking. Casey was wealthy. She and Eric each probably had a different car to drive every day of the week. Casey dressed business casual, wearing office attire by Gucci, Prada, Ferragamo, and a few other notable designers. But she didn't overdo it. Sometimes she could be in something as simple as St. John or Calvin Klein, but those red bottoms always let one know she wasn't that average girl living off of a receptionist's salary. Clearly Casey didn't need to be working anywhere. So Sasha couldn't help but wonder why she chose to spend her days, and sometimes long nights, in the office. It didn't make sense to Sasha. For now, though, she wasn't going to fish. She simply made a mental note to weasel that topic into a future conversation.

"So Eric turned out to be the exception basketball husband, huh?"

Casey looked to Sasha. "Let's just say I turned out to be the exception basketball wife," she said. "But anyway, thank you for all the compliments and for making me feel better, Sasha," Casey said. "You're a sweet girl. And I can tell you're genuine, which I guess is why I just told you all my business." Sasha chuckled. "But I'm glad to meet someone real for a change. I could use a friend like you in my life."

Even though Sasha had not come to Atlanta to make friends, it looked like the powers that be had other plans for her. She guessed He figured she'd need people to look out for her in this strange town the same way Dorothy had needed the Tin Man, the Lion and the Scarecrow. Just like Dorothy, though, Sasha was in for the adventure of her life. Unfortunately, there was no yellow brick road to follow. She'd have to make her own path, and getting off course could lead to more drama than she ever expected.

Chapter 5

"So how are the people down there?" Sasha's mother asked through the phone receiver.

"Ummm, different," Sasha said, and then let out a chuckle. "I must say that I've met some pretty colorful and over-the-top characters. But this one girl that I work with, Casey, she seems kind of regular. She's somewhat of a free spirit."

"Free spirit or high spirit?" Sasha's mother asked. "Because you know high spirit is just another word for a hoe."

Sasha laughed. "Mom, stop it. That is just mean."

"No, that is just the truth," she said. "And sometimes you have to watch out for those free spirits, too. They can be so naïve and gullible and end up getting you into a mess with their simple selves."

"Dang, Ma, why you sound so bitter?"

"I don't know. I'm trying to let you be grown, but you're my baby. You are who you are and I don't want any of those folks down there in that big city influencing you negatively."

"You know me better than that. I'm the same today as I was yesterday."

"Yeah, well, it's tomorrow I'm worried about."

Sasha heard a knock on her front door.

"Ma, I'm going to have to call you later."

"Everything all right?"

"Yes. It's just that someone is at the door."

"You want me to stay on the phone with you to make sure it's not some serial killer or rapist coming to—"

"Ma, if you're trying to scare me back to Ohio, it's not going to work." Sasha laughed. "I'll call you tomorrow, okay?"

"All right," her mother said regretfully. "I love you."

"I love you, too." Sasha ended the call and then headed over to her door while mumbling, "My mother and that ID Channel." She shook her head and laughed.

"Girl, you look hot!" Casey exclaimed as she stood outside Sasha's apartment door.

It was Saturday night, and after numerous invites from Casey to hang out, all of which Sasha had initially declined, she finally accepted Casey's invitation. Sasha figured the girl was not going to let up until she did.

From the looks of things, Casey was more than ready to hit the town. Sasha, on the other hand, wasn't. Her phone call with her mother had set her back some, but the real reason she was running behind schedule was the fact that she'd been unable to tear herself away from her sewing machine. She'd purchased the most beautiful piece of fabric for a jumpsuit she was making. It was just starting to really take form.

The one time she did tear herself away from the sewing machine was to do a little online research of some of the other fashion talent in Atlanta. Who knew? One day she might decide to collaborate, so she wanted to know everything she could about who was who in the fashion industry in Atlanta. People were both flattered and impressed when their reputations preceded them, so Sasha wanted to make sure she was familiar with the names of all the right people. It helped that Norman was very knowledgeable in this area as well. But Sasha couldn't depend on him to make all her introductions.

Casey didn't even wait for Sasha to invite her in. With her eyes glued to Sasha's figure in a one-piece, black shorts-romper, she entered.

Sasha hadn't seen Casey's abode, but she imagined she could fit her apartment inside of it several times over. Still, there was no apprehension from Sasha about having someone of Casey's financial status in her modest apartment. After all, this was the same chick who had grown up in a trailer park.

Casey didn't pay a bit more attention to Sasha's living arrangements. She was too busy checking out Sasha. Casey went behind Sasha, eyeballing her from the back head to toe.

"Well, thank y—" Sasha couldn't even finish her sentence. The whack on her behind completely stunned her. With a hand resting on each cheek of her bottom, Sasha turned to face Casey. Sasha was staring at the girl as if she'd lost her mind. "For real?" Even though Sasha didn't feel as if Casey was coming at her sexually but patting her butt in a girlfriend kind of way, they weren't at that point in their relationship yet. There was still a velvet rope around Sasha's comfort zone.

"I'm sorry," Casey apologized, still ogling Sasha's body. "I couldn't help myself. I had no idea you were hiding a J-Lo booty up under them suits you be wearing at work. And those legs." Casey bent down and ran her hands down Sasha's long legs, bronzed with a shimmering scented lotion Sasha had slathered them in. "They're the color of the caramel apples I get at amusement parks." Casey stuck her tongue out and made a licking sound.

All the chatter at the office water cooler for the two months Sasha had worked there was justified. Casey's tongue made Miley Cyrus's look like an inchworm. Sasha now understood why bets had been placed on how long Casey's tongue was. Of course all this conversation was heard in passing. Sasha didn't get caught up in mess . . . or gossip.

Sasha slowly bent down so that she was now at eye level with Casey. Sasha rested an elbow on each of her knees. "Thanks for the compliment, but if you lick me, we are both going to know exactly how many inches your tongue is when I pull it out your throat." Sasha did a nice-nasty smile and then stood up erect. She brushed down the front of her shorts, flattening any wrinkles.

Casey stood up, chuckling. "My bad," she said. "But just so you know, if you did decide to make good on your word, it wouldn't be the first time the cat's had my tongue. If you know what I mean?" Casey winked and stumbled.

Sasha had to help Casey catch her balance. "Just how many drinks did you have before showing up on my doorstep?" Sasha shook her head while throwing her fist on her hips, realizing that Casey had to be somewhat tipsy. If her out-from-left-field words weren't a sign, that glossy look in her eyes was a dead giveaway.

"Oh, who cares?" Casey shooed her hand. "It's not like I'm driving."

Sasha was a little confused. "Then who's driving? I thought you said Paris was going to meet us out." Sasha must have missed the memo that she was supposed to drive. She began looking in the direction of her open front door to see if maybe Paris was coming up in the rear.

Without Norman's approval, of course, Sasha had agreed to hang out with Paris. Even when Sasha informed Norman that Casey would be there as well, he still turned his nose up at the idea. Norman knew of Casey, but had never really had enough interaction with her to form an opinion of her. He knew Casey was the wife of a baller and that the couple was paid and did everything big. It didn't help Casey's case any that she was friends with Paris. Sasha even invited Norman to join them as well so that he could see for himself that it wouldn't be so bad.

"Chile, please," Norman had spat. "If I wanted to hang out with someone who looked like that thing, I got a whole list of real drag queens I can call up." He even said that spending time with the wives of ballers wasn't his cup of tea. He had said it with such distaste she wondered what he had against those women.

Sasha had taken that as a no and left it alone. So now it would just be the three girls, who couldn't be more different from one another. Sasha, the college graduate with major business plans for herself. Casey, the petite, beautiful, yet somewhat green baller's wife. And Paris the . . . well, Sasha hadn't quite been able to form a description just yet, but she was sure once the night was over she would come up with something.

"Paris is meeting us out," Casey said. "As a matter of fact, she's waiting on us. Let's go." Casey walked over to the door, doing a good job of keeping her balance in her Jimmy Choo Tartini Square Pavé crystal and suede pumps.

"Just one second." Sasha held her finger up and headed toward her bathroom. Her Alice + Olivia Dita mirrored leather pumps were not quite as expensive as Casey's shoes, but they still kept them company on the shelves in stores like Saks Fifth Avenue. "I was about to put on this new Moonstruck 3D Fiber Lash stuff."

"You wear fake lashes?" Casey called out. "Yours look so natural."

"That's because they are," Sasha said from the bathroom. "See, come and look."

Casey made her way to the bathroom where Sasha demonstrated to her how to put on the mascara set she used to extend her own natural lashes.

"See, all you have to do is put on your regular mascara, which is optional. Then you put on the gel base from the Moonstruck kit, then the fibers. And *voilà!*" Sasha turned to show Casey the results.

"Oh, my God. Your eyes are poppin'. They look like fake lashes."

"Umm, hmm. But they are not. This mascara is just enhancing my natural lashes." Sasha tucked her cosmetic bag away under the bathroom sink. "All right. Now I'm red-ta-go." She turned off the bathroom light, grabbed her clutch and keys, then she and Casey headed out the door. She locked the door behind them as they exited the apartment building and headed down the walkway to the street.

"Well, damn," Sasha said, stopping in her tracks as they approached a vehicle. "A Hummer limo for a regular girls' night out?" Sasha questioned as she eyeballed the black Hummer limousine. The driver stood at the back door with it opened for the ladies to climb in.

"This is how my baby Eric does it for his wifey," Casey said, the first to climb in.

In the short little black dress Casey was wearing, Sasha could see all her glory. At least Casey wasn't going out like one of those drunken reality TV housewives with a tampon string hanging out. And let the church say amen to the fact that Casey didn't dress like this at work. Her work attire was always very conservative, and Sasha had never heard a bet placed as to whether Casey wore panties or not.

As Sasha stood there waiting for Casey to completely climb in, she realized that the only times she'd been in a limo was for prom and the time she was a member of her cousin's bridal party. Never had she or any of her friends randomly hired a limo just for a night out on the town.

"You coming or what?" Casey poked her head out of the door.

Sasha exhaled. "Sure. Wouldn't want a Hummer limo to go to waste, now would I?" Sasha climbed inside where she was greeted by a glass of Champagne that Casey had poured her.

"Drink up," Casey said, tossing back a glass of her own. "You need to catch up with me."

Sasha accepted the glass after taking a seat across from Casey. The limo door closed behind them and within seconds they pulled off.

"The bar is stocked with everything you can think of," Casey pointed out as she prepared herself a shot. "I'm sure you'll graduate from Champagne by the time the night is over."

"I'm a lightweight, so maybe not." Sasha took a sip from her glass.

Her tipsiness getting the best of her, Casey leaned in and said, "I'm sure there are a lot of things you weren't into before moving to Atlanta, but trust me when I say this town has a way of making you something that you aren't." Casey leaned back and toasted up her shot before throwing it down her throat. "Mark my words."

Sasha placed her glass to her lips and cautiously took a sip. Casey's words almost sounded like a warning. Surely there was a cautionary tale to go along with it, one that Sasha would have never guessed in a million years.

"Turn down for what?" Casey shouted as she approached the bouncer outside of the club, Sasha on her heels, observing her surroundings.

Besides Marty's Bar, Sasha hadn't been out drinking in Atlanta, so she had no idea what type of place Casey had taken her to. She figured it had to be pretty high class if it warranted a limo transporting them to it.

"As always, it's a pleasure, Mrs. Cortz," the bouncer greeted Casey.

That was Sasha's first sign that wherever they

were, Casey was a regular. That kinda sorta made Sasha feel somewhat safe. She couldn't imagine Casey frequenting a place that was trouble, if not for her own reputation at the firm, for her husband's, who was a local celebrity, as well as recognized as a role model to young sports fans across the map.

Sasha noticed the few men who were outside of the establishment. A couple of the men were smoking cigars, looking quite sophisticated. There was one thing Sasha could say about Atlanta; it may have been known for its PYTs, also known as Georgia peaches, but the men were equally juicy.

"The pleasure is always mine." Casey took her thumb and dipped it right into the single dimple on the bouncer's left cheek.

Sasha watched as the hard-core, three-hundred-pound, muscular man almost turned to mush right there before the women's eyes. He blushed while extending his hand for Casey and Sasha to enter. By the time Sasha was in front of him, his smile was gone and he wore the same hard look he'd worn when they'd first walked up to the club.

Once Sasha and Casey made their way through the doors, they landed in a small, dimly lit foyer. A woman with legs for days, dressed in a black miniskirt suit, greeted them. Her hair was in a bun that sat atop her head. Studious-looking black framed glasses made Steve Urkel look like a geek, but they made her look like every man's fantasy. You know, the secretary type woman who pulls her hair out of a bun, removes her suit, and is left wearing nothing but a man's white, crisp dress shirt and fuck-me pumps. That was her all day.

The woman's fire red–polished nails tapped on

the clipboard in her hands. "Mrs. Cortz," the woman said, "your VIP section awaits you. Right this way." She opened the huge black metal door and all of a sudden the small foyer room that had been stone quiet with the exception of the woman's voice was now filled with bass and lyrics from the latest "it" rapper.

The woman looked over her shoulder to make sure Casey and Sasha were following behind her as they entered the club.

"Well, I'll be dammed," Sasha let slip from her lips as she looked around the room. Within seconds she felt as if she'd been zapped from one world, Earth, to another, the planet of Ecstasy.

The room was pretty much just as dim as the foyer had been. The red, royal purple, and yellow lighting did brighten it just a tad more. Sasha could see silhouettes, but not the full facial features of the patrons who sat in oval booths with high backs like Sasha's favorite ride at the state fair back in Ohio. A small, fancy, crystal-like modern lantern was the centerpiece on each table. Everything about the place whispered incognito while it screamed sex.

Topless waitresses with tasseled nipples to match the lighting color scheme pranced about with trays of drinks and food. From what Sasha could see, there was no bar area nor bartenders. In the center of the room, though, was a round lit-up stage. It had poles like a carousel, but no horses . . . just women. All kinds of women. Every shape, size, height, race, and complexion. The same way a carousel had a variety of pretty horses donning beautiful, colorful saddles, these women had donned such eye catching costumes. The ceiling of the round stage had white lights. It was clear that the only thing that was to be seen was the featured entertainment. After all, that was the most visible thing in the room.

The hostess led them through the club, up a few stairs, to an area that looked more like a sitting room than one of the booths on the lower level. Sasha was so preoccupied by what was going on around her in the club that she didn't pay much attention to where she was walking. She bumped into a waitress as well as a gentleman heading back to his table. By the time the woman who'd led them to their spot extended her hand for them to sit, Sasha was exhausted.

She had seen so many people of different races, shapes, sizes, and choice in hairstyles and clothing. She didn't want to stare, but she could have sworn she'd passed a cross-dressing couple. Yes, the person dressed in men's clothing had feminine features while the person dressed as a woman had manly features.

She felt like she'd just accompanied Alice on her fall down the rabbit hole and was on a real live trip. The only difference was that Wonderland was made up. This right here was real, and from the look of things, as the already dim lights dimmed down to almost pure darkness, it was about to go down.

The music cut off and even the lights on the carousel dimmed to darkness. Suddenly the rap music was replaced by familiar carnival music. Sasha heard a mysterious Vincent Price–sounding voice boom through the speakers that were stationed throughout the room.

"Ladies and gentlemen, the moment you have been waiting for has finally arrived."

Sasha watched Casey get all excited as she began bouncing her knee. "Here we go," she said to Sasha, who wouldn't necessarily describe the emotion she was feeling as excited.

For about two seconds the entire venue went black, then the center stage lit up just like a carousel at night. Except for the music, there was dead silence in the room, as if the pope were about to speak at the Vatican during Holy Week.

Sasha looked down at Casey's hand on her knee. She squeezed Sasha's knee with excitement, like she knew what to expect. Sasha, on the other hand, sat nervously because she didn't know what to expect.

As the stage spun, on one of the poles appeared a woman in a get-up fit for a New Orleans Mardi Gras parade. Feathers, sequins, sparkles, and rhinestones covered her nude-colored costume. She was as still as a statue and a masquerade mask covered her face. Her appearance obviously excited the crowd: they began to whistle and howl.

Casey cheered, elbowing a stiff Sasha. Sasha looked over at Casey, realizing she was signaling for her to join in on the whooping and hollering as well. Sasha squirmed just a tad in her seat. She felt like a fish out of water, and even if her discomfort showed on her face, Casey was too far gone to have recognized it anyway. If she had, she sure didn't give a damn, because she was steadily trying to get Sasha to join in on what she considered fun.

Sasha, out of courtesy, simply smiled and gave a fake little clap, all the while mumbling, "Lord have mercy. What in the hell have I gotten myself into?"

Chapter 6

After the moving carousel stage, which was the only thing lit up in the dark room, did a complete 360 with the woman clinging to a pole, the floor lights flickered; then came the sound of a smooth R & B thug song. The woman slowly wound her body up and down to the music. It took a minute before Sasha realized the dim houselights were now back in business, all while Miss Thing handled hers on that pole. She was tall and thick. Sasha had to give ole girl her props. She was working those poles as she intertwined her body in between them, landing in awkward and acrobatic positions.

A server carried over a tray full of appetizers and set it down. Unless Sasha had missed Casey placing the order, this must have been part of the VIP treatment. Casey's little skinny butt was the first to dive into the delicacies. She grabbed a chicken wing. For all the alcohol she'd guzzled thus far tonight, Sasha figured the petite girl was going to need more than just a chicken wing to soak up all that liquor.

Strip clubs had never been and were not a place that Sasha frequented. She'd been to a male revue before as part of a bachelorette party she'd attended, but she'd never been to a strip club in which the featured dancers were females. Why would she? She didn't get down like that. She barely had time for a man in her life, one whom she was attracted to, let alone the female of the species, to which she had no attraction to at all. Sasha had to admit, though, that she couldn't tear her eyes away from the show taking place before her. It wasn't just the typical striptease act. This woman was performing. She was putting in work, and she deserved every single dollar some of the audience members began to walk up and place on the stage.

"This is nice, eh? She's good, right?" Casey said, popping a jalapeño bite into her mouth.

"She is working it!" Sasha said. "The girl is bad." Not wanting to seem like she was not too into it, Sasha grabbed a nacho, broke it in half, and popped one of the halves in her mouth.

"Good, I was hoping you would say that." Casey stood up. She looked around until she spotted one of the servers. She made eye contact with the woman and then waved her over.

Once the waitress approached their table, Sasha witnessed Casey say something in her ear. The music prevented Sasha from hearing what Casey had said. After a few seconds, the woman walked away and Casey sat back down.

"Here, drink up." Casey poured Sasha a drink

from one of the chilled bottles that sat in an ice bucket in the center of the table. They'd already been in place prior to their arrival. "Bottle service, baby." She handed Sasha the drink she'd poured her.

Sasha took a sip. She frowned. "What is this?"

"Never you mind." Casey laughed. "Just drink. Have fun. Let your hair down. We have a designated driver so you can get white girl wasted if you want." Casey guzzled down her own glass full of the alcohol. "I know I am." She then began to bounce and dance as the music changed into a rap song. Next she turned her attention back to the lone woman on the stage. "Don't stop, get it, get it," Casey cheered.

Sasha looked down at her drink. She then looked over at all the fun her coworker seemed to be having. "Oh, hell. Why not?" Sasha said as she looked down at the drink again, frowned, preparing herself to throw it back. The strong liquid rushed down her throat, feeling like it had left a trail of fire. Sasha coughed a couple times.

"Here. Chase it with this." Casey handed her a bottled water and then focused back on the night's featured entertainment.

Sasha darn near drank the entire bottle of water down. She covered her mouth, let out a small belch, and then felt much better. She shifted in her seat a little bit to get comfortable, then watched as the dancer bounced all over that stage like she herself was a horse on a carousel. As Sasha watched the woman dance, something about her moves seemed so familiar, but before she could even think about it anymore, the woman's dance was over and paper bills were floating to the stage.

Sasha watched as the woman accepted some cash right from patrons' hands, adding in a little flirting with the twist of her hips, the licking of her lips, and the shimmying of her shoulders.

"I'm going to head to the bathroom," Sasha said to Casey.

"Hold up," Casey said. She once again stood and summoned over the server whom she had called over just moments earlier.

Sasha watched as, once again, Casey said something to the woman and then turned her attention back to Sasha. "She's going to take you."

"Come with me." The server grabbed Sasha's hand and maneuvered her through the club, up a small flight of steps, and then down a short hallway. At the end of the hallway was a door. The server cracked the door open and then stuck her head inside.

Sasha watched as the server made certain there was no one in there. She opened the door and then stepped to the side to allow Sasha to enter.

Sasha stepped in thinking she was going to immediately see a toilet and a sink. Instead she saw a seating area with a sectional couch. There was one of those square suede storage table things next to the couch, and a mobile bar on wheels with two barstools. It was lit with purple lightbulbs from a small two-tiered chandelier that hung on the ceiling in the middle of the small space.

Sasha looked around the love shack. "Bathroom," she said to the server. "I needed to go to the bathroom." *Not the damn Champagne room,* she thought.

"Right that way." The server pointed to a door right past the bar.

"Okay, thank you." Sasha headed for the door. She knocked, not knowing if it was a single bathroom or one with stalls.

"It's okay. No one is in there," the server said.

Sasha opened the door and entered the single bathroom. It actually reminded her of her own bathroom at her apartment. It was private, clean, and actually smelled good. As Sasha lined the toilet seat with toilet paper, she looked around to see if she could spot where the air freshener was hiding itself. She noticed a flower-shaped oil refill plug-in air freshener.

After using the bathroom, Sasha went over to the sink, where a touch-free soap dispenser spit soap into her hands. "I need one of those in my life," Sasha told herself. It was weird that the most comfortable space Sasha had been in the entire club was the frickin' bathroom. She couldn't imagine that any patron who had to go to the bathroom would be escorted to that one. The line for the bathroom would probably end up looking like the line outside the club. She was sure there was a more public bathroom elsewhere in the club; one that did actually have stalls. She chalked this up as another VIP perk.

After rinsing her hands and drying them, Sasha exited the bathroom. "Jesus!" she screamed at the figure that lay across the sofa. Even though there were only royal purple bulbs lighting the room, Sasha recognized the performer by the clothes she wore. "My goodness. I wasn't expecting anyone to be out here." Sasha's hand rested across her heart, which was beating ninety miles per hour. "I'm all finished." Sasha let the woman know the bathroom was all hers.

The woman stood.

Not wanting to be a hater, Sasha thought she'd compliment the woman before she made her way back outside the room and rejoined Casey. "You killed it out there tonight. I mean, girlfriend, you worked it."

Without saying a single word, the woman walked over to an intercom box on the wall. Sasha stood confused as she watched the woman play with the dial. Sasha practically jumped out of her skin when a slow tune wailed out of the box. Before Sasha could say or do anything, she stood and watched as the woman sashayed over to her. She stood in front of Sasha and began slow winding her body. She repeated some of the exact same dances Sasha had just seen her perform on stage, still in full costume, masquerade mask and all.

"Oh, okay then," Sasha said, not knowing what to do.

The woman began to circle Sasha before she stopped right behind Sasha. She wasn't touching Sasha, but she was close enough that Sasha could feel the dancer's body heat. All sorts of words and thoughts danced around in Sasha's head. Should she tell this woman to go on somewhere? Should she tell her she didn't get down like that; that she was only there because a friend had brought her to the club? What to do? What not to do?

"Uhh, so, uhh," Sasha stammered as the dancer made her way back in front of Sasha.

The next thing Sasha knew, the woman had bent over and was shaking her rump, then she did a quick split to the floor. A thump could be heard even over the music.

Sasha turned in her knees tight and covered her

own womanhood, just imagining how it had to have hurt to drop it like it was hot. But the woman was not fazed as she picked it right back up again and began twerking.

At this point Sasha couldn't do anything but start looking around the room for some hidden cameras. No way was this really happening to her. What the hell had Casey given her to drink to make her hallucinate like this? It was time to get the hell up out of here.

"Look," Sasha said, "I know this is how you pay your bills, and I am not mad at you." Sasha dug into her clutch. "I don't know how much a trip to the Champagne room usually costs, but a sistah was just trying to go take a pee." She pulled out a twenty-dollar bill. "But here's a twenty for your efforts."

The woman shook her head, refusing to accept Sasha's money. "It's paid for already," she said softly and seductively.

"Huh? What?" Had Sasha really just heard this woman right? "Paid for? But I didn't—" Sasha's words trailed off as a lightbulb went off in her head. "Casey's VIP treatment." The lightbulb in Sasha's head was not purple, though. It was red!

Upon hearing Sasha's last comment, the woman nodded and smiled. She then took Sasha by the hand and escorted her over to the couch. More like dragged her, because Sasha was not a willing participant. She was fine watching a dancer flip on the pole, but a lap dance was a little much.

"Whoa, hold up. Wait a minute. I'm sorry, but . . ." Sasha's words trailed off as she tried her best to keep her feet planted on the floor. She stayed in shape and all, but she was no match for the stallion. The next thing Sasha knew, the woman had sat her on the couch and stood in front of her as she began to remove feathers and shoes and stuff. Everything but her mask.

Every time Sasha tried to get up, the woman seductively pushed her back. Sasha tried to chuckle it off, but now she was getting pissed.

"Excuse me!" Sasha didn't want to read this broad and go toe-to-toe, but she wasn't about to get raped in this VIP room. This was not *Law and Order SVU: Atlanta Edition*. Before Sasha could say another word, the woman removed the mask from her face. There was no longer mystery behind her eyes. Any words Sasha was going to speak were now caught in her throat. But finally one word was able to escape.

"Paris?"

"Duh!" Paris said, then walked over to the intercom and turned the music off. "Child, I told Casey you would be too uptight for this to work out." She wiped her hand across her forehead, glad to have that itchy mask off of her face.

"Casey," Sasha said, sitting on the couch shaking her head in disbelief. "That girl set this whole"— she raised her arms and then let them drop— "thing up?"

"It was supposed to be fun. You were supposed to let your hair down, relax and enjoy yourself," Paris said, flopping down on the couch next to Sasha. "But I'm so glad you didn't." She lifted her leg and began removing her stiletto pump. "Child, my dogs are killing me." Paris began rubbing her feet. Sasha guessed they had to be about size eleven.

Sasha just sat there watching Paris, not quite

sure what she should say about all this. This situation was both weird and awkward. But something did pop into her mind. "You said you weren't a stripper."

"Huh?" Paris asked, so engaged in rubbing her feet down that she hadn't quite heard Sasha's comment.

"At the charity fund-raiser, you told me you weren't a stripper." Sasha didn't like being lied to, so she wanted to get to the bottom of what this woman's issue was.

"I'm not a stripper. Honey, I'm a dancer," Paris clarified. "That down there," she pointed her finger downward, "is art. And on top of that, it's work. And I get paid whether these cheap-ass niggas who only wanna give a bitch a dollar for doing backflips do so or not. Tips is just extra on top of what the club pays me to perform. Strippers live off of tips and drink money. You feel me?"

Sasha didn't reply. She gave Paris a slow smile, hoping her expression wouldn't give her thoughts away. She didn't feel Paris, not one hundred percent anyway, but if she was going to be running into her everywhere she went, she was going to have to find a way to play along. Maybe dancing in this club was not what Paris ultimately wanted to do for a living, but it was what provided the seeds to plant the dream and get it growing. After all, that's what Sasha's job at the law firm was to her: just a stepping stone. Sasha could feel a girl who was working to get ahead.

That last thought alone changed Sasha's entire perspective on Paris's situation. "You know what? I do feel you," Sasha said, surprising herself that her opinion had shifted just that quickly. Rightfully so.

Sometimes women had to do what they had to do to get things popping off. Too bad Paris didn't own her truth, though, because at the end of the day, that girl was a stripper.

"Ladies," said a voice coming from the door.

Both Paris and Sasha looked to see Casey stumbling through the doorway.

Casey was snapping her fingers, wiggling her body, and had the hugest smile on her face. Once she looked at Paris and Sasha sitting over on the couch like two duds, she instinctively got the boo-boo face. She threw her hands on her hips. "Hey, I came to see how my little surprise private party turned out, but this don't look like no party. What's going on?"

"Girl, I told you it was too soon," Paris said. "You gotta break her type in slowly." Paris nodded to Sasha.

"Break? Who gives a lap dance in a damn bathroom?" Sasha questioned, snapping her neck back. "And my type would be?"

"The type that takes life so serious . . . all the time," Paris shot back. "Why? I don't know, because nobody ever makes it out alive anyway, so just chill. Besides, you are a long way from home. Don't nobody know you here. It was just going to be a dance. I wasn't trying to get with you or anything. Hell, I dance for anybody for a dollar. It just so happens that Casey paid a hundred of 'em." She laughed. "It was a freebie for you," Paris said to Sasha. "So just turn up."

There was that "turn up" crap again. First Casey had said it and now Paris. Was that really all the people in Atlanta were about? Turning up? Drinking? Clubbing? Sasha could only handle so much!

"Look, ladies," Sasha said, pushing herself up from the couch, "I appreciate you two trying to show me a good time in Atlanta. I just wasn't expecting all this." Sasha raised her hands. "Or that." She pointed to Paris, who rolled her eyes and sucked her teeth. "Perhaps I'm not the right one for this little threesome."

"Did somebody say threesome?"

All eyes were once again at the doorway, but this time it was Eric entering, snapping his fingers and dancing a jig.

"Oh, Lord, you in on it, too?" Sasha asked Eric. Suddenly a weird feeling took over Sasha. Things were starting to feel less and less like a girls' night out and more and more like the freaks come out at night. "Somebody tell me what's really going on?" Sasha spat, standing from the couch.

Eric frowned as he looked to Casey. Casey slightly shook her head. Eric cleared his throat and clasped his hands together. "What?" he said to Sasha. "We were just giving you a warm ATL welcome. They don't do it like this back in Ohio?" he asked, surprised.

"Actually, they don't," Sasha confirmed. "But just so that we all have a clear understanding, just what is it that y'all do here in ATL, or were about to do?"

Paris, Casey, and Eric gave each other quick looks, communicating something Sasha couldn't quite pick up on. Finally, Casey stepped in, taking Sasha by the arm.

"Nothing, we just wanted to have a little fun," Casey said, as she led Sasha to the door. "Sometimes we can be over the top, if you haven't noticed."

"Oh, I've noticed," Sasha confirmed. Even right

down to Norman, everyone she seemed to be-
friend was over the top in some form or fashion.
Perhaps she would have to ultimately get with the
program, but it wouldn't be tonight. Too much
had happened in too little time and none of it left
a good taste in Sasha's mouth. But she wasn't going
to hold it against them. After all, she couldn't fault
them for wanting to show her a good time, and she
had had fun, up to the bathroom ambush. They
were all still in the getting to know one another
phase. She'd give them time and about two more
chances to get it right. But since she didn't see
them being able to right tonight's wrong, she said,
"I hate to call it a night so early—"

"Then don't," Casey pleaded. "Come on, you
came out for a girls' night out with me and Paris,
so let's have one. Come on." Casey put her hands
up in the air in surrender. "No more surprises. I
promise."

Paris let out a huff. "Well, while Laverne and
Shirley figure it all out, I'm 'bout to go back downstairs and make me some money." With one shoe
in hand and one shoe on her foot, Paris limped
over to the door. "I'll be up to hang with y'all after
my set." She looked back at Sasha. "We good?"

"Oh, absolutely," Sasha assured her. "You were
just doing your job, which apparently involves ac-
costing people while they're peeing. Now go on
and strip . . . I mean dance," Sasha said, correcting
herself.

"Humpf, not afraid to throw a little bit of shade,
I see," Paris said. She then looked at Casey. "I like
her." She slipped on her other shoe and then extended her elbow to Eric. "Come on, boss, escort
me downstairs."

"My pleasure." Eric kissed his wife good-bye on the cheek, nodded at Sasha, and then left the room with Paris on his arm.

After watching them take a few steps, Sasha turned to Casey and said, "Boss. Really? Your man owns this place?" That would explain the VIP treatment for sure.

"Something like that," Casey said. "He has an image to uphold. He's a role model to the youth, you know. What would it look like him owning a place like this?"

Casey winked, took Sasha by the arm, and escorted her back to the VIP section. Sasha couldn't get past the fact that Eric owned this sex circus, Paris was one of the performers, and Casey was the ringmaster. Sasha wondered why Casey and Eric had the club when Eric made plenty of money playing basketball. What if someone found out and sold the story? Why risk their reputation? Maybe Sasha should consider finding herself some new friends; she didn't want to get dragged through the mud with Casey and Eric if anything came out.

Suddenly the words of Sasha's friend's warning back home popped into her head. *You'll be running back home to be with all your friends, because I don't see you making any new ones down there. You'll never fit in.*

Sasha would do anything not to let those words ring true, even if it meant getting caught up in a life that had never been part of her life plan. Sasha enjoyed partying, and she had fun with Casey. Maybe she could take on the friendship in moderation, whether it fit into her business plans or not. Like they say, some of the best things in life are those that are unplanned . . . and unexpected.

Chapter 7

Come Monday morning, there was a chill between Casey and Sasha as they stood in the break room. Even though the room wasn't any larger than fifty square feet, it was as if they were an acre apart. They could see specs of each other, but nothing was in full view because neither woman would hold her eyes on the other long enough to get a complete visual.

Sasha hadn't talked to Casey since she'd left the club at around one in the morning. Sasha rode home in the limo alone, Casey opting to stay at the club with her husband and Paris. The last time Sasha had seen Casey, she was so far gone off that liquid courage that she probably had slept until her alarm clock woke her up this morning for work.

"Hey," Casey said to Sasha while sipping her coffee, avoiding all eye contact with Sasha.

Whether that thing going on between them was mutual awkwardness, Sasha didn't know. She could only speak for herself, and things felt awkward as hell for her. When she had left the club, she had insisted everything was all good. Casey had mirrored the same sentiments. But Sasha wondered now, since Casey had no alcohol in her system and had let the situation marinate, if she still felt the same way.

"Hey, yourself," Sasha said, clearly noticing how Casey was avoiding looking at her. Any other day Casey might have given Sasha the once-over, then complimented her on her outfit, but not today. Sasha hated that evidently things had already changed between the two of them.

Sasha had really liked Casey, too. Casey had never done anything to Sasha to make her feel any other way about her. Of course Sasha sensed that some ole freaky-deaky was going on with her and the mister, but that was their private business. Granted, Sasha couldn't remove the fact that if she'd stayed in that Champagne room five more minutes, they would have made it her business. When Eric had entered the room, the way he was licking his chops and practically salivating had not gone unnoticed by Sasha. If Sasha had to guess, he wanted to show her a good time all right. Either that or he wanted to see her having a good time. Voyeurism was a possibility. But then again, both he and Casey were pretty buzzed. Alcohol is known to be somewhat of an aphrodisiac. But something told Sasha that it didn't take much gin to get them to engage in some out-of-the-box sexual experiences. After all, look at the club he owned . . . and Casey brought her friends to.

Sasha wasn't tripping over the whole strip club thing. She'd personally never had a lap dance before and wasn't into that type of thing, especially from another female. But different strokes for different folks. She was certain there were some things in life she had done that others wouldn't.

She had tried not to appear as though she was lame and enjoy the night. But that didn't mean she wanted Paris to give her a lap dance. Sasha wasn't a square. She'd been out. She'd seen girlfriends get drunk and dance on each other. But Paris wasn't her girlfriend, no matter how one decided to define it. The fact that Casey had been coming from a good place and that it had all been in fun is what allowed Sasha to brush it off. The two women were just getting to know each other. They'd learn each other's ways, personalities, and definition of fun soon enough. Even though Casey had taken Sasha way out of her element, she still wanted to form a friendship with her. For one, her friend's words stayed settled on her mind. For two, she was in a new town where they did things differently than what she was used to. This was normal here. She was normal, right? Being taken out of one's element didn't necessarily have to be a bad thing unless Sasha insisted on seeing it that way. In this particular case, Sasha wanted the glass to be half full.

With that thought in mind, Sasha decided to cut the tension in the air and just act like her usual self.

"I'm glad to see you here this morning. The last time I laid eyes on you, you were standing on the table with a drink in each hand shaking it up as if you were the feature act." Sasha laughed. "You sure do know how to have a good time." Sasha patted Casey on the shoulder as she walked over and grabbed a mug.

"For real?" Casey said, a smile forming on her lips. "You're . . . you're not mad at me?"

Sasha turned to face Casey before she poured herself a cup of coffee. "Mad at what?" Sasha faced the pot and poured herself a cup. "I can honestly say that that was the most exciting ladies' night out I've had in all my life." And Sasha wasn't lying about that the least bit.

"Oh, good." Casey exhaled and visibly relaxed into her usual self. She then walked up behind Sasha and hugged her.

Sasha was a little taken aback. She wasn't expecting all that. Besides, Sasha wasn't really the huggy-feely type. She forced a smile on her face then finished preparing her coffee after Casey released her.

"I was so worried," Casey said. "That's why I didn't call you over the weekend. I thought you were gonna cuss me out." Casey laughed. "But Eric was right. He said you seem like a genuine chick and that if you were pissed, you would have let it be known."

"Well, your husband is a good judge of character. That's exactly how I roll. If I have an issue with you, then you are the person I'm going to speak on the issue with and I'll have no problem telling you about it to your face. So if I say we're good, then we're good. And you and I," Sasha said before taking a sip of her coffee, "are good." Sasha meant every word.

"I guess I should have listened to my husband. I worried all weekend for nothing," Casey said. "But that still doesn't keep me from wanting to go ahead with my little makeup get-together."

"Makeup get-together? Oh, Lord." Sasha rolled her eyes. "What in the world is a makeup get-together? Does it involve Mary Kay cosmetics or something?"

Casey laughed as another fellow employee entered the break area. Both Casey and Sasha greeted the coworker, but that was their cue to walk and talk back to their respective desks.

"But anyway," Casey continued. "Like I said, I thought you were mad at me, so I wanted to make it up to you with a little makeup get-together in your honor. Not makeup as in cosmetics, but makeup as in—"

"I get it, I get it." Sasha nodded. "But there's no reason for us to make up. No harm, no foul. I told you we're—"

"Good." This time it was Casey who cut Sasha off. "I know, I know. But let me do this. It will be a more mellow type of experience. Something I think is more up your alley. Just give me the chance to get it right this time. Plus, I want you to see that I'm not always the buck-wild chick you saw the other night. I know how to turn it down and keep it classy."

Sasha was looking doubtful. It wasn't that she didn't trust Casey. Casey had presented herself as nothing but classy up until the other night. Even then Sasha didn't hold that against her. Now if she acted all rah-rah up in the workplace, that would have been a different story. But she'd been out in a nightclub. She was supposed to be able to let her hair down. Sasha just prayed that next time she didn't pull a Britney Spears and get it all shaved off.

"Come on," Casey pleaded. "Nothing big. It will be at my house. Just a few of my husband's and my friends."

"Hmm, well," Sasha thought out loud.

"Pretty please, that way I'll know for sure we're good." Casey batted her lashes.

"Why are you standing there looking like you are trying to get your husband to purchase you a Birkin bag or something?" Sasha laughed while Casey held her pleading position, now even clasping her hands in prayer mode.

"Oh, alright," Sasha gave in. "But no lap dances." She pointed an accusing finger at Casey.

"Scout's honor." Casey held up her right hand and saluted.

The two chuckled.

"I'll text you everything," Casey assured Sasha.

"Okay, girl," Sasha said as she started walking in one direction and Casey in another.

"I promise. Just a little happy hour at my house," Casey threw in for good measure.

Sasha raised her hand to let Casey know she could quit pleading her case. She was accepting the invite. Besides, what could possibly happen in Casey's living room with just a few of her and her husband's friends?

Her husband. That thought made Sasha stop in her tracks. She couldn't help but remember when she'd replayed the entire night to Norman how he'd acted when he found out that Eric had shown up on the scene at their ladies' night out. Norman had thought the whole evening had been comical, up until the part about Eric popping up. That seemed to have made Norman a tad uneasy. Although he didn't just come right out and say anything negative about Eric, Norman's entire demeanor and attitude had shifted and he began questioning Sasha about Eric's presence. He asked her why he was there, and not with a turned-up nose, but with concerned eyes. That in itself concerned Sasha to some degree. Not enough to really speak on it and drum up something that really wasn't there.

Besides, even though she hadn't known Norman that long and vice versa, she couldn't see him allowing her to put herself in a position that would cause her any arm. On top of that, from what Sasha had seen from Eric, he came across as a pretty cool dude. Harmless. But still, there was just something about Norman's reaction that gave her pause . . . or maybe just made her curious.

"You okay?" one of the paralegals asked Sasha, seeing her standing in the middle of the hallway.

Sasha shook herself out of her daze. "Oh, uh, yeah. I'm fine," she assured the paralegal, then made her way to her desk while taking a sip of her coffee.

A few minutes later Sasha received the text, as promised, from Casey. The gathering was to be this upcoming Thursday, 6:30 p.m. at Casey's house.

Eric and I can't wait to see you again were the words that ended the text.

Sasha couldn't explain why, but all of a sudden a part of her wished she hadn't agreed to attend the gathering. A part of her wanted to take heed of Norman's unspoken warning, urged her to text back, telling Casey she couldn't make it. Then there was the part of her that killed the cat every time: curiosity. So without pondering over it any longer, she replied back to Casey.

I'M THERE!

Hopefully she'd made the right decision. The last thing she needed was one more "I told you so," from Norman or a final *meow* from the curious cat.

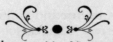

Sasha sat on the stool by Norman's clothing rack waiting in anticipation. Her knee was bouncing while her intertwined fingers tapped her knuckles.

"Chile, will you relax? She's going to love it. Trust me," Norman said. "When I came over to your house and saw you working on it, I knew exactly which one of my clients would slay in it!" Norman snapped his fingers.

Sasha had finally finished the jumpsuit she'd been working on. She couldn't believe one of Norman's clients was trying it on. Sasha prayed the woman liked it. Norman hadn't told his client that the actual designer was sitting right there with them, so Sasha knew that the woman's opinion was going to be genuine.

The curtain that enclosed the dressing area in Norman's in-home studio opened.

"Oh, my God! I just love this little jumpsuit number right here!"

Norman's client, Jessica, spun out of the dressing area and to the front of the full-length mirror like the Tasmanian devil.

"This fabric." Jessica fingered the soft, silky fabric. "It's so light, comfy, and carefree."

"And with these right here." Norman held up a pair of six inch stilettoes that only someone with Jessica's shorter than average height could pull off and not look like an Amazon.

Jessica grabbed the gold strappy shoes from Norman's hands. "Yasss!" she exclaimed. "That's it. I don't even need to try on anything else. This is what I'm wearing to the class reunion." She set the shoes down next to her and continued admiring herself in the mirror. "I'll take it."

Norman looked to Sasha with saucer eyes and a pleased look on his face.

"Yes!" Sasha lipped to him.

Norman in turn lipped, "I told you." He then continued fussing over Jessica.

"I have a standing lunch appointment with my mother," Jessica said, "so, Norman, can you ring this up for me?" She headed back into the dressing area. "Oh, wait." She stopped in her tracks. "How much is it?"

Norman looked stumped and Sasha knew why. When he'd asked her to allow him to present the piece to his client, the two had never discussed the cost.

"You know what? Never mind." Jessica shooed her hand and pulled the curtain closed. She then said through the curtain, "If you have to ask, then you don't need it. And I need this jumpsuit in my life, yes, Lord."

Sasha pumped both fists in the air. She could not believe this. She'd been in Atlanta all of three months and had already made a sale. She'd lived in Ohio all of her life and not one person had ever purchased anything from her. Oh, she'd made items for others before, but no one had offered to pay her. They may have purchased the material and supplies needed, but Sasha had never been paid for her services. She'd never sold one of her pieces and been paid.

"Thank you so much, Norman." Sasha stood from the stool and threw her arms around Norman's neck. "You have no idea how grateful I am to you."

"Chile, it ain't nothing," he said. "Besides, I should be the one thanking you." He then leaned in and whispered, "You cut that crotch area of that jumper just right. Ever since Jessica got her dick removed, it's been a bitch finding the right cut that doesn't make her look like she still has one."

Sasha's mouth about dropped to the floor.

"I know, right," Norman said, in an even lower whisper than before. "Trust me, I was sick, shocked, and depressed all at the same time. I mean, you should have seen that dick." Norman spread his hands a foot a part. "Girl, I begged her ass to ask the doctor could I have it."

"Ewww, Norman," Sasha said, scrunching her face up.

"Girl, not for that," Norman said. "I was gon' bronze that shit. But instead we had to have a funeral for it. May the biggest dick I've ever seen in my life rest in peace." Norman then turned toward his register. "How much you charging for that thang?" He went on back to business as usual.

All Sasha could do was shake her head while saying, "Priceless." Not the jumpsuit, not the moment, but Norman. He was indeed priceless.

Chapter 8

Walking into Casey's home, for Sasha, was like walking into the mansion where the charity event had been held all over again. She almost felt like her little Honda brought down the property value by being parked in their driveway. Even upon pulling up into the circular driveway, it looked more like an all-inclusive resort in Cancun, thanks to the Mexican-style stucco accent. Not to mention the beautiful landscaping. Sasha felt like she had driven to a small, private island somewhere, and not just because the drive from Sasha's place to Casey's was about an hour. Sasha had already learned that nothing in Atlanta was close; there were so many suburbs and sections of town. Come on, two downtowns? Never mind that one was referred to as Midtown. It was two downtowns as far as Sasha was concerned. From the look of things, Casey and Eric even had a town of their own.

After ringing the doorbell, Sasha was greeted by

the housekeeper, who was dressed in the typical black-and-white uniform.

"Sasha?" the housekeeper said with a Spanish accent.

Sasha nodded, surprised the housekeeper knew who she was. "Yes."

"The others are expecting you." She smiled and moved to the side so that Sasha could enter.

This must have meant that Sasha was the last one to arrive. How else would the housekeeper have known who she was? As the housekeeper closed the door and then led Sasha through the foyer and into the sitting area, she hoped the other guests didn't take her for a diva attempting to be fashionably late. It was only 6:45. So she'd gotten turned around a couple times. Hopefully everyone would understand that she was still new in town and had to learn the city. Or in this case, the island, because this joint was in the boondocks for real.

"Sasha, you made it," Casey greeted as she walked over to meet Sasha at the entry of the room. "I was just about to call you to make sure you weren't lost or anything." Casey gave Sasha a hug. When she pulled away, she gave her the once-over. "Oooh, look at you. What's that? Donna Karan?" She pointed her index finger up and down the length of Sasha's body.

"Actually it is." Sasha smiled. Norman had been right insisting that she borrow a Donna Karan original that had been created specifically for one of the clients he was working with.

Sasha had never even been one to borrow her best friend's clothes when she was growing up, let alone borrow a stranger's outfit. But Norman had convinced her that she really wasn't borrowing. In fact, the celebrity client had not even worn it yet. Sasha's body would be the first the suit hugged.

"Besides, celebrities borrow stuff all the time to wear on the red carpet," Norman had added to make Sasha feel even more comfortable about wearing the suit. "Just don't let anything happen to it. You fuck up the dress, then you're fucked."

"Me?" Sasha said. "But you're the one who is responsible for the safekeeping of your garments."

"True, but in the court of law, I will lie like O. J. and say you stole it off my rack when I turned my back." He pointed to his serious facial expression. "Straight face like O. J. You know I'll do it. I'll be in the courtroom like Johnnie Cochran talking about, 'If the suit fit, that bitch did that shit.'"

Sasha laughed so hard she got a cramp in her stomach.

"Oh, you go ahead and laugh, but mess up that dress and watch an Oscar performance of a lifetime. I will throw you under the bus and roll over you twice before I mess up my reputation in this business. Folks gotta know their stuff is safe with me."

"Then if it's all like that, maybe I shouldn't borrow it." Sasha had intended on wearing one of her own pieces in the first place. Sasha's aesthetic wasn't formal, though. It was dinnerwear, after-five, and Kentucky Derby, but not red carpet, which is what Norman had insisted she wear. She valued Norman's advice.

"Trust me, hunty, you are going to the Cortzes'. I don't care if the only guest there is Stevie Wonder, you better go looking your best in the top-of-the-line, latest high-end fashion. Betchu that bitch Casey gon' be snatched." He snatched the air and snapped his fingers. "I have a saying," Norman continued. "I don't care whose castle it is, you make sure you are the belle of the ball."

Norman hadn't steered Sasha wrong to date, so she couldn't see why he would start now. The way Casey's eyes lit up as she walked around admiring every inch of the Donna Karan suit, Norman had not yet been made out to be a liar.

"Sasha, you are wearing the hell out of this suit," Casey said. "If you weren't six feet tall, I'd have to borrow it myself." She laughed.

"Thank you," Sasha said, definitely feeling as if she'd made Casey proud, not that she was a people pleaser. She had to admit, though, Norman was indeed right. It did feel good being the belle of the ball in someone else's castle. She looked around the grand room with its vaulted ceilings.

"Come on. There's someone I want you to meet." Casey grabbed Sasha's hand and pulled her over to the sitting area where there were two gentlemen.

Sasha looked around slightly puzzled. Where was everyone else? From the way the housekeeper made it sound, all the guests had already arrived. Sasha quickly thought back to whether there had been any other cars in the driveway. She had been so mesmerized by the beautiful home that she hadn't paid much attention. There may have been one or two cars parked out front. She wasn't sure.

Sasha tried to listen to see if maybe there was the sound of music or chatter coming from another area of the house. Maybe that was where the real action was going on, but she heard nothing. Casey had said it was just going to be a small get-together, but as Sasha noticed the candles lit throughout the room, she realized there was a dif-

ference between a small get-together and an intimate one. And this looked more intimate.

Once the two gentlemen saw Casey and Sasha
approaching, they stood.

"Sasha," Eric greeted, extending his hand.

"Good to see you again, Eric," Sasha said as he
leaned in and kissed her on the cheek.

Eric looked rather lavish in his deep royal blue
suede cigar jacket. "It's always a pleasure to see
you." Eric then turned to the gentleman standing
next to him. "And this here is my boy, Terrance."

Sasha looked over at the larger-than-life being
that stood next to Eric. Eric was a nice size guy,
being a tall guard on a basketball team. But dude
next to him looked like he could break Eric in
half. If it was true that muscle weighed more than
fat, ole boy was tipping the scales.

"Sasha, this is my teammate and best friend, Terrance," Eric introduced. "Terrance—"

"Sasha," Terrance said, cutting off Eric. He extended his hand.

Sasha took note of how he'd taken over the introduction. He didn't need another man doing
for him what he could do himself.

"I've heard quite a bit about you," the tall, dark
cocoa man with a neat and freshly trimmed goatee
continued.

Sasha slowly slid her hand into his. He lifted it
to his mouth and placed a soft kiss on it, staring at
her the entire time, not even blinking.

Once upon a time Sasha would have been turned
off by his intensity. Some wanna-be Idris Elba guy
had performed this same scene back in Ohio once,
leaving his disgusting slobber on Sasha's hand. She

supposed it was his way of showing her what he could do to her lower set of lips if given the chance. She didn't want his big, crusty lips on any parts of her body. There was nothing attractive about a man with crusty lips. Malik Yoba might have had a tad of ash on his in some of the episodes of *Empire*, but he was fine, classy, tranquil, and elegant. The fool who had tried to play smooth operator with Sasha had reminded her of Jerome from *Martin*. He had been trying way too hard and his tactic didn't come off as natural at all. There had been nothing genuine or smooth about this kiss. But this Terrance guy, he was no Jerome or Malik Yoba. As a matter of fact, with a quick once-over, once Sasha was able to pull herself away from his hypnotizing eyes, she saw he was unlike any man she had ever met before.

"It's good to see you again," Terrance said, letting go of Sasha's hand.

She looked down at her hand, which had definitely just been kissed by a prince rather than a frog. Perhaps Sasha was coming to this conclusion a little too fast. She'd only been around him all of one minute. But he just came across so natural, not as if he was trying too hard, but hardly trying.

Sasha rubbed the back of her hand. It was dry. Yes! She wouldn't have to worry about excusing herself to hurry up and get his saliva off of her hand before it dried up and left a breath odor.

"And you look just as stunning as you did the first time I saw you." Now it was Terrance who was giving Sasha the once-over.

"Well, thank you," Sasha started, trying not to blush, her eyes smizing—the term Tyra Banks coined, which meant smiling with one's eyes—at this handsome fellow in front of her. She was able to come up for air out of his compliment just long enough to realize what he'd said. "Have we met before?" Sasha asked in a confused tone.

"He was at the charity event," Eric interrupted.

Sasha thought back long and hard. She didn't recall seeing him at the event, let alone being introduced to him. He was not easy to forget. Unless someone had slipped something in one of her drinks that erased from her memory portions of that evening, there was no way she had met him and didn't remember.

"I remember you introducing me to Paris," Sasha said to Eric, "but not Terrance."

Even though Sasha was looking at Eric, through her peripheral vision she saw how quickly Terrance's head shot in Eric's direction. Sasha looked to Terrance to see him giving Eric a look as if he couldn't believe his friend had introduced a woman like Sasha to a woman like Paris. Sasha had to admit that she felt flattered. See, Sasha never had to think she was too good or better than folks when she had other people who thought it for her. Sasha was humbled that it was obvious she came from good stock.

"That's because I didn't introduce you to Terrance," Eric replied to Sasha. He turned to Terrance, giving him the opportunity to take over the conversation.

Realizing Eric was waiting on him to speak, Terrance turned and said to Sasha, "I asked him who you were once I saw you heading out. Eric offered to make the introductions, but I figured since I hadn't been able to get you to notice me earlier that night, I definitely wasn't going to get you to say hello."

Sasha smiled, even though she had no idea what this man was talking about.

Noticing Sasha's confusion, Terrance clarified. "When you entered the party, you walked in. You were looking right at me, or so I thought. I waved, but you just kept it moving."

"Oh, no," Sasha said. "I promise I must not have noticed you."

"Ohhh, man." Terrance grimaced, grabbing his gut as if Sasha had just punched him in it.

"Oh, no, I didn't mean it like that." Sasha grabbed his hands to get him to stop overreacting. "It's just that I was feeling out the space we were in. The place was fabulous and had all of my attention. I'm so sorry. I would have never been so rude as to completely ignore someone trying to greet me." She let go of his hands and her eyes begged for him to believe her. She remembered Paris saying that when she first met Sasha she thought she was going to be all stuck-up and funny acting. That's the last thing Sasha wanted anybody to think about her, especially this man. She wasn't desperate, she wasn't dying to get people to like her or to be accepted into the in-crowd, but she wasn't a rude bitch, either.

"I was just joking, I know what you meant." Terrance laughed.

"Well," Casey said, "now that you both clearly acknowledged one another,"—she looked to Sasha—"Sasha, this is Terrance." She then looked to Terrance. "Terrance, this is Sasha."

"Nice to meet you, Terrance," Sasha said with a nod.

"Same here," Terrance said, returning the nod.

For the next few seconds the two just stood there, then Casey jumped in.

"Well, dinner should be served in a few," Casey said. "Sasha, come over to the bar with me and let's get you a drink." Casey looped her arm through Sasha's. "We'll be back, fellas," she said to the men, and then led Sasha over to the bar area.

Who the hell was that man, Sasha couldn't help but ask herself. She knew his name was Terrance. She knew he was Eric's best friend, but that's all she knew. Eric and Casey seemed like decent people, but might have had a little world of their own that they lived in. Was Terrance, perhaps, a part of that world? Not knowing the answer to that, Sasha didn't know if she should play it safe and keep her distance, or get to know this man, who clearly, by the way he looked into her eyes while kissing her hand, wanted to get to know her.

Meow was the only answer Sasha could hear in her head. And trust, that sound wasn't coming from the curious cat.

Chapter 9

"You really didn't have to walk me to my car," Sasha told Terrance as they made their way down Casey and Eric's walkway. Her mouth said it, but deep inside, she was oh so glad he'd offered to walk her to her car. That gave her a couple more moments in his presence. His conversation inside the house had been simply delightful. He didn't come off as some Simple Simon jock, but instead had dreams and goals beyond just hoop dreams. He'd shared with Sasha how he was taking a couple online marketing, accounting, and investment courses. After she shared her dream of opening up her own boutique, he even offered her some tips. He was dropping so many nuggets about entrepreneurship and investing in one's own business that at one point, Sasha pulled up the memo feature on her phone and actually took notes.

Sasha was quickly drawn in by his intellect. Even if he was just trying to impress her, she still appreciated that. And anybody who had the knowledge to help her get closer to accomplishing her goals, she was all for it.

Terrance could have just as easily sat back as if she was supposed to fall at his feet. But no, he realized Sasha was the kind of girl he had to work for. She was glad to know he recognized that.

Sasha could see that he was a successful go-getter who still wasn't satisfied, instead wanting and striving for more. This was evident when he shared how even though he played pro ball, he had other career ambitions. As a matter of fact, he'd already flipped five houses, doubling the money he'd originally invested in them.

She never expected to be bitten by the attraction bug so hard. Terrance was fine indeed, but it was his mind that had her tipsy with fascination. She'd seen tons of handsome men during her tenure in the ATL, but there was something about Terrance that simply captivated her. He'd been the first and only man, in Ohio or Atlanta, to take her mind off business for more than five minutes and allow her to dabble into just a pinch of pleasure. They'd talked a little business while getting to know each other, but even staring into his eyes while he shared his wisdom, for Sasha, was pleasure.

"Oh, but I did have to walk you to your car," Terrance said. "That's how my momma raised me. My mother told me what she expected of a man, and my father showed me what was expected of a man."

Sasha's eyes widened and her heart danced a little jig. But she didn't want to get ahead of herself so she asked, "Are your parents still together?"

"Yep, going strong after being together for thirty years."

"Oh, wow. That's amazing!" Sasha said, and she meant it . . . in more ways than one. Although finding a man, let alone a husband, had been the last thing on Sasha's mind, like everything else in her life, it didn't mean that she hadn't planned it all out. And one of the things on her list of marriage material was a man who had been raised by both parents and that, God willing, his parents were still together to this day. "I didn't have too many friends coming up who were raised in two-parent homes, including myself." Sasha began removing her keys from her clutch as they approached her car.

"Yeah, my household was like a rare gem, especially in the hood," Terrance replied. "When my friends came to my house and saw my dad, they looked at him like he was an alien or some type of foreign object." He chuckled. "Their eyes would be all bucked. They'd walk up to him and be like, 'Can I touch him?'" He reached out as if he was going to touch Sasha's arm. "'Is he real? Is it a real live . . . fa . . . fa . . . father.'" He laughed. "They could hardly say the word."

Sasha chimed in with laughter of her own. "Stop it. You wrong for that." Her laughter ceased. "I know you play basketball, but I didn't know you were a comedian also." Sasha stopped once they approached her car.

"Yeah, well, there are a lot of things about me that you don't know."

He said the words with a hint of mystery in his eyes, enticing Sasha to find out more.

Terrance removed a strand of Sasha's hair that the slight evening breeze had blown onto her cheek.

"But prayerfully, all that is about to change." He stood looking into Sasha's eyes.

Sasha was still stuck on the fact that he'd said the word "prayerfully." Bingo! That was another check on her list: a man who loved the Lord. He could have said any other word. He could have said "hopefully." But no, he'd said "prayerfully." Was it possible that God was about to interrupt her own life plans so that she could start living the one He had in store for her?

"And just how would all of that change? Me not knowing things about you?" Sasha played coy.

"It would change by you agreeing to go out with me," Terrance said. He waited on her response, still looking her dead in her eyes.

A man who was direct and to the point. A man who knew what he wanted. A man who didn't waver and could look at things straight on. Check, check, and check!

"Well, I don't recall you asking me out." Sasha was usually forward and straight to the point as well, but she had to admit that she was indeed enjoying this little game of cat and mouse. She wanted to play a little longer, which was also out of character for her. She recalled Casey having said one time that dealing with a baller can bring a woman out of her usual character. Was this what Casey had meant by the words? For Sasha, being out of character didn't feel so bad.

Terrance took Sasha's hands into his. "Miss Lady, would you be ever so gracious as to allow me to indulge in your company by donating just a couple hours of your time to a common folk like myself?"

Sasha giggled and blushed. Who was this girl

and where the hell had she come from? Sasha was usually in serious mode. Although she didn't feel the need to party and have fun 24/7, she did crave happiness and contentment. Fun was temporary. Happiness was the real deal. But right now, even though living happily ever after with a husband and a couple of crumb snatchers was way down low on the totem pole, it still was part of her goals.

"Well," Terrance said, "will you go out with me?"

Terrance might as well have been asking Sasha to marry him as far as Sasha was concerned. That's what it felt like to her. She wasn't into the dating thing to the point where she'd have to juggle multiple men, and then eliminate them according to her man checklist. She didn't have time for that, and she especially didn't have time to waste. Just last week she'd attended a free three-evening seminar put on by a nonprofit organization with a mission to create more minority business owners. It focused on the different aspects of real estate such as leasing property versus buying land and building. There was a focus on budgeting for remodeling, upgrades, or moving into a turn-key business. That's something she could have missed out on if she was more into dating than preparing for her future. So going out on a date wasn't to be taken too lightly in her world.

"You know what, never mind." Terrance released Sasha's hand. "Don't go out with me."

Sasha swallowed the lump in her throat. The one in her stomach felt like a rotten apple with worms residing in it. Chills ran through her body. Her blood felt like it was draining to her feet and her heart started pumping quite a few beats more per minute than usual. Was this what rejection felt like?

"Just meet me out," Terrance suggested instead. "Somewhere casual, public; you know, like two friends would do." He leaned into Sasha. "'Cause I really do need a friend in my life right now."

Terrance had to have been placed strategically in Sasha's life, and not just by Casey and Eric. This was divine. Sasha always said that her future husband would be her present friend. She wanted to break out in a praise dance like her grandmother used to do back in the day. This was it; Sasha didn't need any more signs, miracles, and wonders, or any more checks on her list. She'd be a fool not to give this man a chance to see where things could go from here. She'd been in charge and complete control of her life up until this point. Switching up gears a little and letting her girlfriends, Miss Destiny and Miss Faith, take the wheel for a minute might not be such a bad thing at all.

"So just that quickly I'm in the friend zone?" Sasha said teasingly, not quite ready to bow out of the game of cat and mouse just yet. And she was doing pretty good hiding the fact that on the inside she was screaming and hollering that he hadn't actually recanted his invitation for her to go out with him; he'd simply altered it a bit.

"That's not what I meant," Terrance said, looking downward as he shoved his hands in his pants pockets and bit his bottom lip. He looked like a shy little schoolboy.

Sasha had to bite her bottom lip to keep from telling this man how freaking much she was digging on him. Maybe initially, at the charity event,

he hadn't stood out and made such a grabbing
and lasting impression on her, but he was definitely
making up for it now. Perhaps that just hadn't been
the time or the place the two were supposed to connect. In this moment, though, everything felt perfect.

"Well, just what exactly did you mean?" Sasha
was being all seductive, in a subtle kind of way. She
hoped it didn't come off as trying too hard, because in all actuality, she wasn't trying. This man
was just bringing out a whole other side of her that
was definitely genuine. So genuine that Sasha wished
she could hit a mute button. She didn't want the
man to think she was a desperate ho.

"I'm a gentleman," Terrance said. "I don't want
to come off all strong and move too quickly as if
I'm just trying to get in your drawers, when I really
just want to get to know you."

Either Sasha was a totally bad judge of character
or this guy was good; Oscar-worthy good. It didn't
feel like he was running lines as if he'd been study-
ing them for months. His words were like a mouth-
watering meal Sasha didn't want to end.

Sasha stared at Terrance for a moment in an attempt to read him. Once she was sure she'd com-
prehended the words on the proverbial pages, she
spoke. "So you're trying to escape the reputation
of a baller when it comes to relationships, huh?"

Terrance's eyes widened. Sasha concluded that
was a result of him being surprised she had read
his mind.

"It's like a plague, you know," Terrance answered.

Sasha nodded. "Yeah, I know. Well, I don't actually know personally." Sasha nodded back toward
the house. "Casey's the only person I've ever known

to date a pro ball player. Any other observations have been just from reality shows."

"Awww, man." Terrance washed his hands down his face. "I guess I'm doomed then, because those shows find the most cheating cats in the business and then put their wives on the show so that everybody else can see how much pain the guys are causing them by traveling all the time, getting with groupies and cheerleaders."

"Then that's all just for show? That's not really how it goes down?" Sasha asked. For the first time it was registering that Terrance wasn't just some fine-ass, nice gentleman. He was a pro ball player, and yes, they had reputations of being lowdown, dirty, cheating, having babies on the side heart-breakers. That was too much drama. Sasha didn't do drama. And unlike the many people who claimed that they didn't do drama but always seemed to be caught up in it, Sasha *really* didn't do drama. She couldn't help it, though, if the people around her did do drama. She might not participate in it, but a little drama voyeurism never hurt anybody. After all, that seemed to be what life was about these days, people benefiting in one way or another by other folks' drama. But allowing someone like Terrance in her life could be too close for comfort.

"Some of what they show on television about us is for show," Terrance admitted, "but I must confess that some of it is the truth. But I think that's for the guys who get in these exclusive relationships with women, even get married, without being honest with themselves about who they are and what they are and are not capable of."

"So let me guess," Sasha said. "You are not one of those men?"

"Do I look like one of those men?" Terrance asked in a tone almost as if he was testing Sasha.

A test already? Sasha thought to herself. She imagined that he wanted to know what she saw—what she thought—when she looked at him. After all, she had those same unspoken questions about him.

"I know exactly what I want and when I'm ready for it." He licked his lips as he gave Sasha a quick once-over.

Sasha subtly twisted her thighs together to try to suppress the throbbing between her legs. But she quickly stopped, as she could have sworn she heard the sound of a wave hitting the shore thanks to the wetness forming between her legs. "Umm, so anyway, back to us meeting out . . . as friends." Sasha cleared her throat, swallowed, and tried to maintain her composure. "Umm, I think I'd be down for that. I'm still in the process of making new friends here in the city."

"And you can never have too many friends." Terrance shook his head.

"So, uh, why don't you just give me your number and I'll call you one day to see if you have some time to—"

"Well, hell, I have time now," Terrance said, cutting Sasha off.

Sasha opened her mouth to speak, but honestly didn't know what to say. Although Terrance was being pretty straightforward, he wasn't coming off like a perv. His tone wasn't aggressive, just very matter-of-fact. He didn't play around, waste time, or mince words. His actions validated exactly who he said he was. He was like the male version of . . . well . . . her!

Words didn't come out of Sasha's mouth, but a chuckle did. It was one of those "Boy, stop playing" chuckles. But as Terrance stood there staring at her, he was doing anything but playing.

Sasha snapped her neck back. "You serious? I know you don't expect me to just go out with you tonight, the first time we've ever laid eyes on each other."

"Correction, the first time we've ever been introduced, because I'd definitely already laid eyes on you," Terrance said. He gave Sasha a side-eye glare. "What's wrong, you scared? Afraid of what I might think of you if you agree to go out with me after just one night of being formally introduced? You one of those people who care what everybody else thinks and lives your life accordingly?"

Okay, Terrance had definitely struck a nerve with Sasha with his last comment. If there was one thing Sasha had never done in life, it was to allow the opinions of others to influence how she lived. The fact that he even thought that about her made her want to prove him wrong, and so she did.

"I can do whatever I want, when I want. I'm my own woman, so if I wanted to go out with you tonight after just meeting you, hell, I would. It's no different than a chick meeting some dude in a bar and then sitting there all night and drinking it up with him." Sasha was pumped and in pure sista-girlfriend mode. Her hands were on her waist and her head was snapping on her neck.

"Oh, yeah?" he said in a challenging tone. Sasha couldn't quite tell if he was being sincere or just playing along. "So let's go, then. I know the perfect spot where we can grab a couple drinks and just chill."

"Fine," Sasha said, more like she was accepting a challenge and not an offer for a drink. If Terrance had been using reverse psychology, it had worked like a charm. And Sasha didn't care. A part of her wasn't yet ready to leave Terrance's presence.

"Fine, then, follow me." Terrance spoke in a "you win" tone.

And perhaps he was winning right about now. But in life, just like in the game of basketball, the game could shift at any time.

"I will," Sasha snapped, then used the key fob to unlock her door. She opened her door as Terrance made his way toward his car. "Wait, aren't you going to tell Casey and Eric that you're not going back in to stay? They think you're just walking me to my car."

Terrance looked back at the house. "Nahh," he said. "They'll know the deal."

"The deal?" Sasha said. There was no telling what Casey and Eric might think *the deal* was. She didn't want any misunderstandings. No matter how honest her intentions, Terrance was a pro ball player and she was someone who just met him. Now here they were riding off into the night together to hang out. That could be looked at all kinds of ways.

"I didn't mean it like that," Terrance said. "Look, if it will make you feel better, I'll just shoot Eric a text or something." He then turned back around and walked to his car.

A little smile appeared on Sasha's lips. She was *sooooo* glad he'd decided not to go back in that house and tell them a thing. In spite of what Sasha had just said, deep down inside, she did care to some degree what people thought about her. She didn't want it to look like she'd gone home with the first man she'd met in Atlanta, because that wasn't the case. This wasn't any different than her going out to have a drink with Norman within minutes of her first time meeting him . . . Okay, maybe just a little different. But so what? And besides, it wasn't like she and Terrance were going to either of their homes. They were going out for a drink, and she'd probably just get a cappuccino or something. She'd had enough alcohol for the night.

Sasha got settled in her car and started it up. She waited until she saw the lights from Terrance's Range Rover before she threw her car in drive. She then proceeded to follow him. Sasha hadn't really mastered the streets of Atlanta yet. She still used her GPS eighty percent of the time. She hadn't asked Terrance what bar they were going to, and she probably wouldn't have known it had he told her. She couldn't keep up with Atlanta's night life. There were bars and restaurants for days.

As Sasha followed Terrance, a couple times she had second thoughts about proceeding with the evening with him. Each time she wanted to renege, though, she reminded herself that it was nothing more than two friends out grabbing a drink, and then she'd be wholly back on board again. It was when they pulled up to a huge black gate that Sasha began doubting her decision again.

"What kind of bar is located in a gated community?" she asked herself as she watched the gates open and Terrance drive in.

It hit Sasha that Terrance was Eric's buddy. Eric did own that freaky-ass strip club. Was it possible that Terrance was into that type of thing as well,

even though he never gave her that impression?
On the flip side of the coin, Sasha was Casey's
friend. It was possible that Terrance was thinking
the same thing about her. This could be bad, all
bad.

She checked out her surroundings as she followed Terrance inside. At first all she saw was landscaping. Just looked like grass and trees. As they
drove up a hill, she could see what she initially
thought was an apartment building. It only took
her pulling up behind Terrance into the circular
driveway to realize that this was no gated community. This was no apartment complex. This was Terrance's home!

"Oh, hell no!" Sasha let out, shaking her head.
What was this fool trying to pull? Perhaps he had
taken her for some young and dumb groupie. It
was an understatement that Sasha was getting hot
up under her collar. And here all this time she'd
pegged him as the perfect gentleman—God sent.
He wasn't nothing but a wolf in sheep's clothing . . .
who knew how to dribble a ball.

Terrance got out of his car and began making
his way to Sasha. She was mad, but that cool glide
of his made parts of her a little glad and jumpy inside. She still had the right mind to run over his
smooth ass for trying to play her stupid. But she
managed to calm down by the time he arrived at
her window. She felt she needed to give him the
benefit of the doubt, to explain himself and apologize if need be. Perhaps he'd just left his wallet
and needed to run inside and grab it real quick.

As Sasha went to roll her window down to talk to
Terrance, he already had his hand on her door
handle opening it up for her. He stood there hold-

ing the door open for her with one hand while extending his other arm for her to exit the car.

"Ummm," Sasha said as she began looking around. "This doesn't look like a bar or any kind of club to me." She looked back at Terrance, awaiting an explanation.

"Who said anything about going to a bar?" Now he was looking just as confused as Sasha. "And I didn't peg you for the clubbin' type. Seems like you're above the club life."

This man knew how to make a woman, in this particular case, Sasha, feel like, not just a dime, but a rare coin. But she still needed to be cautious.

"I didn't want to offend you by taking you to some random club or something," Terrance continued. "I thought you would prefer something like, I don't know, the bar I have in my home."

Sasha looked at him to see if he was for real–for real. "So what was all that talk about meeting up in a public place? This is as private as it gets." Sasha pointed down the hill. "Private gate." She pointed at the house. "Private home. Private bar."

"On some occasions I entertain others at the bar," Terrance explained. "So I'd like to think of it as publicly exclusive."

Sasha let out a harrumph. "You got the wrong one, baby." She went to reach for her door to close it, but Terrance grabbed her hand instead.

"Please don't be that way," Terrance pleaded. "It's . . . it's not that private. I mean, yes, it's my private home, but we won't be alone."

"Oh, really now?" Sasha said, putting one hand on her hip. "So what you got up in there? Your entourage, your posse, so that once you're through with me they can have a turn? Ain't no fun if your homies can't have none? Is that what you're used to, because let me tell you—" Sasha's finger was just a-pointing.

"Okay, wait a minute now," Terrance said, letting go of Sasha's door and putting both hands up for her to tone it down. "You're going a little too far." His once smooth tone now had an edge to it.

Sasha was a little taken aback. She pulled her neck back in disbelief. All night Terrance had spoken with her in a very respectful tone.

When Sasha's eyes locked with Terrance's, he seemed to have recognized the alarmed look in her eyes. "I'm sorry," he apologized. He'd brought his tone down several notches.

Sasha relaxed her shoulders, thankful for his apology and the fact that he had some self-control. That enabled her to have some as well, because if he thought he was going to stand there and read her, he had another think coming.

"Now I've been nothing but respectful to you," Terrance continued in a civil tone. "I haven't accused you of being anything other than what you've shown yourself to be, which is a nice, respectful lady. Now what if I started talking to you, insinuating that you are some gold-digging ho? Took you to some hole-in-the-wall bar, or even a strip joint or something, and then expected you to put out? You'd be offended. Well, I'm offended at the way you are coming at me. I've not done a single thing to make you think I'm some kind of perverted rapist or something. You might not be a gold-digging ho, but maybe you are one of those stuck-up chicks who went to college and thinks she's better than everybody else who might not have a fancy degree. Well, I'm here to tell you that no, maybe I didn't get a college degree. But I went to college, and you know what? I went on an academic scholarship, not a basketball one. I could have graduated and became the owner of my own *Fortune* Five Hundred company if I'd wanted to. But I loved ball. It was my life. So I did what made me happy at the time and what I thought was the best thing for my family. I entered the draft. Yes, I had to drop out of college to do so, but I—"

"Whoa, whoa, wait," Sasha said, stepping out of her car. She had really hit a nerve with Terrance. She thought earlier tonight she'd heard him mention something about playing offense on his team. Well, somehow her words had him playing defense in their conversation.

It was apparent to Sasha that he was truly hurt by the inferences she'd made about his character. That explained why he'd taken offense and had gotten a little loud just moments ago. And he had every right to be. Him insinuating that she could be stuck up alone had pissed her off, because that's not who she was. So she could only imagine how he must have felt with her practically calling him a rapist.

"I'm sorry. I didn't mean to come off like that," Sasha apologized. "That's not who I am, either. I don't say things to intentionally hurt people." Sasha hadn't meant to hurt him. She was simply trying to be cautious. She was still trying to read who he was without getting lost between the pages. But after what she'd just witnessed, she felt she could close the book. Terrance was the real deal, and he had too much to lose and too much at stake not to be. She couldn't imagine he'd jeopardize his life and livelihood by being some creep or jerk.

Terrance stood there looking at Sasha. Behind his eyes Sasha could see that he was still a little hurt, but there was some anger there, too. This is not how Sasha wanted the night to end. This was not the bad taste she wanted to leave in Terrance's mouth.

"Let's just go inside and have that drink, okay?" Sasha suggested, hoping to turn things around. She could have very well hopped in her car and gone home, but a final impression as a bougie bitch was not what she wanted Terrance to have of her.

Sasha stared at Terrance, who stood there looking as if now he was the one debating whether he wanted to continue his evening with Sasha.

Sasha closed her door and hit the button on her key fob to lock it. It was habit and not that she thought anyone would steal her little Honda from this mansion. If the inside resembled the luxurious outside, she was certain he had vases in there that cost more than the value of her car. She looped her arm through Terrance's. There, now he had no choice. He was too much of a gentleman to fling her arm loose and leave a lady standing there on the curb.

As he stared at Sasha, a little smile forced its way onto his lips. "Come on, woman," he said as he began walking to his doorstep, "before you make me . . ." He was now in a joking mood.

"Before I make you what?" Sasha wanted to know as she walked to his doorstep arm in arm.

He chuckled.

"You're laughing, but I'm for real," Sasha said. She then stopped in her tracks, forcing him to stop in his. She slightly jerked Terrance to face her. "Before I make you do what to me?" she asked, seductively looking into his eyes.

"I didn't necessarily say I was going to do something to you."

"Oh, you didn't?" Sasha played dumb, placing her index finger on her chin as if thinking back.

"Nope," Terrance said, enunciating the *p.* "Must have been wishful thinking on your part."

"Wishful thinking?" Sasha shot back.

"Yeah, you wishing I was going to do something to you."

Sasha tucked in her bottom lip and blushed. "Come on, let's go." She walked past Terrance, leading the way to *his* house.

"Oh, you got the key or something?" he jokingly asked her.

"Nope." Sasha said the word in the same manner as Terrance had just said it. "Must have been wishful thinking on your part."

"Touché." Terrance laughed, then made his way past Sasha to open up the door.

Once inside, Sasha tried not to appear material struck; after all she'd been in mansions and luxury homes since moving to Atlanta. Norman had taken her to some amazing homes and had even allowed her to play his assistant as he dressed a client for a video shoot. But Terrance's place put them all to shame. It was huge. Gigantor! The foyer was the size of her entire apartment. The ceiling was something only Spider-man could have gotten to. Even he might have run out of web navigating it.

"Lovely," Sasha said, looking around. She could have sworn she'd heard her voice echo.

"Thank you. My mother did it. She lives here, too, you know."

A slight but noticeable frown appeared on Sasha's face. She felt a couple kinds of ways about that. For one, it was definitely not a check on her list, but a big red X. A man who lived with his momma was a cause for immediate elimination.

"I'm just joking." Terrance laughed. "Not about my mother decorating it. She owns her own interior design company. I'm joking about her living with me."

"Oh," Sasha said, relieved. Terrance had a sense of humor and Sasha liked that about him. She'd just have to get better at figuring out when he was joking and when he was for real. In her opinion, Terrance was like one of those books or movies she'd have to read or see twice. The second time around perhaps she'd pick up on some things she'd missed the first time. Kind of like what she had to do with the movie *The Sixth Sense.* She's missed both the obvious and the not so obvious the first time she'd seen the movie. By the second time, she knew exactly what to expect and to look out for.

"You act like you were disappointed." Terrance leaned into Sasha's ear. "Like you were afraid my mother was going to catch us doing something we weren't supposed to be doing."

Sasha was speechless at Terrance's comment, but only because he was right. But no way was she going to voice that that was exactly how she was feeling. It wasn't necessarily that his mother would catch them doing anything R-rated, just catch her there in his home, period . . . after having just met him. Damn, why was she so hung up on and not able to shake the whole going out—or home—with a man on the first night of meeting him?

"Come on," Terrance chuckled. "Let's go."

Sasha went to follow him, but was startled by a voice that came from behind them. It was the voice of a woman, an older woman. Did this man's mother really live with him? That would make him a liar. Big red X, and again, cause for immediate elimination as a husband prospect.

"Mr. McKinley, good evening. Can I get anything for you?"

Sasha quickly turned and faced the short, older black woman who was walking from the opening at the other end of the foyer. The woman wore a black dress with a white apron.

"Oh, no, Miss Hart," Terrance said. "You can retire for the evening." He looked to Sasha. "I think I'm taken care of for the night." With that Terrance turned and continued walking.

Sasha smiled at Miss Hart before following Terrance. Miss Hart didn't return the gesture; she simply shook her head and gave Sasha a look that said, "Another one bites the dust."

All Sasha could think about was the hashtag made popular by Beyoncé, #dusttosidechicks. But she wasn't a side-chick. She wished she could have stood there and defended her honor to Miss Hart, but Terrance grabbed her by the hand and pulled her along. He led her down a staircase and into what might as well have been a nightclub.

"I can only imagine how many parties have gone on down here," Sasha said, admiring the burgundy-and-gold color-coordinated room. It had a couple of booth seats, tables, a bar area, and both a juke-box and a DJ booth in addition to a stage. "And it's even fully equipped with a stripper pole. Nice," Sasha said, both playfully and sarcastically.

"Oh, so you do a little stripping?" Terrance teased as he walked over behind the bar.

"I thought you knew," Sasha played along. "What girl who went to college didn't have to do a little stripping to pay off her student loans?" Sasha began laughing. "No, but really, I don't have nothing against a chick who's gotta do what she's gotta do." Sasha made her way over to the stage while Terrance prepared them each a glass of wine. She went over to the pole and looked at it for a moment. She then touched it. After thinking for a second, she quickly snatched her hand away as if the pole was hot. "This thing been cleaned?"

Terrance laughed. "That's what Miss Hart is for."

Taking his word for it, she reached out and touched it again. Sasha held the pole with one hand and then slowly began to walk around it. Next she put both hands on it. She got so wrapped up in the fantasy of it all that she didn't even realize Terrance was watching her every move.

Terrance carried the two glasses of wine over to the jukebox, which was at the end of the bar. He sat the glasses down on the bar while he punched in a couple songs. He then turned, picked up the glasses of wine, and made his way over toward the stage just as the music came on.

Sasha turned to look at him once the music filled the air.

"I hope you like R. Kelly," Terrance said, extending her glass of wine to her.

Sasha was standing there looking like Terrance's mom had actually caught her doing something wrong.

"Why you looking like that? All guilty? Like you're doing something you're not supposed to be doing?" He took a sip of his drink while still extending Sasha's to hers. "Woman, you're grown. Now take this drink and get your dance on."

Sasha smiled, giggled, and looked down at the drink. "No, I'm good." She'd told herself she was not going to drink any more tonight. "But what I'm not good at is dancing." She walked down the steps from the stage. She'd been dragged to a pole dancing class or two with her friends, but she couldn't quite get the hang of it.

"No, stay up there," Terrance said, sitting down at one of the tables in front of the stage. "You don't have to dance or anything, not unless you want to. Just stay there because on a stage is where someone like you belongs. On a pedestal." He leaned forward with a serious and intent look on his face. "Yeah, you're different. You're a star. You stand out. There ain't nothing about you that's average." He sipped his drink and said, "Nah, you don't belong out here with the rest of us ordinary folks. You're not regular at all."

Sasha was mesmerized by the way he was reading her. These were internal thoughts that Sasha had had about herself ever since she could remember. No, she wasn't conceited or felt she was better than the rest of the world. But she'd seen so many people content with an average life; just making it day by day and living a routine life. She couldn't do it. Ordinary and regular would not be the life she lived.

"You just want to see me do some dirty dancing," Sasha said, giving him a playful side-eye.

"That too." He raised his glass and extended hers to her again. "Drink. Nothing like a little liquid courage."

Sasha was a tad parched, she reasoned. Besides, in looking around the room, she didn't see a cappuccino machine. So what other choice did she have? It had taken very little convincing from Terrance or herself to make Sasha reach for the glass of wine and sip.

"Dance." Terrance sipped from his own glass while looking up at Sasha.

Sasha took another sip of wine. She was going to need some courage all right. She closed her eyes and allowed the wine to slither down her throat. In doing so the music infiltrated her being. Slowly she began to rock her hips back and forth. Forth and back. Back, back, forth and forth like an Aaliyah song. She didn't even realize it, but she was smiling. Once again she did ring around the rosey with the glass of wine in hand, taking sips until it was all gone and another song was now playing.

Terrance stood and took the empty glass from her, refilling it. Sasha watched the deep plum wine funnel into the glass.

"That wine is delicious," Sasha said as she accepted the offering.

"It's the best bottle I have," Terrance said, now refilling his own. "I've been saving it for—"

"Let me guess," Sasha said, tipsy enough to be feeling herself. "You've been saving it for something special."

"No, not at all," Terrance said, shaking his head.

He took a sip of his wine, keeping his eyes glued to Sasha over the rim. "I've been saving it for *someone* special."

Once again, Sasha's insides melted. If this man kept it up, she'd be a puddle of caramel right there on that stage, or butt naked in his bed . . . whichever came first.

Not able to accept the compliment the same way she'd been accepting glass after glass of spirits, Sasha shrugged it off. "I bet you say that to all the girls."

"What girls?" Terrance asked on a more serious note. "Not all ball players have hoes in every area code, you know."

Sasha looked Terrance dead in the eyes. "No, I don't know." She sipped her wine. More like guzzled, because now the glass was half empty. "You want me to believe that a fine-ass brother like yourself, with a job that pays millions, not married, no kids . . ." Sasha paused and hiccupped. "You don't have any kids, do you?"

"Not even a maybe baby," Terrance assured her.

Sasha couldn't help but stop and mentally check off one more thing on her list. No babies, which meant no baby momma drama. Yasssss! She had to keep her excitement at bay. "Well, that even makes you more of a catch. So why haven't you been caught?"

Sasha watched as the proverbial wheels in Terrance's head turned.

"Fear," he said plainly and simply.

"Fear?" Sasha questioned. "What are you afraid of?"

"It's not me who is afraid." Terrance finished up his wine and sat the empty glass down on the table.

He then made his way up to the stage. "It's you," he said to Sasha in her face, then eased his way behind her.

"Me?" She went to turn around, but his body pressed behind hers and wrapped around her prevented her from doing so.

"You heard me," he leaned down and said in her ear. "You. Women like you, you're afraid to just take me for who I am. You're afraid that I'm going to turn out to be the last man, or even your father. Afraid to just take me at face value and just . . . well . . . let me love you."

For a minute there Sasha had thought she'd peed herself. Or hell, maybe she'd even come. Something was running down her leg. But she looked to realize that Terrance's words, his presence, his aroma had weakened and hypnotized her. While he was pouring out his heart, the little bit of wine she had left was pouring out of her glass, down her leg and onto the stage.

"Damn it!" Terrance snapped, realizing Sasha had wasted the expensive wine.

"Oh, no!" Sasha said, jerking around, now facing Terrance, and staring at the mess she'd made. "It's going to mess up my shoes." Why of all days had she worn those midnight-blue suede pumps? She looked up at Terrance. His facial muscles were tight. She hoped she hadn't ruined the mood with her clumsiness. She'd already ruined her shoes, that was for sure.

Terrance stared at the spilled wine as if he was counting down his anger. Sasha couldn't blame him for being upset. Let someone come spill some red wine up in her spot, carpet or no carpet. Sasha swallowed hard as she waited to see how Terrance was going to handle things.

"I'll just go get some napkins and clean this up." Sasha went to move, but Terrance grabbed her by her arm.

"No," he said as he continued to stare down at the mess. He then looked up at Sasha.

She watched as his eyes softened before he spoke again.

"Let me," Terrance insisted as he kneeled down. He began removing Sasha's shoes, one by one, as she balanced herself on the pole.

He didn't appear mad. That was a good sign for Sasha. But she felt bad. She couldn't let this man clean up after her like this.

"I'm so sorry. Let me clean this up." Although Sasha was sure that Miss Hart had cleaned up more than her share of messes, there was no need to bother her for this one. Sasha was used to cleaning up her own messes. No one had ever run behind her and cleaned up after her.

"I'll clean it up," Terrance said. He grabbed Sasha's bare foot. He looked her in the eyes as his tongue began licking traces of the wine that had spilled on her leg.

"Terrance," she said, but that's all she said. There was no "don't" or "stop" behind her plea. And so he didn't stop.

A moan escaped Sasha's mouth as she gripped the pole so tight that her hand was starting to sweat. Terrance's tongue danced all up her leg as he lifted it over his shoulder and began to lick and kiss her thighs. He definitely wasn't mad. Sasha no longer had any doubts about that.

"Terrance, I—"

"You're afraid?" he asked in a challenging tone, already hip to Sasha's reaction to a challenge.

"N . . . no," Sasha stammered. "I'm not afraid."

Sasha figured that when she didn't say anything else, Terrance took that as permission to proceed. He began placing kisses on Sasha's womanhood through her panties. He had managed to lick dry the spilled wine that ran down her leg, but now he was indulging in a whole other kind of wetness.

"Umm, umm," Sasha moaned at the heat of Terrance's tongue emanating through her panties. The wineglass dangled between her two fingers before it dropped to the floor.

The crashing sound and the music were the sound track for the sensual display the two were engaging in. Terrance rubbed the leg that he had thrown over his shoulder with one hand while he slipped her panties to the side with the other. The flesh of his tongue was now on the flesh of Sasha's clit. Sasha grabbed the back of Terrance's head and just began to guide it. He was already coming in for a landing; she might as well guide the plane.

"You taste so good," Terrance said. "Like fine wine . . . No pun intended."

"Don't stop," is what Sasha said out loud although in her head she was saying, "Shut the fuck up and don't stop." Dudes were good at screwing up a moment by talking too damn much or saying the wrong thing. She was on the verge of climaxing. No way could she let this moment be in vain by allowing him to mess up the mood by using his mouth in all the wrong ways.

"Mmmm." Terrance was slurping and slapping as he ate the kitty, and Sasha was purring like she was a kitty; a kitty being stroked just right. The faster his tongue flicked and sucked, the more and louder she meowed until she erupted in his mouth.

"Oh, uh, ah," Sasha said as she now gripped the pole with both hands. Her eyes were still closed as she allowed the sensational feeling she'd just experienced to marinate.

Terrance took Sasha's leg off of his shoulder and stood up. He began kissing her neck. She had barely been able to come to grips with how good his tongue had felt on her private parts, and now he was putting it to work on her neck.

Sasha could feel Terrance's hardness against her. Then it hit her. *I hope this nigga don't think I'm 'bout to return the favor. Didn't nobody tell him to eat my pussy.* That raunchy thought stayed in her head, but she meant it and would unleash it if he dare tried to put his dick in her face.

"I've tasted you, now I want to feel inside of you," Terrance whispered in her ear before tracing it with the tip of his tongue.

Sasha's body tightened with sexual tension. The irony of it all was that the first song Terrance had played on the jukebox was coming to pass. Her mind was telling her no, that giving up the cookies to this man on the first night would have her singing Lisa Lisa and the Cult Jam's hit song. But her body's reactions were screaming yes.

She hadn't been intimate with a man in almost a year. She needed this. Hell, she deserved this. And besides that, no one would ever have to know. What was so wrong with Terrance just being the guy she went home with and screwed? It wasn't like she was going to marry him or anything, even though he was making the cut according to her checklist. She couldn't marry him now. No way could she humiliate herself by having to share stories with their children of how they'd met . . . and had sex on the first night.

Five minutes later as Sasha scratched her nails down Terrance's bare back as he thrusted in and out of her, she realized that she'd just thrown all her inhibitions out of the window. Oh, and that thought about her not wanting Terrance thinking she was a desperate ho . . . that was out the window, too. But little did she know, now there was one other thing dangling on the window's ledge as well: her dreams.

Chapter 10

"Okay, bitch, what's his last name?"

His last name? Even when Sasha had called her mother up to tell her about the nice basketball player she'd met, her mother hadn't quizzed her as much as Norman was now quizzing her.

Sasha sat on her couch with her feet tucked under her. She eyeballed her cell phone, which was right next to her on the end table. Since arriving to Atlanta, Sasha had saved up some of her coins and invested them in a nice living room suite; well, a partial one, anyway. The entire set she'd eyeballed in the store consisted of a couch, loveseat, chair, ottoman, a coffee table, two end tables, and some throw pillows that had been situated on the display for show. Sasha had only gotten the couch and one end table. She was going to go back and get the chair and ottoman once she'd saved up enough money. The store clerk who'd assisted her suggested she apply for a credit account so that she could take everything home that she wanted that day. But that wasn't how Sasha did things. She refused to get pulled into the black hole of living off of credit. If she couldn't afford to pay for it now or within the next thirty days, she wasn't getting it. She knew that once she was ready to open her own boutique, she'd have to take out credit then, so she had to make sure she had credit score swag by keeping her credit on fleek.

"I see you looking at that phone," Norman griped. "You better not pick it up and try to Google that man's last name."

Sasha bit her bottom lip. She'd been busted, because that's exactly what she had been about to do. "Uggghhh." Sasha buried her face in her hands. She was embarrassed and humiliated.

"Umm, hmm, you just ought to be hiding your face in shame. Not only do you sleep with the man on your first date—"

"It wasn't really a date," Sasha corrected, removing her face from her hands. Ironically, it was as if she was about to save face, her own, to some degree. "We were just out grabbing a drink . . . at the same place."

"Even worse," Norman snapped. "You sleep with a man the first night you see him—"

Once again Sasha cut Norman off. "Was introduced to him. Remember I told you that he saw me at that charity event?" Sasha nodded as if that made the scenario all the better.

"Whore, for real?" Norman tilted his head to the side, smacked his lips, and sucked his teeth.

"I am not a whore," Sasha said adamantly.

Norman tilted his head in thought for a moment. "Yeah, you right. You ain't a whore. A whore got enough marbles to get paid for giving up the cookies. You just a plain ole ho!" Norman said. "I thought you had a better business sense than that." He frowned. "You been running around here scoping out other boutiques to see how they have their stores set up, how they are running their businesses and what not. You've been going to business seminars, sketching, tagging along with me on my gigs; all in the name of being Miss Business Entrepreneur Extraordinaire. And you don't even pull out your tin bucket to collect when you hit the jackpot? Or should I say when you let the jackpot hit you?" Norman pretended he was humping and smacking ass. "Pow! Pow! Pow!"

Sasha looked around for something to throw at him. She wasn't about to risk destroying her iPhone. Damn, why hadn't she just splurged for the matching toss pillows that had decorated the couch in the store? She could have definitely stood to toss them right about now. "I knew I shouldn't have told you." Sasha crossed her arms and pouted.

"I know you don't call yourself being mad at me, girlfriend," Norman said. "You know I speak the truth. You only told me because you wanted me to confirm the truth that you were feeling about yourself, which is that you're a ho."

Sasha couldn't help but let out a laugh at Norman's bluntness. "You are so stupid."

"No, you are. You don't give it up to a baller the first night and don't get shit but a damn drink and reputation as a jump-off in return. If you think he's not gonna tell everyone around town about tapping your fine ass, you're crazy."

"What was I supposed to do, sleep with the man and then ask him to pay my car note?"

"Absolutely not," Norman said. "You're supposed to sleep with the man and then ask him to pay your car note *and* your rent." Norman exhaled. "I can see you have a lot to learn if you plan on hoeing around Atlanta."

"Well, I don't plan on hoeing around Atlanta," Sasha said, offense now reflected in her voice. "I hadn't planned on sleeping with him; it just happened."

"Just happened, huh?" Norman said, not completely buying it. "First Casey takes you to a strip club, then she introduces you to a guy you decide to screw immediately?"

"Yes, it just happened," Sasha said, then cast her eyes downward. After a couple seconds she looked back up at Norman. "And I wanted it, too. Is that so bad?"

Norman's face transformed as if he was coming to a realization. "Oh, my Lord Jesus, Mary Mother of God." Norman stood up and stared at Sasha. "You done caught feelings for the dick." He snapped his fingers. "Just that quick . . . and on the first hump!" Norman began pacing. "What in the world am I going to do with you?"

"Not just his dick, but I'm digging on him," Sasha said. "Terrance is a really nice guy." Sasha looked down.

"I can't take all this puppy-dog sadness," Norman said. "Yes, if I wanted I suppose I could spend the next few minutes beating you up, or I can be your gay boyfriend and comfort you."

Sasha looked up at Norman, hoping he chose the latter. She was out of cocoa butter to rub on the bruises that came with one of Norman's tongue whippings.

"Oh, princess," he said as he went and sat next to Sasha, putting his arm around her. "It's okay.

Nectarines come to Atlanta all the time and get caught up before they've earned their peach fuzz. It's happened to the best of us, trust and believe. Sexing a baller will give you some fuzz. It's how half the girls in Atlanta get down at some point."

"But now that you've put everything in perspective, I do feel stupid," Sasha said. "And I am a ho." She made a face as if she'd just eaten something disgusting. "I don't even know his last name." She whined as she allowed her head to drop on Norman's shoulder.

"Chile, you don't need me to beat you up. You're doing a fine job of it yourself." Norman exhaled. "But if it will make you feel any better, his name is Terrance McKinley."

"McKinley, yeah, that's it!" Sasha said excitedly. She now remembered Miss Hart calling him Mr. McKinley. In that moment she felt even more ashamed that she knew his housekeeper's last name and not his.

Norman continued on. "His position is starting point guard. He plays offense, too. He attended Florida State for his freshman and sophomore year of college. Very smart. Was actually one of very few, if any, college basketball players drafted to the NBA that were on an academic scholarship instead of a basketball scholarship. Chose to throw his name in the hat for the draft after his sophomore year. His mom had learned she had breast cancer and he wanted to guarantee the family had the money to save her life."

It touched Sasha that Terrance had been willing to do whatever it took to save his mother. He probably would have gotten to that part in his rant last night outside his house if Sasha hadn't cut him off.

"He lives a hop, skip, and jump from Buckhead. Signed a new contract with the league last year for several million dollars. Has a few endorsements under his belt, which is mad money, so he's not struggling. Never been married, no kids, not even a maybe baby. There. Now you know pretty much everything you need to know about the man you slept with." Norman shrugged.

Sasha's eyes burned a hole through him as he spoke.

He looked down at her as her head still rested on his shoulder. "What?"

"I'm afraid to even ask how you just happen to know so much about Terrance." There was a look of pure fear in Sasha's eyes.

Norman stared at her for a moment, then busted out laughing. "Oh, no . . . You think . . . Chile, please." He pushed her head off of him. "He is not my type."

"Whether or not he's your type is not my concern," Sasha said. "It's whether you're his type that gives me pause." Sasha swallowed, hoping, waiting, that Norman would put her mind at ease.

"The man's not gay, if that's what you're wondering. He's not bisexual, either. He's not looking for a woman to be his beard, either."

"Beard?" Sasha questioned.

"Chile, yes; that chick, that trophy, that arm piece that a man uses to project to the world that he's a heterosexual knowing all the while he's allergic to fish."

Sasha nodded her understanding. "Well, you know so much about him, I was just wondering if he, you know, ran in the same crowd as you."

"That would depend on which crowd you were

referring to," Norman said. "Call me the melting pot of Atlanta. Honey, I can mix in with the best of them. But the crowd I know ya boy from is Atlanta's elite. I've dressed him before."

That fact didn't put Sasha's mind at ease.

"Not like that, silly girl," Terrance said, swatting her leg. "His publicist hires me from time to time to make sure he's crisp when he has a photo shoot or television interview or something. I do my research on my clients. The way I dress them has to be cohesive with who they are as a person. You know what I'm saying? What a person wears is an extension of who they are. I have to be on my A game. So he either keeps his shenanigans real close to the chest, unlike ya boy Eric apparently, or he's not a closet freak. We hope."

Sasha learned something new from Norman every day. But the one thing she was truly glad she'd learned was that the man she'd had a one-night stand with was straight.

"So let me ask you something," Norman said. "Was there at least protection involved when you let a complete stranger hit it?"

"Uhh, yes," Sasha said, rolling her eyes. "There was a whole vending machine full in the bathroom."

"Bathroom!" Norman shouted. "I thought you said he took you to his place." Norman stuck his finger down his throat and made a gagging sound. "Not only did you screw this man on the first night, but on a bathroom floor?" Norman shook his head. "I can't." He stood up. "I'm out of here." He pretended to be looking around for his things. "I know I have some ho-ish ways, but you, sweetheart, take the cake. Even the backseat of his car I can understand. But a damn public bathroom floor . . . with vending machines full of prophylactics!"

"He did take me to his place," Sasha was quick to say.

Norman threw his fists on his hips. "And just what kind of room in somebody's house has a bathroom with a goddamn condom vending machine in it, huh?"

"The barroom with the stripper pole." Sasha had said it matter-of-factly, oblivious to how it sounded to someone who didn't know the setup.

Sasha's response only put Norman in that much more of an uproar.

"Stripper pole?" Norman spat. "I told your ass not to hang around that damn Paris, didn't I? You just wouldn't listen. Now that trick got you stripping, screwing on bathroom floors and God knows what else." Norman closed his eyes, put his head down, and continued shaking it.

Sasha had to laugh at how dramatic her friend was being.

"This shit is not funny," Norman said, looking up at Sasha. "You'll get a reputation as a ho and then no woman is gonna want you dressing her man!"

"It wasn't like what you are making it out to be. It wasn't in some strip club or anything like that. It was in the privacy of his own home. I mean, yeah, I got a little intrigued by the stripper pole he has installed at his house. I busted a move or two, and then one thing led to another. But we didn't get down on the bathroom floor. You've got too much imagination!"

He moseyed back over to her and sat. "Okay, you've got my attention. Do tell."

Sasha could see that now it was Norman who was getting intrigued by her replay of the night before. "Well," Sasha said teasingly and excited to know that for the first time since she'd met Norman, he genuinely seemed interested in the goings-on of her life. Not that anything outside of her daily norm was usually going on. "Like I told you before, he brought some wine over to me. I just happened to be on the stage on the stripper pole at the time. I was just trying it out, not trying to give him a striptease or anything like that."

"So you were fully dressed?" Norman asked curiously.

"Absolutely," Sasha assured him. "I stopped dancing to take the glass, and he asked that I keep dancing, which I did." Sasha blushed proudly. "I guess I must have learned a thing or two from Paris, because I got him so riled up that—"

"He started throwing money at you!" Norman exclaimed excitedly as he began bouncing up and down on the couch, clapping his hands. "I knew you wasn't plumb dumb. I knew you didn't give it up like a ho without getting something valuable. Yes!" He pumped his fist.

Sasha hated to disappoint him. "No, that man did not start giving me money." She rolled her eyes.

Norman sucked his teeth and allowed Sasha to continue.

"He actually gave me something much, much better." Sasha started staring off, squirming and licking her lips.

Norman bit down on his manicured nail. "Ohhhh, it must have been good if it put that type of glow on your face." He then gasped. "He ate the ill nana," Norman guessed.

Sasha nodded and smiled.

"Oh, yes! That's my girl. At least get that thang topped off." He pointed to her private area.

"Right," Sasha said proudly. "Give your girl some kind of credit." Sasha was glad that it seemed as though she was redeeming herself with Norman.

"Wait, not so fast," Norman said, bringing the mini celebration to a halt. "Do you owe him one?"

Sasha frowned, confused by Norman's question.

"Do you owe him one, bitch? Or did y'all sixty-nine?"

"Sixty-nine?" Sasha's wheels turned as she tried to figure out what Norman was asking. "Owe him one or did we do a sixty-nine?" she pondered out loud until it all came together. "Ohhh, did I just let him do me or did I do him?"

"Yes," Norman said.

To Sasha, he was looking as if he was glad his poor country girl had been able to figure things out and do the math on her own.

Sasha laughed. "I did not return the favor, if that's what you mean."

"That's exactly what I mean." Norman sighed. "So at least you know he ain't gon' be running his mouth about how the new girl in town screwed him the first night. Because your ammo is that he ate the pussy on the first night. Which is worst? If he puts your business out there, then he'd take the risk of you firing back and putting his out there. I know he's not willing to lose his player card for that."

Sasha thought for a moment. "You're right." She

shrugged. "I guess." It was a double-edged sword as far as she was concerned. Either way it went, though, the woman always seemed to be the only one with a sliced-up reputation when all was said and done.

"Anyway," Norman said, "you let him do you on the floor and he was strapped up," he recapped. "Now for the most important part: was it good?"

For the first time during her and Norman's entire conversation, Sasha truly had no shame or hesitation in saying, "God, yes! And if I had to make the same choice all over again, I wouldn't deviate one little bit. So if that means I'm a ho, then ho, ho, ho, merry Christmas!"

The two grabbed hands and chuckled while Sasha continued giving Norman the sticky, icky details about her encounter with Terrance. About an hour later, Norman had heard enough. "Well, girl, let me get on out of here so I can go through my phone address book and see who I can get to strip and sixty-eight me tonight." Norman laughed.

"What?" Sasha said, scrunching her nose up. "I had no idea a gay man could be turned on by heterosexual sex stories. I thought you were just being your usual nosy self."

"Girl, bye. I tuned that little kitty-cat of yours right on out," Norman said. "I was vicariously living through you; imagining it was myself instead." Norman stared off. "I always wondered what Terrance's man parts were like ever since I accidentally grazed it while fitting him in some Ralph Lauren slacks."

"Get on out of here," Sasha said, standing up from the couch and walking over to Norman. "You are bound and determined to have me looking at this man a whole other way." She began pushing Norman to the door. "Go, go, go."

"I'm going, I'm going." Norman made his way to the door and then stopped. "And for the record, you are not kicking me out. I said I was leaving first."

"Whatever suits your boots," Sasha said, then opened the door. "I'm about to sit here and chill."

Norman looked to Sasha in a motherly manner. "Now don't take this the wrong way, and I'm not trying to be cruel or rain on your parade. But I don't want you sitting around here waiting on Mr. NBA to call you back. That's not how it works. Ballers hit it and quit it, baby." Norman stood in the doorway. "So move on with your life and find the next man in Atlanta to eat your pussy."

Sasha shook her head and rolled her eyes. "You are so—"

"Honest," Norman said. "I'm honest. I'm painfully honest; the truth hurts, but it hurts so good. And my honesty is why you'll keep me around. Because trust me, love, if you haven't learned already, you soon will, that in this town, honesty and trust are as rare gems as any." Norman winked at Sasha and then left, throwing her a wave over his shoulder.

All Sasha could do was watch her friend walk away with a smile on her face. As far as she was concerned, honest was her middle name. No, she wasn't as blunt and abrasive as Norman. She didn't practice keeping it real to the extent that it hurt someone's feelings. Norman, on the other hand, couldn't care less. He was like the momma who told her child he or she was ugly before the rest of the world got a chance to. That could be appreciated to some degree. And if Sasha knew now what she would soon find out, she would truly bask in having a friend as honest, truthful, and loyal as Norman. Because it wouldn't be long before she would become acquainted with the polar opposite.

Chapter 11

"That must have been some impression you made on ole boy," Casey said as she, Sasha, and Paris walked the mall.

From what Sasha could tell, she and Paris had hit the mall just to do a little window shopping, but clearly Casey had her husband's black card, because she was buying up everything that shimmered bright enough to make her stop and do a double take.

"Why did you say that?" Sasha was quick to ask. Her heart began beating a gazillion miles per minute. Or maybe it had stopped. She wasn't sure at this point. She wouldn't be sure until she found out exactly what Terrance had told Casey and Eric about the night she'd met him.

Sasha and Casey hadn't really talked much about it in the three days that had gone by since Sasha and Terrance's bathroom floor rendezvous. Technically, it wasn't on the bathroom floor per se. They'd only stood on the floor. It was up against the wall that Terrance had commenced laying the pipe on Sasha. But Sasha wasn't about to pass on such details to Casey. She was cool and all, but they weren't yet I-feel-like-I've-known-you-all-my-life-and-can-tell-you-anything cool.

Sasha had, of course, thanked Casey for the wonderful evening. Casey had asked Sasha her opinion of Terrance. Sasha had shared that he seemed like a nice guy, but she didn't go any further than that. If anything, she wanted to see what unsolicited information Casey would offer. It was possible that Casey had been doing the same to Sasha. Maybe Casey was fishing to see whether Sasha would be honest with her or not. But then again, Casey could be just a tad on the dizzy side sometimes. Unlike Paris, whose mouth was unfiltered on purpose—just because she wanted to be nicety—Casey's mouth was unfiltered by accident. She talked just to be talking, and if what she was saying was a truth that could be hurtful or offensive, then so be it. Again, unlike Paris, though, Casey was always apologetic if she realized her words had harmed someone. Sasha had to admit, Casey's and Paris's differences balanced things out. Sasha liked the balance. It allowed her to stand in the center of the teeter-totter without worrying about falling.

Even before Norman had instilled in Sasha the value of honesty, she'd always respected and expected it in any relationship she was in, be it a friendship or a romantic relationship. So Sasha had to be mindful when speaking to Casey about her night with Terrance. She carefully walked the fine line of being guarded versus being dishonest in her answers.

Being guarded was not telling Casey that she'd jumped Terrance's beautiful, strong bones . . . and loved it! What Sasha also was not telling Casey was that she'd been doing exactly what Norman had ordered her not to. She'd been waiting by her phone to see if by some farfetched chance he'd call her. As crazy as it sounded, even if he didn't want to call to ask her out on a date or to just talk, damn, wasn't her lady jungle worthy of at least a booty call? Or had her stuff been out of commission for so long that she didn't even know how to please a man anymore? At the moment, Sasha would have much rather opted to have pulled off from his house and left an impression as a bougie bitch rather than a bad lay.

"Eric says Terrance has asked about you every time he's spoken with him," Casey said. "In practice or out."

"Oh," Sasha said, more relaxed. Terrance hadn't called her, but at least he'd asked about her. Still didn't pull out the dent in her ego.

Both women looked to Paris as she choked on the frozen slushy drink she'd been slurping.

"You okay?" Casey asked Paris.

Was Sasha less of a friend because she was more interested in getting back to the subject matter of Terrance rather than seeing if Paris was choking to death?

"I'm good," Paris said, patting her chest.

"So what exactly does—" Sasha attempted to pick up the conversation where it had left off before Paris's choking spell, but Paris interrupted once again.

"Y'all not talking about Terrance McKinley, are y'all?" Paris asked. Her eyes darted and blinked back and forth from Casey to Sasha.

"Yes, Eric's best friend, Terrance," Casey confirmed. She, on the other hand, didn't bat an eye as she replied to Paris matter-of-factly.

"Bitch, you know I know who Terrance is," Paris said, rolling her eyes.

Sasha's eyes were now darting from Casey to Paris. Paris had put a little stank on the word "bitch" when she said it, so she didn't know how Casey was going to react to that.

Accepting the word "bitch" as a term of endearment, Casey simply continued on. "He's crushing on Sasha here." Casey winked and then playfully elbowed Sasha.

"Girl, stop," Sasha said playfully, trying not to blush. Paris's intentional use of the B-word toward Casey was no longer on her mind. "I met the guy once."

"Yes, but he's talked about you a million times since," Casey confirmed.

"If she made that much of an impression," Paris interjected, "then why isn't he calling her up himself to tell her? Seems childish to be sending messages through his best friend." Paris poked out her lips and rolled her eyes. "Sasha, girl, you's a business woman. You ain't got time for boys and games in your life. Not even the game of basketball, and especially not with someone like Terrance." Paris pursed her lips and rolled her eyes.

"Okay, let's bring it down to a sensitive level," Casey said. "I think Sasha should be able to form her own opinion of Terrance. Don't you, Paris?" Casey looked at Paris all bug-eyed.

Paris simply let out a harrumph, tooted out her lips, and rolled her eyes. Her usual.

Sasha wasn't sure if she should remove and put away the sunglasses she was wearing on top of her

head, because shade had just been thrown. Or was
Paris asking a legitimate question and making a legitimate concerned statement based on her perception?

"You know how these guys are," Casey said,
shooing her hand. "They want folks to think they
are these hard players, but underneath they all
sensitive and shit." Casey and Paris shared a hand-
slapping *hee-hee* moment.

Sasha concluded that no shade was being thrown,
just the women vocalizing their observations and
own experience with men. But Sasha didn't throw
all men into the same pile and she wouldn't throw
Terrance into it unless he showed her something
different.

Still, with their personalities, these women made
it hard for a sister to determine if they were hating
or congratulating. With Paris, it was one of those
cases of "That's just how she is."

"Besides," Casey continued on with the conversation, "Terrance claims that the *somebody* who says
that Terrance is a really nice guy didn't give him
her phone number." She then cleared her throat
and proceeded walking, staring straight ahead.

Sasha had never given Terrance her phone
number. She was supposed to get his so she could
call him up to see if he had time to connect, but
the time had turned out to be right then and
there. That instantly changed the way Sasha had
been feeling about things. There was after all a
genuine chance that Terrance didn't think she was
just some piece of ass, or that her ass wasn't worthy
of him having another piece. No, that wasn't the
reason at all why he hadn't called her.

Sasha used the back of her hand to wipe off the

proverbial sweat beads from her forehead as she thought to herself, *Whew, my reputation in this town is still intact!* That added a little pep to her step. Sasha's chest puffed all out and her shoulders lifted.

"What?" Casey said. "Why are you all of a sudden walking around the mall like a peacock?" Casey asked. "Oh, I get it. You like him, too!" Casey exclaimed, a little bit too loud.

"Shhh," Sasha said, placing her index finger on her lips. "You loud."

"And you feeling Terrance," Casey said, "or just feeling the fact that he's feeling you."

Sasha could not hide the relief she felt inside, not to mention the boost to her ego. She smiled and blushed.

"Oh, yeah, she's feeling him all right," Paris said, not sounding like she was experiencing even a tenth of the excitement Sasha and Casey were. "Her true redbone features are telling on her." Paris pointed to Sasha's face. "Look at her cheeks turning all red. The child is flustered." Paris began fanning herself as she looked to Casey. "I must admit this whole conversation has me a little hot and bothered as well." She shot Casey a knowing look that went unnoticed by Sasha. Sasha was far off in La La Land.

Sasha didn't deny Paris's statement. That would have been being dishonest. Because she was definitely feeling Mr. Terrance. And although she didn't confirm it vocally, her actions spoke volumes.

"If you're really feeling him," Paris said in a serious tone, "you better not play games. No pun intended, but he will bounce that ball right to the next court. You keep doing the fake-out moves and the clock is going to run out without you ever getting your shot. Terrance ain't gon' stand around and watch you dribble. That gets boring."

Sasha poked out her lips in thought for a moment. Was Paris trying to say that Sasha was boring, too boring to keep a man? But never mind that; there was something more important Sasha wanted to do regarding Paris's word and the means by which they were delivered. "If I didn't know any better, I'd swear that you were speaking from experience."

"I am," Paris was quick to say.

Sasha's stomach sank. Her face mirrored the effect. Was Paris trying to say what Sasha thought she was trying to say? Had Paris had her own personal experience with Terrance? Because Sasha did not do leftovers. It was an unspoken rule that no matter how close or not close a woman was with a chick, she did not get with someone whom anybody in the clique had kicked it with. It didn't matter if the kick-it session included sex, just a movie, or even a couple phone calls. Nobody wanted to bring their man around someone whom, even if just for a hot second, he had been interested in. And no woman wanted to break bread with another woman who'd had her man first. That was too much power for any woman to have over another.

"Paris," Casey said under her breath almost in a seething manner.

Casey nodded her head toward Sasha while giving Paris a commanding look.

Paris turned to Sasha. "Child, fix your face," Paris said to Sasha. "You gotta remember where I work at," Paris reminded her. "I see these situations go down on a regular."

Sasha's emotions decreased from ten back down to zero upon Paris's clarification.

"Men will be men," Paris schooled. "Like Kanye said, a man can't be in a room full of hoes and not cheat. And these ballers are surrounded by hoes every day of the week. Hell, the average Joe is surrounded by 'em too! But if you gon' get with a man whose going to cheat, you might as well at least get with one that can pay for your pain and suffering."

Casey agreed with a nod.

"Why deal with a broke jive-ass nigga versus a rich jive-ass nigga that can at least provide you with a plush lifestyle?" Paris sucked her cheeks in and then released them with a popping sound.

"I hear what you are saying," Sasha said. "But no amount of money in the world mends a broken heart. I'm just not sure if I'm willing to take the chance . . . to take the risk."

"I speak from experience when I say—" Casey started to give Sasha a little insight on the life a baller's girl has to lead—how thick her skin must be—but Paris cut her off.

"Child, life is a risk," Paris said, pitching her empty drink container into the nearest receptacle. "Ask Casey. She took a risk, and look how things panned out for her." Paris looked to Casey. "You're living the fairy-tale life. Right, Casey?"

Sasha detected something about the way Paris was looking at Casey that made it seem like Paris knew something that Sasha didn't know. It was as if Paris didn't want Casey to truly confirm that she was living a fairy-tale life, but was more like turning a knife that was in Casey's heart.

It was possible that once again Sasha was reading Paris wrong. But that last comment was as conde-

scending as all get-out. And once again it had
seemed to go right over Casey's head as she eagerly replied to Paris's line of questioning without
a second thought.

"I wouldn't trade the life I'm living for the
world, Paris," Casey said with a smile as she looked
forward.

Sasha sensed that a minute ago Casey had been
prepared to share some other aspect of her life as
a baller's wife. But now it was almost as if she purposely was not going to voice such; not in front of
Paris, anyway.

Casey looked to Sasha. "I have everything I
need, want, and then some. After all, it could be
worse." She looked to Paris. "I could still be popping my pom-poms somewhere. Or even worse, I
could have to survive and pay my bills by working
in a strip club, but instead, I own the strip club the
strippers work at."

Without a doubt, Sasha was certain that was
shade and then some. Casey had shot Paris dead in
the heart with her words. But with Casey being
Casey, she was probably none the wiser of how perfect her aim was. Or was she?

"I'd rather still be stripping, or even shaking
pom-poms for that matter, rather than having to—"

"Anyway." Casey cut Paris off quickly, then faced
forward again. She'd put down Paris's livelihood
so unapologetically that it wasn't even funny. She
didn't look at Paris, she didn't offer the standard
"No offense" or anything. She kept strutting down
that mall like she'd simply just told them how the
weather was outside.

Well, Sasha wasn't sure how the weather was outside, but now she knew undoubtedly that it was

shady as hell in the mall. For the first time Sasha felt a little uneasy about the company she was keeping. Casey and Paris shooting invisible bullets at each other, although quite entertaining, was also slightly disturbing. Friends didn't do that to one another; not real friends, anyway. Fake friends, perhaps. Friends for show. Frenemies, maybe. Two people struggling at being cordial, even. But real friends? Not in Sasha's book. And the thing was that these two had known each other a few years. So if this is how they did each other, God only knew what they would do to her. But right now, thoughts of Terrance trumped cattiness. She was not going to let her mind get all discombobulated trying to figure out what these two ladies were doing when she could be figuring out what she was going to do about Terrance.

"You know what, ladies?" Sasha said. "I think I'm going to call it a day. I want to go home, do some sketching, and make a few phone calls to some spaces I've seen for lease."

"Oh, wow!" Casey said excitedly. "You're already to the point where you're ready to open up shop? I'm so happy for you. I'm going to be your best customer!"

Sasha smiled at just the thought of Casey keeping her word. "No, not yet," Sasha said with a positive attitude.

Hearing how excited Casey seemed to be for her made Sasha rethink her last assessment about how Casey might operate as a friend. The fact that Casey could celebrate another friend's growth and success was a sign that she was a true friend indeed. And just to think, Sasha had almost had the girl pegged all wrong.

"I just want to have some idea of how much certain spaces in different areas would cost me," Sasha said.

"Yeah, honey," Paris agreed. "Like they say, 'Stay ready and you won't have to get ready.' "

"That's all I'm saying," Sasha agreed.

"And that's all the more reason why you need to be linking up with money bags," Paris said.

Sasha didn't know what Paris was talking about. The puzzled expression on her face reflected as much.

"Mr. Basketball Player," Paris clarified.

"Oh, no, honey," Sasha was quick to say. "I'll leave the gold digging for someone else," she declared emphatically. "I've worked too damn hard to just have somebody write me a check in exchange for coochie. And I've got a degree to prove it."

"And you got student loans to prove it, too," Paris reminded her.

Sasha didn't have a rebuttal for that.

Paris kept going. "You can have that fool pay off your student loans and buy you a storefront with just the interest on his real money. He won't even miss it. Trust me."

For two tenths of a second Sasha wanted to agree and even considered entertaining Paris's thought. But it quickly exited her mind . . . or perhaps it was evicted. "Naaa." Sasha shook her head. "I want to know that I did this all by myself. That I reached my dreams with hard work and not a hard dick."

Casey laughed.

"Oh, okay," Paris said, twisting up her face and giving Sasha a see-if-I-ever-try-to-help-your-ass-again look. "Then you just scurry on along and go chase your dream, girlfriend," Paris said with an attitude.

Sasha made a face as if she'd bitten into something sour.

"What's wrong with your face?" Paris was quick to ask, not missing Sasha's expression.

Sasha went to open her mouth, but it was Casey's words that were heard.

"There's still a couple more stores I want to hit up." Casey looked to Paris and looped her arm through Paris's, which was on her hip. It was a subtle attempt to hold Paris back, as if sensing she was about to pop off. "What about you? You hanging with me?" she said to Paris.

As Sasha watched the two interact as if just a moment ago they weren't playing the dozens, she reconsidered Sasha and Paris's relationship. Perhaps after all they were more like sisters: able to fuss and fight but then move on because when all was over with, they loved and cared about each other. Sasha could accept that. Sasha was too busy analyzing her friends' relationship to pay any attention to the way Paris was staring at her.

Paris kept her eyes glued on Sasha, giving her the up-and-down look, while she replied to Casey. "Naw. I need to hit the road, too. I need to check in with my baby and handle mommy duties before I go to work tonight."

"Baby!" Sasha exclaimed. "You have a child?" Sasha went from being bent out of shape with Paris to being totally shocked by Paris. She had to have heard Paris wrong. She refused to believe for one minute that Paris had a child tucked away somewhere. In all this time, she'd never seen a child or heard Paris mention one. Maybe she was talking about her pet dog or something. Sasha knew several people who treated their pets like they were their children or something. Yeah, that had to be what she was talking about. A nice little shih tzu that she had to go home and feed and take out for a poop before she went to work.

"Yes, I am somebody's mommy," Paris confirmed. Her demeanor softened with the thought. "I have a six-year-old son who is the most handsome and brilliant little first grader in all of Atlanta."

"Oh, okay," Sasha said, and she left it at that.

Inside she was wondering how she could know a person for months and not realize they had a child. What does that say about one as a parent? All Sasha knew was that growing up, she stayed on her mother's hip. If Sasha's mother was at the store, then Sasha was right there with her. There wasn't any "Can you watch my child while I go to the grocery store." Neither was Sasha's mother one to dump her off at a neighbor's or relative's house either. If Sasha's mother was at home, then that's where one would find Sasha as well.

If there was a PTA meeting, if Sasha had a concert, play, or what have you, her mother was right there. Sasha's mother might have gone out every now and then with a girlfriend or two. It wasn't on the regular to the point that a person saw her in the streets and going out of town to party so much that they had no idea she had a child at home she could have been taking care of instead.

Sasha's insides were boiling over with inquiries she wanted to address to Paris regarding having a son—like why he was never with her. Like how she could spend so much time on the streets of Atlanta with a child at home. Luckily, Sasha had been taught to think before she spoke. As the words she thought in her head formed into complete sentences, she recognized that Paris could easily take them as shade. Now she understood exactly how Paris and Casey's earlier conversation had so easily turned into shady acres. Neither had thought before they'd spoken. Sasha would definitely be the exception in the trio.

"I guess I'll just finish hitting up the mall solo then." Casey sighed, then said to Paris, "Well, tell little Tory I said hello."

It relieved Sasha to know that at least Casey was aware of the fact that Paris had a son. Sasha didn't think she'd have been able to bite her tongue had Casey shot out, "What son?" That would have been too much. That would have taken the cake for sure!

"I will, lady," Paris said. She then leaned in and gave Casey a hug before the two separated. "All right, girlie girl," she turned to Sasha and said. If she'd been feeling some kind of way about Sasha just a moment ago, talk of her son had dissolved those feelings.

"You take care," Sasha said with a wave as she and Casey watched Paris walk away.

"I had no idea she had a son," Sasha said. "He's never with her."

"He's *sooooo* cute, too, with his little chocolate self," Casey cooed.

Sasha noticed how much Casey's eyes lit up when she talked about Paris's son. There was a longing there. "You like kids, huh?" Sasha said.

"Girl, I *loooooove* kids!" Casey said.

"Then you better tell that husband of yours to give you some," Sasha said with a smile and a pat on Casey's arm.

A melancholy expression appeared on Casey's face.

"Oh, I'm sorry," Sasha said, realizing she'd touched upon a sensitive subject unknowingly. "Can you not have any kids of . . ."

"Oh, no," Casey said, shaking her head to correct Sasha. "I mean I can, but I can't."

Sasha wasn't sure what Casey was trying to say.

Casey looked down, taking a few seconds to get her thoughts. "Eric said we can't, not with the lifestyle we live."

"Lifestyle?" Sasha asked.

Casey's head shot up. "I mean, well, you know, all the traveling we do from state to state. Dream vacations to other countries. You know. Not to mention he could get traded at the drop of a dime. If our kid was in school, we'd have to pick up and leave. That could be devastating. You know what I'm saying?" Casey let out some nervous laughter and then spoke again without giving Sasha a chance to respond. "Well, anyway, I'm going to, uh, you know, get back to shopping." She began backpedaling away from Sasha. "Good luck with, you know, the boutiques. The sketches or whatever." She turned forward and hurriedly walked away.

Sasha stood there dumbfounded. This afternoon with the girls had mentally exhausted her. If she didn't know any better, she would think both Paris and Casey had this other life they were living. Maybe not a secret life, but just one they kept tucked away nice and snugly. She hoped she didn't find herself caught up in either one of them.

Chapter 12

"You got me feeling all schoolboyish," Terrance said to Sasha as they strolled through Centennial Park.

Sasha chuckled as she looked down at her sandal-covered feet. "Why you say that?" She looked over at him; ironically, she was blushing like a school-girl.

"I'm hinting around to my boy about how much I'm digging on you, hoping he'll tell wifey and wifey'll tell you, then you'll call me, blasé-blasé."

Sasha laughed. "Well, isn't that just how it went down?" Terrance did finally tell Eric to have Casey pass on his phone number to Sasha, which she did . . . which led to the call that led to now.

"My point exactly!" Terrance expressed animat-edly. "Once I found out that Casey had given you my number, you had a brotha waiting around by his phone to see if you were gon' call and thangs."

Sasha watched Terrance overexaggerating in both his tone and his hand movements. Perhaps that was his way of making light of the fact that

Sasha had him doing some ole chump stuff. Little did Sasha know, he'd do it again if it meant things would end up how they did today: her agreeing over that phone call to go out with him. This time they really had opted for a public place to meet at.

Once again, Sasha chuckled. She knew the feeling Terrance was describing all too well, because that was exactly the role she'd played after her and Terrance's first encounter . . . before realizing he didn't even have her number to call. That thought brought about a question in Sasha's mind.

"A man so blunt and as forward as you, and with all the resources and connections you have, seemed like you could have figured out how to get my number."

"Oh, I had your number, but—" Terrance stopped and looked over at Sasha, who ceased her stride as well. "Don't think for one minute I don't have pull in this city."

Sasha loved the way Terrance was coming across. Not arrogant or overconfident, just sure of himself. She looked away and began walking again. She didn't want Terrance to see her as turned on by his demeanor as she was. She feared her cheeks were as red as the flames shooting through her body. "Then I'm even more confused," Sasha said. "If you had my number, why didn't you use it?"

"Because I wanted *you* to give it to me. Me getting your number and calling you doesn't necessarily mean that you would be receptive to the call. But you giving me your number yourself puts my doubts at rest."

Sasha tilted her head to the side. "Hmmm, you don't come across to me as a man of many doubts."

"Because I'm not," Terrance assured her.

Sasha noticed how he stayed a couple steps behind, as she purposely stayed two steps ahead. She didn't want the slight view of her black, sexy panties peeking through her white skirt to be missed. By the time this date was over, Sasha wanted to make sure that Terrance sent the designer a thank you card, because if the material had been just slightly thicker, he'd have been denied the visual treat.

"But when it comes to women," Terrance said, "a brotha would be lying to himself and the rest of the world if he claimed not to have some doubts as to how y'all operate."

"How we operate, huh?" Sasha repeated. "Well, do you have any doubts now?" Sasha raised an eyebrow as she glanced over her shoulder at Terrance.

"About what? Giving you my number?" Terrance shook his head. "Nah. I know you wouldn't have taken it if you hadn't planned on using it. I haven't known you for but a week or two, but I know you don't play games. I can't imagine you allowing even just a minute piece of paper to clutter your desk or your phone. You don't keep unnecessary things around. Like I said, you ain't one to play or be played with. Tell me if I'm wrong, but I bet when you were a kid you had not a single friend at recess because you don't play."

Both Terrance and Sasha laughed.

Terrance got serious and then tucked his bottom lip in while gazing at Sasha, who had slowed her pace slightly, allowing him to catch up with her just for a moment.

"Looks like you're very observant, Mr. McKinley," Sasha said, "because you're right; I don't play." Sasha abruptly stopped and faced Terrance.

"So if you think I'm one of those groupie chicks who you can play to the left, or if you think I'm a gold digger just 'cause I let you get it day one, or if you—"

Sasha's words were silenced by Terrance's tongue slipping into her mouth, after he'd pulled her mouth to his by cupping the back of her head. Sasha had never been one to display affection in public. As a matter of fact, she turned her nose up at couples who couldn't afford to get a room and therefore forced the public to witness their sensual regard for each other. But at this moment she didn't give a damn! The diva ho inside of her—nickname given by Norman, of course—wouldn't have minded Terrance bending her over the nearest park bench and hitting that from behind. But she'd already done the dirty deed standing up in a bathroom. And although Terrance appeared not to have lost any respect for Sasha, she wasn't willing to take the chance of lightning striking twice. So this time she'd keep her legs closed and her knees tight. But what harm was a kiss?

"You are the best kisser in the whole wide world," Terrance said to Sasha. He'd stopped kissing her, but was still so close that his lips grazed hers when he spoke.

"And how would you know?" Sasha asked, staring passionately into Terrance's eyes. It was then that she thought she'd noticed one of his eyes were crossed. But then again, maybe it was her eyes crossing because they were so close and she was trying to stare at him. "You kissed every woman in the world?"

"Yes," Terrance started, "because in my opinion, baby, you are every woman." Terrance went in for another passionate kiss. This time Sasha grabbed him by the back of his head and caressed it while their tongues danced.

"Get a room, why don't you? There are kids in the park, for crying out loud!" a jogger said as he passed Sasha and Terrance.

The two parted while laughing.

"He's just jealous that he's not the one kissing you," Terrance said, wiping Sasha's lip gloss off his mouth. "Anyway, you sure you don't want to go to a restaurant, grab something to eat?"

Sasha quickly put her hands up and shook her head. "Oh no," she said. "Nowhere where there is a bathroom, especially with the way you got me feeling now."

Terrance laughed, even though Sasha couldn't have been more serious. "And how do I have you feeling?"

Sasha thought for a moment, then she said, "Boy, you got me feeling some kind of way," and on that note, Sasha began walking away again with the hugest smile ever on her face. It got even bigger when she didn't feel Terrance walking immediately behind her. Those lacy black panties were surely doing their job.

"What's the matter, can't keep up with me?" Sasha shot over her shoulder, knowing darn well Terrance preferred not to.

"I can keep up. It's just the view from where I'm at. Ump, ump, ump." He shook his head.

Sasha put a little dip in her hips.

"See, now you are playing," Terrance said. "I guess I had you pegged all wrong."

Sasha turned and faced Terrance as she continued walking backward. "How so?"

"You do like to play." He licked his lips and nod-ded, almost knowingly.

Sasha raised her eyebrows, gave Terrance a naughty look, and then turned forward and con-tinued strutting. After a couple strides, Sasha shot Terrance a glance over her shoulder. He was rub-bing his hands together, watching her every move. He stared at Sasha as if he were the lion and she his prey. Now looking straight ahead, perhaps Sasha should have kept her eyes on the lion a little longer.

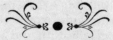

When Sasha walked into her apartment after her first official date with Terrance—their first night together didn't count, for Sasha had already killed it in her mind and buried it in ho heaven as Norman had instructed her to do—she was still definitely feeling some kind of way. She was having a hard time categorizing the date as good, bad, or in between. It was good in the sense that Terrance had shown her the best romantic afternoon possi-ble. What woman didn't enjoy a nice stroll in the park on a beautiful day; not to mention the bou-quet of flowers he purchased for her from a ven-dor along the way? Then of course there was the Ferris wheel ride and the ice cream cone. They each had removed their shoes long enough to get their toes wet in the fountain. It was something straight out of a romance novel. And it couldn't have been written any better had Brenda Jackson, the queen of romance novels, penned it herself.

Terrance had truly outdone himself as a gentle-man extraordinaire, making any other date Sasha had ever been on comparable to an ordinary trip to Mickey D's. But it had been bad in the sense that Terrance exposed some things about himself on this date that did not line up with Sasha's list. She'd have to erase a couple mental checkmarks. Come to find that Terrance didn't love the Lord as much as she'd thought after all. During their walk in the park they'd copped a squat on a bench to chat it up. When Sasha had asked, Terrance couldn't even remember the last time he'd been to church. Sasha didn't hold that against him. Although she'd gone to church on occasion with her mother, that was the gist of it. She didn't serve on the usher board or anything like that.

When Sasha had asked Terrance if he prayed regularly, his response was, "You know it; right before every game."

"Ugh," Sasha said out loud just thinking about it. Not being able to check something off the list of what her man had to have felt equivalent to having to check Terrance out of her life. But he was so cute. He was so handsome. He was so sexy, caring, attentive, and kind. The brotha was smooth. What else could she say? The good definitely outweighed the bad. And the very good . . . well . . .

Sasha flung her purse onto the couch and then flopped down right beside it. She really had to think this thing through. To the average person this might not have been serious, but need it be repeated that Sasha wasn't the average person? Everything in her life had to line up as planned. Getting off course with even the slightest little matter could mean her entire life taking a detour, which could lead to pure disaster. It was no secret that sometimes when people got off course in life, it could either be hell getting back on course, or the person could stray completely from their vision altogether. As fine as Terrance was, Sasha just didn't know if she could risk all she'd worked hard for . . . for love.

She let out a *tsk* and flung her hand out as she stood up from the couch. "Love? I don't even know if I like him, and here I am thinking about love." She could try to fool herself all she wanted about Terrance, but the fact that he was occupying so much of her mind space was a pure sign right there that she liked him all right.

"Okay, so I like him," she admitted to herself. "Now what?"

The "now what" was the fact that she needed to justify keeping Terrance on her list even though he didn't meet everything on her husband material list.

Okay, well, loving the Lord didn't necessarily mean one had to be up in church every Sunday, did it? Was it possible that finding a church home together was something they could add to their list of things to do, or even go on a date to church? Sasha posed these questions to herself silently in her head. She'd never done so much talking to herself in her entire life since moving to Atlanta to live by herself. She decided to table the one-sided conversation until after she showered and changed into her nightclothes.

Fifteen minutes later, Sasha climbed into her bed and back into her head. Thoughts of Terrance and the whole church issue were still on her mind. Yes, Sasha had attended church with her mother back in her hometown. But in the six months she'd been in Atlanta, she certainly hadn't bothered to find a church home. Perhaps it was the fact that choosing a church in Atlanta was just as difficult as choosing a place to grab a bite to eat. The franchises were endless. Perhaps she and Terrance could find a church home together, one they'd ultimately join and even get married in some day.

Sasha popped up in bed as sweat beads formed on her forehead. She looked around the room, her eyes landing on the digital alarm clock that rested on her nightstand. It was 10:53 p.m. That was just two minutes since she'd climbed in the bed and lain down. Not long enough to fall into a deep sleep and start dreaming, which only meant one thing. She hadn't actually been dreaming, she'd been daydreaming about actually marrying Terrance. And all this after only one date.

"No!" Sasha scolded herself, whipping the covers off of her and jumping up out of bed. The daydream now felt more like a nightmare in Sasha's mind. She had daydreams about fabrics, designs for what the marquee outside her first boutique would look like . . . not men. Okay, so after seeing the movie *Magic Mike* perhaps she did have a couple daydreams about being pulled up on stage by the male strippers and being pumped in the air. But that was different. She was now fantasizing about one man in particular. Now not only was she visualizing being pulled on stage by male strippers, but it was at her own bachelorette party.

"No!" Sasha yelled out to herself again, this time even spanking the back of her own hand. "Bad girl." She shook her head. "Get it together. Girl, get your thoughts together." As Sasha paced, she regretted the day she'd signed the lease to her apartment even more. She should have never settled for a place without a tub, because right now more than anything she needed one of those long bubble baths to get her mind right. Instead she'd have to settle for a shower . . . a cold one! Because that was the only thing that was going to cool her down when it came to Terrance. Either that, or the shade that was about to be thrown her way about the man of her daydreams from one of her so-called friends.

Chapter 13

Sasha was surprised when Paris sent her a text asking her if she wanted to meet out for a Saturday afternoon brunch. What was so surprising was that it hadn't been a group text that included Casey; not only included Casey but had been initiated by Casey. Usually the only time Sasha ever met up with Paris was when Casey set it up. Even though it caught Sasha off guard, she still accepted the invite. She and Casey weren't joined at the hip. There was no good reason why Sasha couldn't hang out with Paris without their mutual friend being present. Sasha saw it as an opportunity to form a relationship with Paris outside of the one they shared with Casey. After all, Sasha had nothing against Paris. She really liked her and thought she was a hoot. There was never a dull moment as long as Paris was around. Of course she'd never share how she really felt with Norman. He was far too territorial. But he didn't give Sasha the blues about hanging out with Casey half as much as he did when it came to Paris. But Sasha wasn't going to let Nor-

man's *thing* with Paris keep her from hanging out
with the girl.

As Sasha approached the club–like pizza restaurant, she hoped there would be no awkward moments trying to keep up a conversation with Paris.
Up until now the only thing Sasha knew for sure
that she and Paris had in common was the fact that
they were both friends with Casey. Hopefully that
wouldn't turn out to be the only thing, or else this
would make for one long outing.

When Sasha walked in, she was greeted by the
hostess. Sasha was in the process of asking for a
table for two when she saw Paris already sitting at a
table.

"Never mind," Sasha told the waitress. "I see the
other member of my party."

The waitress smiled and nodded as Sasha made
her way back to the table Paris was sitting at. As she
approached the table, she noticed that Paris was
sipping on a mimosa.

"You started without me?" Sasha jokingly
asked. She was about to open her arms for a hug.
Perhaps it was an Atlanta thing, but Sasha had
taken note that every time the three of them met
up, they always greeted one another with a hug,
did the once-over, and then complimented each
other on something such as their hair, shoes, or
outfit. Strangely, Paris didn't even stand up, let
alone open her arms to embrace Sasha for a hug.

Although Sasha thought it odd, she didn't take
it to heart. Maybe it was really just a Casey thing
and since Casey wasn't here, Paris didn't feel the
need to do it. Sasha would have these girls' MOs
down to a science soon enough.

Once she realized that Paris wasn't going to open

her arms for a hug, Sasha pulled out her chair and sat.

"Thank you for inviting me." Sasha looked around at the chic spot. "Mimosas and pizza. Nice."

"Umm hmm," Paris said with her lips pushed out and her eyelids low. "Nice," she mocked Sasha. "So I guess I better appreciate the niceness of this here place." Now she looked around. "Because not everything is nice. I mean, some people try to make like they nice, but then the minute you turn your back they talking about you like a dog."

An immediate chill rushed through Sasha's being. This time there was no confusion or question about it. Miss Paris baby was throwing shade and snowballs. Call her Ice Queen because Sasha was frozen; at least her words were frozen in her throat anyway.

"Can I get you something to drink?" The waitress wearing skimpy, tight black shorts with a tight black tee shirt approached their table and addressed only Sasha. Paris's glass was still more than half full.

Sasha didn't even want to respond to the waitress. She wanted to respond to what Paris had just said, but decided not to ignore the waitress. "I'll have what she has. A regular mimosa please," Sasha said to the waitress, but the entire time she stared Paris down.

"So you want what I got, huh?" Paris let out a harrumph. "Figures," Paris mumbled under her breath. She then mumbled so low that Sasha couldn't make out, "Half the tricks in Atlanta want what I got . . . or should I say had?" She rolled her eyes and crossed her arms.

Paris wasn't returning Sasha's glare. Her face

was still all contorted while she looked around, kicking her foot that was across her leg. Sasha was filled with anxiety and couldn't wait to get back to the conversation at hand to see what had Paris's G-string up her ass.

"I'll be right back with that drink," the waitress said, then walked off to fill Sasha's order.

Sasha jumped right back in. "You were saying something about people not being nice," Sasha said to Paris. "I could be wrong. I could just be all up in my feelings, but I felt as though you were directing your comment toward me." When Paris, still with twisted lips and now with one eye half closed and fluttering, just sat there wobbling her head like she was half listening to Sasha, Sasha continued. "Do we have a problem?" Sasha asked, a little louder than she'd wanted to. But the way Paris was sitting there looking at her as if she was a non-muthafuckin-factor was too much for Sasha to be quiet about.

"Oh, are we getting loud?" Paris asked with a smirk on her face that was egging Sasha on to let the inner ratchetness out. Paris uncrossed her arms and leaned in across the table while looking directly into Sasha's eyes. "I don't have a problem, but apparently you do. From what I hear, you have a problem with me being a mother." Paris then leaned back like she'd just dropped the mic after one hell of a performance.

Does she think she just checked me? Sasha thought to herself. She then shook off all the heated feelings that were building up inside of her. She had to keep it cool, calm, and classy. She was not going to let this city or anyone in it take her out of character. "A problem with you being a mother? Are you serious right now?" Sasha clearly had no idea what left field Paris had gotten her information from . . . not at first, anyway. Then it hit her; her mind went back to that day in the mall when Paris mentioned that she'd had a son. Sasha had been dumbfounded and shocked. Clearly she hadn't been able to hide her reaction and now Paris was calling her on it. "Is that why you invited me here today? To have a sit-down like we on the *Mob Wives* reality show or something?" Sasha asked. "It's not even that serious," Sasha assured Paris. "So the expression on my face when you mentioned that you had a son was that of a little surprise, doesn't mean I had a problem with it. I mean, what reason in the world is there for me to have a problem with you being a mother?" Sasha sucked her teeth. This was nonsense. Folks couldn't even make facial expressions anymore without someone getting all sensitive?

"Girl, bye," Paris said figuratively while waving her hand with a literal goodbye motion. "Don't even try to play stupid now that you in my face. Especially when you had a whole lot to say behind my back."

"Trust and believe that there is nothing I've said behind your back that I can't say to your face," Sasha said as the waitress came and set her drink in front of her.

"Are you two ready to order yet?" the waitress asked as she looked back and forth from Paris to Sasha.

It was obvious she could sense that she'd interrupted a very intense encounter. "I'll give you

ladies a few more minutes to look at the menu,"
she said, feigning a pleasant smile and then walking away.

"So is this what you invited me here for?" Sasha
picked the conversation right back up from where
she'd laid it down.

"That's exactly why," Paris confirmed. "It sho'
wasn't to break bread with yo ass. I'd already let
the situation fester long enough. The next time I
see you out with Casey, I at least want us to be cordial, so you need to be checked before that situation arises."

Sasha raised her back from the back of her seat.
She shook her head and made a face as if to say,
"Did I hear this girl correctly?" She then said to
Paris, "Check? Who gon' check me, boo?" Sasha
said matter-of-factly, daring Paris to come with it.

"Bitch, please," Paris snapped off.

This conversation had now reached ten, and
fairly quickly. Sasha hadn't even taken a sip of her
drink yet. So one thing was for certain: whatever
was about to go down, she couldn't blame it on the
alcohol.

"How the fuck you gon' try to question people
about me being a mother behind my back, but
then try to play it down when you in a bitch's
face?" Paris said, just as loud as she wanted to be.

"What? Question people?" "People" meant more
than one person. What the hell was Paris talking
about? Sasha only knew a handful of folks in that
town, and trust and believe she didn't have the
time on her hands to run around town with Paris
on her lips. There'd only been one person she'd
ever even mentioned the whole fact of Paris being
a mother to. That's when the lightbulb went off in

Sasha's head. "Casey." The word fell off her lips in disbelief. The next emotion was hurt. Would Casey have gone back to Paris and mentioned their brief conversation that day in the mall? But it was so innocent. Sasha hadn't really said anything wrong. But Sasha had to realize exactly which two people she was dealing with here. Those heifers could throw shade at midnight with no sun in sight. No telling how Casey had relayed the conversation to Paris and how Paris had heard it. Well, on second thought, it was clear how Paris had heard it. She'd heard it in such a way that this brunch was basically nothing more than a meet-me-after-school-at-three-o'clock set up. And that was jacked up, because Sasha was starved.

"Yeah, Casey told me what the hell you said," Paris confirmed. "And if you had such a concern with me having a child, then why didn't you say shit right then and there? I'll have you know that I take great care of my son and I don't need no stuck-up-ass jump-off from the Midwest trying to put anything other than that out on the streets. 'Cause you don't want to go there with me, Miss Thing," Paris shot in a threatening tone. "They didn't stop selling shovels when you bought one. I can dig up the dirt and sling it, too, Miss NBA jump-off."

That was it for Sasha. She'd been stuck at the first time Paris had called her a jump-off, so for her to say it again put Sasha over the edge. Sasha wasn't stupid. She knew exactly what Paris was referring to. Sasha had already been feeling some kind of way after having slept with Terrance on the first night she met him. She did not need Paris fanning the flames, so it was time she pulled out her fire extinguisher. "Look, I had no beef with you. I never questioned anything about your parenting. The only thing I mentioned was that I had no idea you had a son. In all these months I'd never seen him with you or even heard you talk about him. I know if I had a baby, I'd be so proud that the whole world would know it."

"Bitch, I am proud." Paris jumped to her feet. "And everyone in my world does know it. Ho, I don't know you. I don't talk to you like that. You're not part of my world. I'm not whipping out my wallet with baby pictures to show your ass. You're Casey's friend, not mine," Paris clarified. "So, bitch, that's why you didn't know. I can't say the same for you; all of Atlanta knows about you hoing with Terrance."

It wasn't but two seconds until Paris was wearing Sasha's mimosa. That wasn't good. Not only had Sasha been hungry, she'd been thirsty, too, and now there went her drink.

Sasha sat there in shock with her mouth hanging open. No, she hadn't just thrown her drink on Paris. Sasha wouldn't have believed it herself if she hadn't looked in her hand and seen the now-empty glass. What had happened? When? Why?

It was that very last "bitch" that had caused Sasha to just snap. Or had it been "ho"? Either way, Sasha was so regretful—that was until Paris's glass whizzed by her face, grazing her cheek, but not doing any damage. Not even a drop of the little bit of liquid that had been left in the glass splattered on Sasha. Nonetheless, Sasha hopped up out of her seat. It was inevitable that she and Paris were about to go to blows. Unlike when this kind of stuff went down on reality shows, there was no film

crew to break up the fight. As Paris came around
the table—mad that the throwing of the glass had
not done any good and therefore hell-bent on
making sure she got payback with her own two
hands instead of a weapon—a couple of waitresses
intervened.

Just as Paris swung on Sasha, one of the waitresses grabbed Paris's arm while the other pressed
her back into Paris's stomach to push her away
from Sasha.

"Let me go! Get the fuck off of me!" Paris began
to fuss and holler.

"Bitch, please," Sasha said. "You are as big as a
horse. If you wanted to get at me, you'd gallop
your big ass right through them and get me."

Paris looked down at the table for something
else to throw. There was nothing but a table setting. But now a man, the restaurant manager, had
entered the scene and was able to hold Paris back.

"Bitch, fuck with me and your name will be mud
in this city," Paris yelled in anger. "I'll let everybody know you here on a gold-digging mission.
Running through ball players and shit."

"No, ho, that's you," Sasha shot back. "Remember, you're the one who works as a stripper. You're
the one using your body to get coins. And apparently it's really just coins, the kind that make noise,
because real paper dollars would have kept your
car from getting repossessed once upon a time,"
Sasha spat. She couldn't even believe it herself
that she was going tit for tat with Paris. What else
could she do, though? She was not about to sit
there and let Paris think she could bully her. It was
time to resort to playground rules. If a bully hit
you, you hit them back where it hurts: that way

they won't mess with you anymore. Well, Sasha had swung some good punches, but now it was time to hit below the belt for good measure. "I wonder what your son says when he goes back to school after 'Take Your Child to Work Day'. Let me guess, 'Come on class, let's make it rain.' "

Paris's head damn near snapped off her neck. Sasha's words had cut to the jugular. Blood was shooting out of her neck and she couldn't even speak. Sasha was on a roll, though. She wasn't going to stop there. Before Sasha had moved to Atlanta her mother made her buy a gun and take a class on how to defend herself with it. Sasha had learned that if you pull out your gun, you better aim it. If you're going to aim it, you better shoot it. If you're going to shoot it, shoot to kill. In a sense that's exactly how Sasha had used her tongue, like it was a gun . . . a deadly weapon. It was time for Paris to die. That last comment just had to have been the fatal wound.

Surprisingly enough, Paris managed to gain control of herself and not lose it, but instead fire back. "Yeah, boo-boo. I had a rough patch financially. Haven't we all? But right now I'm driving a Land Rover, so now what? Now I'm picking my son up to and from private school in style while your broke ass is riding around in a Honda." She let out her wicked, annoying laugh.

"I'd rather work at a morally decent job and drive a Honda than have to take off my clothes for a Land Rover."

"Bitch, don't nobody take their clothes off, not all of them anyway. And I'll have you know that I don't have a problem in the world doing what I do. Hell, if you got the body, flaunt it."

"You mean gallop," Sasha said. "Your big ass stomping around like a damn horse or some-thing."

"Fuck you, you bony-ass fake bitch," Paris spat, going off in a rage again and having to be re-strained.

"Doug, get her out of here," the manager said to the man who was approaching them. He was wear-ing an apron so he must have been one of the cooks.

"Come on, ma'am. Let's go." Doug was very soft-spoken. He gently grabbed Sasha's arm.

"Y'all can do and say whatever the hell y'all want, just not up in here," the manager said as he began escorting Paris out of the restaurant right behind Sasha. And Sasha and Paris continued throwing verbal jabs at each other all the way until they were outside. "Where's your car, ma'am?" the manager asked Paris.

Paris managed to point while she called Sasha every name in the book.

Doug just stood there making sure Sasha didn't charge Paris or anything. Once Paris was inside her vehicle and had started it up, Doug and the manager headed back inside the restaurant.

Sasha watched as Paris peeled off in her truck. Her window was up, but she could still see Paris's lips moving. She was snapping her neck and point-ing her finger the entire time.

It took a few seconds for reality to set in for Sasha. "What just happened?" Sasha had to ask herself out loud as she stood there in complete awe. She took in a few breaths to try to calm her-self down. She then looked around. She could see people staring at her through the restaurant windows. Her anger turned into sheer humiliation as she hurried off to her own vehicle.

Had she really just had a public argument with someone whom she thought was her friend? Paris had been right about one thing she'd said: that Sasha was Casey's friend and not Paris's. That should have been the first red flag for Sasha; when Paris invited her out to lunch minus the nucleus of their little trio.

Speaking of Casey . . .

It was at that moment when something dawned on Sasha. Paris's whole beef with Sasha seemed to rest on the fact that she thought Sasha was questioning her parenting skills. There was only one place Paris could have gotten an idea like that. But instead of assuming anything, Sasha was going to find out firsthand.

She hopped in her car and drove off. She'd just tangled with one horse, so to speak, and now here she had to go get what she needed to know from yet another horse's mouth.

"Saddle up," she told herself as she exited the parking lot hoping that she didn't have to bust the damn horse in its mouth.

Chapter 14

"**D**id you whoop that trick? Did you whoop that trick?" Norman was bouncing around Sasha's living room waving his arm around in the air as if he were an extra in the movie *Hustle and Flow*, as he sang the hook of one of the more memorable songs from the Oscar award–winning film.

"Will you stop it?" Sasha said, rolling her eyes as she sat on the couch with her feet tucked up underneath her bottom. She was wearing a long spaghetti-strapped maxi dress. She'd changed out of her two-piece pant suit after returning home from her brunch from hell with Paris.

"I'm sorry, but I've been wanting to kick that drag queen in the balls for quite some time now," Norman said. "But in spite of popular belief, I did not wake up like this." Norman ran his hands down the side of his own maxi dress. He showed up at Sasha's doorstep in full Norma gear, informing her that he had been on his way to an afternoon rendezvous. But when he got the phone call from a distressed Sasha, stating that she'd gotten into a fight with Paris, he pumped the heels on his stilettoes real quick. He made a change of plans and headed straight to Sasha's place instead of his afternoon lover's. "My momma taught me to never hit a woman." Norman raised his nose in the air. "That and how to put on my mascara so that it doesn't cake." He rolled his eyes.

Sasha sucked her teeth. "Well, to answer your question, no, I did not whoop that trick. Not with my fists anyway."

A disappointed look was now cast over Norman's face.

"But I beat that bitch down with my words."

Norman smiled and clapped his hands together. Apparently that gave him some satisfaction. Sasha was sure it was not as much satisfaction as learning that she had pulled out a track or two of Paris's weave would have given him. This would have to suffice, though.

"Do tell, blow for blow." He sat on the couch next to Sasha. "And you better make it good, 'cause I literally could have been getting a blow by blow right about now." He looked down at his private parts. "If you know what I mean."

"I know exactly what you mean, and it's TMI, thank you very much." Sasha shook her head.

"Girl, just tell me what the hell happened." Norman was all set for Sasha to spill the tea, especially if that tea involved Sasha dismissing Paris as a potential friend.

He had more than expressed his dislike for Paris to Sasha. Sasha felt it went beyond him being jealous that Paris would steal some of his thunder as Sasha's bestie. After all, they were both loud, over-the-top, funny, and outrageous at times. Casey, on the other hand, was no threat to Norman. He'd told Sasha that she was just a little pussycat, although he brought it to Sasha's attention that she might not be declawed. That he was sure those little claws of hers could do some damage if her back were against the wall. But Paris was the type of level five hurricane that did damage just because she liked the aftermath.

Sasha went on to tell Norman everything that had gone down between her and Paris. She started with the initial text Paris had sent inviting Sasha to brunch. She went all the way to Paris peeling off in her car. Blow by blow details, just as Norman had requested.

"Umpf, umpf, umpf." Norman shook his head. "I can't believe I missed all that good old-fashioned Atlanta sweet tea," he said regretfully.

"Well, you're the one who said that if ever Paris is around, you won't be. So I don't invite you anywhere where I know she's going to be."

"Yeah, well, it was probably better off that I wasn't there anyway." Norman sighed. "God knows I would have snuck in a blow or two." He laughed.

Sasha let out a slight chuckle.

"Oh, there goes a laugh," Norman said, smiling and pointing at Sasha.

Sasha immediately started frowning again. It just didn't feel right to be joking and happy after getting into such a vicious verbal altercation with someone. At the time of the argument, it felt good when Sasha hit Paris with a left and then hit her with a right. Nothing replaced the feeling of being victorious in the ring. But now that it was all shouted and done, Sasha was left to reflect on the aftermath. And that didn't feel good at all. Her only concern wasn't just how Paris's words had made her feel. Yeah, they stung, but Sasha had gone way below the belt. She'd watched enough reality shows to know that she'd hit Paris in the unspoken zone that was never to be treaded on.

"I talked about her child." Sasha closed her eyes and shook her head. "I lose my mind if somebody talks about my momma. I can't imagine if someone put their mouth on my baby."

Norman rubbed Sasha's shoulder. "Cheer up, ladybug. She got off a couple good shots of her own on you." Norman thought for a moment and then chuckled. "That jump-off thing . . ." He chuckled again, but when he realized that Sasha was giving him a side-eye with blades, he silenced himself.

"But come to think of it, she called me a jump-off more than once. And the way she said it, too. It was with such disdain, almost as if she's jealous she's not Terrance's jump-off. Not that I am," Sasha was quick to say, putting her hand on her chest.

Norman looked down. Sasha watched him scan the carpet as if trying to hurry up and come up with something to say. "Yeah, but I know her ass really felt it when you threw it up in her face about her car being repossessed." He looked at Sasha. "How did you even know about that? That happened a couple years ago."

Sasha thought for a moment as she stared straight ahead. She shrugged her shoulders. "I don't know." She looked to Norman. "Didn't you tell me?"

"Un, un." Norman shook his head. "You know this beauty don't talk about that beast. I got ninety-nine things to talk about, but Miss Paris ain't one," he said matter-of-factly. "But, hell, everybody knew about her car being zapped while she was in Walmart shopping." Norman let out a harrumph. "The repo man sure know where to find a broke bitch." He laughed.

Sasha was still focused on where she'd learned that bit of info. "Are you sure you didn't tell me? Because everyone might have known, but you know me," Sasha said, "I don't know everybody. Just you and Casey. I talk to a couple people at work, but not like that. So it must have been Casey."

"Must have been," Norman agreed. "'Cause Paris's show-off ass sure wouldn't have told you." Norman puckered his lips and fluttered his long fake eyelashes. He crossed his legs and then placed both hands on his knees. "Well, well, well, if it ain't Little Miss Casey with a big ole ladle stirring up a nice pot of smelly shit." Norman let out a deep breath. "Who'da thought it?"

Sasha tried to think really hard about who or where else she could have heard about Paris's car being repossessed. That was some kind of underhanded information to have on somebody. So what possible scenario or discussion could have been taking place for Casey to have even mentioned it? Sasha was not one to sit back and talk about someone's business, nor listen to someone else run them into the ground . . . whether the person being discussed was a friend of Sasha's or not. Sasha didn't see the difference between someone running a person into the ground and someone watching or listening to the other person do it.

"No, Casey's not a shit starter,"—she raised an

eyebrow at Norman—"or a shit stirrer. I'm sure she must have just mentioned it in passing or something," Sasha said in Casey's defense.

Norman uncrossed his legs and spread them like a dude, resting his elbows on his knees. "Bitch, who the hell, 'in passing,' "—he used quotation marks with his fingers around the words "in passing,"—"comes out and tells you somebody's damn car got repossessed? Somebody who is trying to underhandedly tell somebody's business, that's who! After all, how the hell Paris find out you said something about not knowing she had a kid in the first place? Come on, Ray Charles. Can't you see that Casey is the common denominator here?"

The opinion Norman had expressed to Sasha that he had of Casey was starting to take on another shape. Sasha wasn't sure; maybe Casey was one to watch. God knows what folks say about the quiet ones. Just because Casey wasn't as loud as Paris didn't mean she couldn't ultimately do just enough damage. A hurricane may leave a more visible sign of destruction, but in some cases, termites can secretly do far more damage.

Sasha had never thought for even a hot second that Casey was trying to play her and Paris against each other. Why would she? Sasha wasn't hardly trying to steal Paris as a BFF from Casey nor was Paris dying to be around Sasha like that. As a matter of fact, had it not been for the fact that Paris had wanted to confront Sasha face-to-face, the two of them probably never would have been in a situation where it was just the two of them. *So what reason could there be,* Sasha asked herself, until something came to her mind.

"You know, Casey and Paris are funny to the point where sometimes they say things that I might think is shade, but it's regular ole conversation for them," Sasha said to Norman. "It's like they don't mean it to come out the way it does or to be taken the wrong way. It's just the way they do things." With Norman not being around Casey and Paris the way Sasha was, Sasha could understand why Norman would think the way he did.

"They throw shade, that's what those heifers do," Norman said, his mind not changed by Sasha's attempt to find reason in Casey's case of diarrhea of the mouth. "And you betta not sit your ass there trying to defend them. You think a big ole oak tree don't know it's creating shade when the sun is shining? Well, that big ole oak tree, who happens to be named Paris, knows when she's creating it. And so does that little bush who stays in her shadow: Casey." He looked to Sasha. "And hell yes, I just threw rocks at both them bitches. I'm very clear about mine."

"Why Casey got to be a bitch?" Sasha said. "I thought we were just hating on Paris."

"We were until you spilled the whole damn carafe of tea. Now that I'm no longer parched, I can see that Casey set you up on the low-low."

"Set me up for what?"

"For drama. To bring the ratchet or hood out of you, I don't know, something." Norman threw his hands in the air and let them drop to his sides. "You said it yourself that you never hook up with just Paris, that Casey is always there." Norman began looking around the room. "Well, where she at now? Where the hell Miss Casey Baby at now?"

Norman went looking behind the couch for Casey. He then went and checked under the lamp on the end table. "Casey, where are you and your ladle at?"

"Actually, she's on her way here," Sasha interrupted Norman's shenanigans. "Or at least she should be here any minute." Sasha looked down at her watch. "I called her when I left the restaurant, but she didn't answer. She sent me a text that she was at some silent auction or something. I hit her back with a 911 followed by 'Paris's and my lunch didn't go so well.' She then texted me back and said she'd be right over after her event was over."

Sasha's cell phone began to ring. She scooped it up from the end table and looked at it. "Speak of the devil." She showed Norman her caller ID screen with Casey's name and picture displaying.

"And the devil appears," Norman said, raising an eyebrow.

Sasha sucked her teeth. "Hello," she spoke into the phone as she put the call on speaker.

"Girl, I'm on my way," Casey said. "I stopped and got us some wine."

Norman snapped his neck. "Bitch know she had that shit on chill since last night, knowing some ish was 'bout to go down," he whispered.

Sasha put her index finger over her lips to shush Norman. "Okay, well, I'm here waiting on you."

"Okay, chick. I'll be there in five."

Sasha ended the call. She leaned back on the couch and could feel Norman's eyes burning a hole into her. "What?" Sasha said, shrugging her shoulders.

"What?" Norman mocked Sasha, her gesture and all. "So you 'bout to just sit over here and have wine with a rat, huh? Well, don't forget the cheese, a rat's favorite delicacy."

"Norman, for real, you really need to stop," Sasha said. "The least we can do is hear what Casey has to say about this."

"Un, un, you can sit here and listen to what Casey has to say." Norman swooped up his purse. "I'm going to get my dick sucked, or suck a dick or something. This pond is just not big enough for me to swim around with you two fishes. And mark my words, Casey is a fish that if you keep around too long, she gon' stink some stuff up real bad, and don't say I didn't warn you."

"Drama queen," Sasha said to Norman.

"Yes, I am a drama queen, and I make it damn clear that I'm a drama queen," Norman said. "And as much as it pains me to say this, I can appreciate Paris, too. Bitch is a snake and she lets you know she's a snake, so if you get bit and injected with her venom, shame on you. But that Casey . . ." Norman shook his head. "I'm not so sure."

"Right, and because you're not sure is why you shouldn't judge her and jump to conclusions about her."

"Why you going so hard for that girl?" Norman asked.

"I'd go hard for any of my friends."

Norman paused. "Friend, huh? If you say so." He flung his purse onto his shoulder. "I guess there's just one more thing I should warn you about the ATL." Norman paused for drama.

Feeding into it and curious as well, Sasha asked, "And what's that?"

"Be careful of that word 'friend.' It's often used interchangeably with the word 'enemy.' "

Norman exited Sasha's apartment, the brisk closing of the door leaving a chill behind. Or perhaps it was his words.

"When you talked about her son, you hit below the belt," Casey said. "Kids are off limits." She picked up her glass of the red wine she'd brought over to Sasha's place and took a sip.

Casey had only repeated what Sasha already knew. It was like pouring salt into a wound. But it wasn't Sasha's wounds that needed to be tended to right now. Sasha had to figure out how Paris had gotten wounded in the first place. Apparently, Sasha's little comment about not knowing Paris was somebody's momma had stung her deep. But when Sasha had voiced her feelings, Paris had been well out of earshot. So how had the words grown legs and traveled to her ears?

"I know what I said about Paris's son and the whole making it rain comment was all wrong," Sasha had no problem admitting. "But what I'm trying to wrap my mind around is how it even got to this point." Sasha picked up her own glass and took a sip of wine as well. "Paris is under the impression that I've been running around Atlanta calling her a bad mother."

Casey set her glass down. "Well, you did make reference to the fact that you were clueless about the fact that Paris was even a parent. Like she'd been running rampant around Atlanta, when she should have been at a PTA meeting somewhere."

Sasha's mouth dropped open. If Sasha wasn't mistaken, Casey was sounding defensive of Paris, like she had a problem with something Sasha had said as well. But on top of that, the words Casey had just spoken had unequivocally *not* come out of Sasha's mouth.

"Wait a minute here." Sasha held her hand up for Casey to pump her brakes. "All I spoke was my truth. I didn't say anything outside of that. So I don't know where you got all that extra stuff from." Sure, Sasha had thought a whole lot of things about Paris having a child, but she hadn't dared let those things fall from her mouth. "Funny thing is about all of this, though," Sasha said, "is that the only person I even shared my thought with was you. So what I'd like to know is how it got carried back to Paris in the first place."

Casey shrugged and picked her glass back up. Sasha watched her sip her wine all nonchalantly.

Casey cupped her wine in her hand. "Well, you know, all I said to Paris was that you said you didn't peg her to be a mother."

Sasha snapped her neck back. "But that's not what I said."

"Well, kinda-sorta you did," Casey said in a singsong voice while tilting her head to the side.

"There is no kinda-sorta," Sasha snapped. "I said exactly what I said, which was that I had no idea that Paris had a child. That's black and white, baby. If I say something, then take my words at face value. There is no reading between the lines. So what it sounds like to me is that you relayed to Paris what you chose to hear and not what I actually said."

Casey seemed a little taken aback. "Look, I did not come over here prepared to have to defend myself. After all, this is a dispute between you and

Paris. I'm just trying to get you two back on track. How the hell did I end up in the middle of it?"

"How did you end up in the middle of it?" Sasha repeated mockingly.

"What? Are you trying to say that I was on some he-said, she-said stuff when I mentioned that to Paris?" Casey seemed hurt and confused by the fact that Sasha would think she was that kind of person. "I promise you, Sasha, that is not who I am." Her eyes became moist. "You can ask anybody, I've never had to defend my character, and it really hurts me to think that I might have to now, because I really like you. I love having you as a friend." Casey put her glass down and wiped the tear that escaped from her eye.

"Oh, Casey." Sasha put her wineglass down and scooted closer to Casey on the couch so that she could comfort her. First Sasha had cracked Paris over the head with her harsh words, and now she'd punctured Casey's heart. Things were going from bad to worse. A tiny part of Sasha was starting to believe some of the folks in Ohio again; that she wasn't going to make any friends . . . that she wasn't even worthy of friends. That she should probably get her country ass out of the big city and haul it back home just as soon as her lease was up.

Sasha couldn't let that happen. She had to make it right, starting with Casey. "I know you wouldn't do something like that on purpose." Sasha put her arm around Casey. "But you have this funny way of communicating and saying things. And not just you. I'm learning that you Georgia peaches communicate on a whole other level than what I'm used to. Some of the fresh stuff that comes out of y'all's mouths would be fighting words back home, but you all don't seem to be fazed by it. Ya let it roll right down y'all's back. So maybe I should just learn to relax and not be fazed either," Sasha surmised.

"So are you trying to say that we throw shade at each other?" Casey asked, not the least bit comforted by Sasha's words.

"Well, yes," Sasha said, not hesitating to share another one of her truths.

"Wow!" Casey said, sounding even more hurt. "It's nice to know you feel that way about me, when all along here I thought I was cool with you." She guzzled down her wine and then refilled her glass with the bottle that was chilling in a Selene on the table.

Sasha put her hands up in defense, closed her eyes, took a breather, and then opened them again. "Okay, look, maybe I'm saying things all wrong, but I don't know how else to say them. All I did with both you and Paris was tell the truth." Exasperated and frustrated, Sasha added, "Is that how it works in Atlanta? People get mad at the truth?" Sasha shook her head and then took another sip of wine.

"I hear you," Casey said, sniffing. "I guess you are just keeping it real, but at the end of the day, that's what we are doing, too."

Sasha allowed Casey's words to sink in for a moment. *"Keeping it real."*

That pricked at Sasha's soul just a bit. She was never a fan of keeping it real if it involved hurting someone's feelings, and clearly that's exactly what she'd done, first to Paris and now to Casey. Was it possible that Sasha was changing and not even recognizing the change within herself?

The fact that Casey had even gone back and told Paris anything was now the furthest thing down the totem pole as far as Sasha was concerned. Sasha was now focused on her own behavior, words, and actions. Sasha was slowly but surely coming to the conclusion that maybe this wasn't about Paris or Casey, but instead about her and who she was as a person. Perhaps they were right where they needed to fit, and Sasha was the square peg trying to fit into a circle.

Sasha put her wineglass down, then removed Casey's from her hand and sat it down, too. Casey shot Sasha a strange look for doing so.

"Look," Sasha turned to Casey and said, taking her by the hands. "I'm sorry. I'm sorry for trying to flip this and put it on you. I said something, it got back to Paris, and she found it hurtful. If I hadn't wanted it to get back to her, then I shouldn't have said it, period, point blank. And even though I hadn't intended for it to hurt Paris, it did. For that, I owe her an apology as well. When you hurt someone, whether you mean to or not, you apologize with no ifs before it or buts after it. So, I'm sorry. Thank you for coming over to sit with me to hear my side of things. That alone shows you are a friend. You could have easily jumped to Paris's defense to go see about her, but you didn't. You're here, so in my mind that counts for something."

Casey nodded and smiled. "I accept your apology. Thank you for that. That really means a lot to me, because God knows good friends are hard to come by. And not only do I want you to be a good friend to me, but I truly do want to be a good friend to you, so if I've done anything—"

Sasha cut her off. "Remember, no ifs before an apology."

Casey nodded her understanding. "Yes, you're right." She cleared her throat. "I apologize for anything I've ever said or done to you that hurt you, that you felt was shade or whatever. I'm sorry."

"Apology accepted," Sasha said with a smile. The two friends hugged each other. "Whew, that was a lot," Sasha said, pulling out of the hug and picking up her drink. "I have been doing a whole lot more drinking than ever since I've moved to Atlanta."

"It be like that sometimes," Casey said, picking up her own glass. "This place is known to change a person."

That was exactly what was happening to Sasha. And since it went without saying, she didn't say it . . . out loud. But Lord knows she was thinking it . . . and feeling it, too. Somehow, she couldn't quite shake the feeling that Casey's tears had been a move to get Sasha to feel sorry for her.

Chapter 15

"Pardon me," Sasha said as she entered her apartment building. There were movers lugging in a bad-ass leather couch. The deep rich brown color was like a pool of chocolate. Sasha could smell the leather without even inhaling deeply. The "new" smell emanated from the furniture like incense. It wasn't even up for debate whether this was real or faux leather. Sasha was surprised she couldn't hear the cow still mooing. The men wore gloves so as not to get their fingerprints on the couch. There were pieces of cloth on the arms of the couch to protect it as well.

Furniture like this belonged in a house with a two-car garage, not some Craigslist apartment complex. *Fools,* Sasha thought. Who else but a fool would waste their money going into debt on that kind of expensive furniture for this glorified college dorm?

It was safe to say that Sasha was hating and full of envy. The honest side of her could envision that set in her own living room. She could imagine sitting there flipping through fashion magazines and being inspired. Only in her vision, the furniture was in her home in Buckhead somewhere. She exhaled. A girl could dream, couldn't she? Perhaps someday her dream would come true. For now, she knew better than to purchase the best bottle of Champagne on the menu and drink it out of a beer mug, when beer is what she should have ordered in the first place. But due to her sixth sense for fashion and good taste, she made sure she always looked like fine wine.

"No problem," said the mover holding the front end of the couch. "You're okay." He looked to his coworker carrying the other end of the couch. "Yo, Karl, hold up and let the lady by."

When the men paused, Sasha squeezed by them through the doorway, and up the steps that led to her apartment. As she arrived at the top landing, she saw a third mover coming down the hall. He nodded a hello and then went to help his coworkers.

"We got it. This is it," Sasha heard one of the movers say.

In the meantime, Sasha was really hating now. Not only had somebody in her building been able to afford such luxury furnishings, but they actually lived on her floor. Now not only would Sasha be able to smell the aroma of her neighbor's dinner drifting through the hall, she'd be able to smell their living room suite, too!

Sasha gave herself a quick pep talk and reminder to stay focused on her own life, not to covet what her neighbor has. Speaking of neighbors, just then Kels and her live-in boyfriend, whom Sasha had literally run into her first day in

Atlanta, walked out of their apartment. Kels eye-balled Sasha while her boyfriend locked their apartment door behind them.

Well, at least the furniture didn't belong to An-gela and Marcus, Sasha's nickname for the couple, as they reminded her of the couple from Tyler Perry's *Why Did I Get Married*. She could hear them arguing on the regular. Kels would probably cut Sasha if she thought for one second that Sasha was trying to covet both her man and her furniture. Sasha chuckled softly to herself at the thought.

"Howdy, neighbors," Sasha said in a kill-'em-with-kindness tone. Even though Kels looked at Sasha like she'd stolen something from her, namely her man, Sasha refused to reciprocate the attitude.

"Umm, hmm," Kels said, twisting up her lips and rolling her eyes.

Kels's boyfriend opened his mouth to speak. Kels snapped her neck toward him. She made him bleed, she'd cut him so deep with her eyes. Those daggers she'd shot at him were no joke. He was bleeding sweat. He quickly closed his mouth and balled his fist. Sasha could see in his eyes just how torn he was. He didn't want to be rude. His mother had probably always taught him to speak to someone when spoken to. He lifted his hand, but then he looked over at his woman and more than likely thought better of it.

This time Sasha had to chuckle out loud. Kels had her man in check.

Kels stopped in her tracks. "Did I miss some-thing? What's so funny?" She looked from Sasha to her man, then back to Sasha again. "You two got some kind of inside joke I need to be let in on or something?"

Sasha stopped and stared at Kels for a minute. This girl could not be serious. But when Sasha saw her nose flaring, she knew it was safe to say she was beyond serious.

"No inside jokes here," Sasha said as she exhaled, hoping to put her feisty neighbor's mind at ease. "Have a good evening, you two." Sasha shook her head as she made her way to her own place, making a mental note that she would never allow a man to make her feel so unconfident and deranged. Because even though Kels might have thought she was a boss chick for having her man on a short leash, she looked more like an insecure, crazy chick.

Sasha looked down at her key ring for her front door key. Once she had it between her index finger and thumb, she looked up. Once again Sasha stopped in her tracks, but this time it was out of fear. She noticed that her apartment door was wide open.

"What the . . ." Her heart rate tripled. All sorts of crazy thoughts ran through her mind. Had someone broken into her apartment? Were they still there . . . waiting to rob, rape, and beat her? Had they taken everything she owned? She breathed in and then out. Maybe there was a problem with the water pipes; they'd burst and the maintenance man was in there fixing them. There was a plethora of things rushing through Sasha's mind like crashing tidal waves.

"Pardon us, ma'am."

"Ahhhhh!" Sasha jumped and grabbed her chest. She turned around to see the movers behind her, still carrying the couch.

"I'm so sorry," the mover carrying the front of the couch said. "Didn't mean to scare you."

"Oh, that's okay," Sasha said, catching her breath. She had a sudden thought. "Can you do me a favor and check out my apartment for me? I think someone might be in there."

"Sure," the man said with concern. "Let us go set this down first and we'll be right there."

"Thank you so much," Sasha said, feeling much more at ease.

"Uhhh, can you step to the side?" the mover asked her. "So we can, uhhh . . ." He nodded to the couch.

"Oh, yes, sure. Certainly." Sasha hurriedly stepped out of the way.

With couch in hand, the movers walked past Sasha and went straight into her apartment. She at least thought they would have set the couch down in the hall before going into her apartment, but maybe they didn't want to take the chance of someone stealing it while they inspected her place for an intruder. Nonetheless, she was going to wait right out there in the hallway. She wasn't going into her apartment until she knew the coast was clear. If she heard some tussling, yelling, and commotion, she'd go run and call 911 to come rescue the movers. But it was not going to be a triple homicide if she could help it.

Only a few seconds had passed when both the movers came out into the hallway, looking around.

"Okay, which one is your place?" the mover asked Sasha.

She looked confused. "Here." She nodded to her open apartment door. "Where you just went in."

The two movers stood there looking confused.

"Where we just delivered the furniture?" the mover asked Sasha, scrunching up his face.

"Delivered the furniture?" Sasha said. "You mean you were . . ." Her words trailed off as she walked directly in front of the movers. They parted to let her through her doorway. Sasha cautiously stepped inside. Sure enough, not only was the leather couch placed in her living room where her old couch had once sat, there was also a matching loveseat. Both the couch and loveseat had beautiful throw pillows on them, and there was a Persian rug placed in the middle of all the furniture. But the most surprising and beautiful thing out of it all was the chocolate accessory sitting on the couch like he owned the place.

"Terrance?" Sasha said in shock. "What . . . what are you doing here?" She dropped her purse and keys on one of the ottomans and began spinning around in a daze. "What is all this? I don't understand how you got into my apartment."

"Mr. McKinley, is everything good?" the mover who had been doing all the talking thus far asked Terrance.

"Yes, gentlemen. As you can see,"—he sensually eyeballed Sasha—"everything is just fine." Terrance stood as he dug into his pants pocket. "Thank you guys for everything. I appreciate it." Terrance pulled out a wad of cash and peeled off a hundred-dollar bill for each mover. He then peeled off a third. "And give this one to y'all's boy," Terrance said, referring to the third mover Sasha had seen earlier.

"Thank you, Mr. McKinley." The silent mover finally spoke. Benjamin Franklin had a way of making people talk. "Any time. Just call on us."

"Thank you," the more talkative mover said to Terrance, then looked to Sasha. "So everything's okay, ma'am?"

Apparently he hadn't forgotten about how frantic Sasha had been just moments ago. Sasha was still stunned at the scene going down before her.

"Uh, yeah, I think. I mean . . ." She shook her head, hoping the words would rattle into place. "I, uhh, don't understand." Sasha looked to the movers. "Guys, I didn't order this furniture."

"I did," Terrance chimed in. "Don't you like it?" He sat comfortably back down on the couch.

"I-I love it," Sasha tried to assure him, only her dragging words didn't sound so sure. She had to pause and think about this. What exactly did him buying this furniture mean? Certainly this brotha didn't think he was going to be camping out at her crib. Is that why he'd purchased the furniture? He wanted to get something he could be comfortable on? Had he actually bought it for himself instead of her? They'd only been dating a little while. She'd been out on ten dates with another guy who barely wanted to pay the restaurant tab, let alone buy her a brand-new living room suite. But what Sasha had to realize was that she wasn't dealing with the average dude. Terrance was paid. He was a baller. This was all foreign to her.

"I knew you would." Terrance smiled. He looked mighty proud of himself for picking out the furniture all on his own. "I knew this was your taste. Not that the furniture you had before wasn't nice, but I just didn't see you all sprawled out, elongated, resting,"—he nodded toward Sasha's body while eyeballing it—"on something like that." He licked his lips. "Not with all that you're working with. Only the best for the best."

Well, he'd confirmed that he had, in fact, bought the furniture to suit her liking. Sasha swallowed. She appreciated the compliment. She appreciated the furniture even more. She hoped she wasn't sounding hard to please or ungrateful. "I appreciate that, Terrance, I really do, but—"

"You really don't like it, do you?" Terrance asked, sounding disappointed. "You just don't want to hurt my feelings. Come on, I'm a big boy. You can tell me the truth."

"No, it's not that at all," Sasha said. "When I saw the men moving the furniture into the building, I was already jealous of the owner, having no idea that you were the owner."

"You are the owner," Terrance corrected. "It's all yours."

Sasha walked over to the loveseat. She was still having a hard time grasping the fact that this man had given her such an expensive gift. Then again, there was always a chance that he hadn't just simply given it to her. Perhaps there were strings attached. Heck, there could even be money attached. She could be wrong in assuming that it was completely paid for. Perhaps he expected her to pay for the rest. She admired it and rubbed her hand down the loveseat. It felt so soft. She could definitely picture herself curled up on it flipping through magazines. She needed more clarity first. "But I can't . . . I can't afford this. What are the payments? Probably about five hun—"

"There are no payments." Terrance cut her off. "It's my gift to you. It's paid in full."

Terrance had confirmed beyond a shadow of a doubt he'd bought this furniture just for her. Sasha's mouth fell open. She didn't know what else to say at this point. She looked to the deliverymen. They each nodded, backing up Terrance's statement that no balance was owed. The furniture was all hers. Sasha put her hand on her forehead and went and sat down on the couch next to Terrance. "Good Lord," she said as she sank into the softness. "This is . . ."

"Yours," Terrance said.

Sasha stared at the furniture, rubbing it. "Thank you, but—"

"I know you are not about to have me have them come pick this furniture back up," he said, sounding slightly annoyed.

Sasha looked from the furniture to Terrance. His tone was a little edgy. She wanted to look at him and see if his facial expression matched. Perhaps his words had come across harder than he intended. That was the second time that his tone had made Sasha bristle.

Terrance looked at Sasha. "I don't offend easily," he started. "But I'm going to take it personally if you don't accept it. I really took a lot of pride in picking this out for you."

That explained why Terrance's tone had sounded on the verge of callous there for a minute. He'd been offended by her rejecting his gift. Sasha could understand that coming from a man like Terrance. He'd probably encountered many women who expected and therefore accepted him throwing gifts their way. He was going to have to get used to the fact that Sasha wasn't one of those women. At the same time, she didn't want to appear ungrateful to the man.

Sasha thought for a moment. She was so torn. What woman in her right mind would want to give the furniture back? Especially not a jump-off, which is what Paris had accused Sasha of being. Especially not a gold digger, which is what Paris, in so many words at the mall that day, had instructed Sasha to be. Sasha didn't want to be labeled as any of those things. So would keeping the furniture make her out to be just that?

"Consider this as a blessing," Terrance said now in a much softer tone, in an effort to be more convincing to Sasha. "My momma always told me that a person should always accept a blessing from God. And more importantly, never block a blessing from God."

Sasha looked to Terrance. She'd heard that saying before. She believed it to be true as well, but there was only one thing. "You ain't God," Sasha said to Terrance.

"True," Terrance said, scooting closer to Sasha. He got right up in her face and then held her chin with his hand, turning her face to him. "But let me be your savior." He then planted a deep, passionate kiss on Sasha's lips. He pulled away and stared into her mesmerized eyes.

"So, uhh, are we leaving the furniture or not?" the less talkative mover asked.

Sasha didn't respond. She simply sat there staring into Terrance's eyes.

Terrance, not taking his eyes off Sasha's, simply shooed the movers out with his hand. They exited, closing the door behind them. Upon hearing the door close, Terrance and Sasha engaged in yet another passionate kiss.

"You taste too damn good," Terrance said, pulling away from Sasha, staring her in the eyes. "It's the truth," he assured her when she returned his stare, her eyes showing doubt.

"And you, Mr. McKinley, taste too good to be true."

"Why do you say that?"

"Because it's how I feel. I come to Atlanta, the first guy I meet is everything a girl could dream of. It doesn't even seem real. It's like I'm living a fairy tale right now."

"See, that's what I meant about that fear factor," Terrance said. "Don't be afraid to let me do what I want to do. Don't be afraid to allow someone to make you feel like a princess in a fairy tale. I mean, I don't get it." Terrance gave Sasha a quizzical look. "You said it yourself; women dream of a man treating them like this, and when a man like me treats you in ways you dreamed of, you can't accept it. It makes me think women want certain things, but then deep down don't feel worthy or like they deserve it when a man does try and do it for them."

Sasha had to admit that Terrance had a very valid point. She'd always looked at herself as someone who deserved to be taken care of. Someone who deserved nice things. Here Terrance was doing it and she was trying to find fault in it. She owed this man an apology and she knew just how to apologize.

Sasha moved to stand in front of Terrance.

After a few seconds of silence he looked up at her. "What?"

"Oh, nothing. I just wanted to thank you."

"Yeah, well, you're welcome," Terrance said in a dry tone.

"You're welcome?" Sasha questioned.

"Yes, you're welcome for the furniture.

Sasha placed her hands on Terrance's knees as she got down on hers. "Oh, but I haven't thanked you yet."

Terrance and Sasha stared into each other's eyes as Sasha leaned into him. Her lips brushed his as her hands moved up his thighs.

"Oh, man," Terrance whispered against her lips, squirming in excitement.

Sasha pressed her lips against Terrance's as her hands worked their way toward his groin. The sound of his pants being zipped up was like the needle scratching a vinyl record.

Terrance looked down at his zipped pants with disappointment.

"Your fly was open," Sasha said, pulling away from him.

"Oh, uh, thank you. Thank you." Terrance looked uncomfortable and disappointed.

"What's wrong?" Sasha asked. "You didn't think you were about to get a blow job in exchange for a sofa, did you?"

Terrance bit his bottom lip.

Sasha burst out laughing, then moved to sit beside him.

"That kiss was my way of saying thank you. No one has ever done anything like this for me."

"You're welcome," Terrance said. "Knowing you, you've probably never let anyone do anything like this for you, which is why I didn't ask, I just did." He kissed Sasha on the forehead.

"You think you know me, don't you?"

"Don't I?" Terrance questioned. "Trust me. I've met those chicks who wouldn't hesitate to furnish their entire house on my dime. I didn't even have to offer it as a gift to them—hell, they asked me." He let out a harrumph. "But you, on the other hand, Miss Lady, I knew if I offered, you'd decline. So I didn't ask. Like I said, I just did."

Sasha turned to face forward. "Speaking of which, how did you 'just did'? How in the world did you get into my place?" Sasha turned abruptly to face Terrance again. "Did you secretly make a copy of my key or something? What else you got up in here?" Sasha said jokingly as she began to look around. "Some little microphones and video cameras?" She looked back up at him.

Terrance laughed. "Woman, you crazy, although that might get us our own reality show."

"I'm serious. You're the one who I found sitting in my apartment when I got home from work today. An apartment you do not have the key for . . . or do you?" Sasha asked.

"No, I don't have a key," Terrance assured her. "I'd never sneak and make a copy of your house key. The property manager let me in."

"What the?" Sasha said, perturbed. "How he just gon' let any ole body up in my spot? You could have been a stalker or a killer or something."

"Well, if an NBA star showed up with ten men named Benjamin, wouldn't you have turned over the key as well?"

Sasha looked at Terrance, once again outdone by all he'd done for her. Terrance winked.

Sasha smiled. "No, *I* wouldn't have. You are

something else." She rubbed the sofa. "I still can't believe you did all this for me."

"Well, believe it, because this is just the beginning."

"Oh, Lord, what's next?" Sasha asked jokingly.

"Well, I was thinking as I sat here earlier watching the movers carry the furniture up." Terrance paused, hoping to pique Sasha's curiosity.

"And what were you thinking?" Sasha said.

"That this type of living room suite belongs in some place much more . . . I don't know . . ." Terrance chose his words carefully as if wanting to impress Sasha, not offend her.

"Bigger, more expensive?" Sasha saved Terrance by finishing his sentence for him. "A house?"

"Exactly." Terrance snapped his fingers. "I mean, the matching chair is still on the moving truck. We couldn't figure out where to put it without making the place seem cramped."

"There was a chair?" Sasha said excitedly, then realizing that Terrance was right, there was no place in her apartment to put the matching chair, her excitement deflated like a Tom Brady football.

"Yep," Terrance said, sounding just as disappointed as Sasha. "It was a final purchase, too, so I can't even get my money back for it."

"So you just let them take it back to the store?"

"No, of course not."

"Oh," Sasha said, relaxing a bit. Prying, she asked, "Well, what are they going to do with it?" Deep inside she imagined him giving it to the real jump-off; her matching chair sitting in some hoochie's Section 8 apartment.

"I figured I couldn't break up a set like this, so if

the entire set won't fit into this apartment, then I guess it all needs to go in a house."

"A house?" Sasha asked. "Whose house?"

Terrance sat up and turned Sasha's upper body to him. He looked her in the face before he dropped his next bombshell. "To your house, or should I say, our house, if you let it be?"

Sasha paused to read the expression on Terrance's face. He had to be kidding. "A house? You bought me furniture and a house to put it in?"

"No—I mean yes—well," Terrance said, trying to put his words together. "Yes, I bought you furniture, but no, I didn't buy you a house."

Sasha exhaled. This bomb-ass furniture suite was more than enough. She couldn't imagine being gifted a house by a man she'd practically just met.

"I was thinking more like my house. Like you move in with me and make it *our* house?" Terrance said.

Sasha lifted completely up off of him. "Are you crazy?" she asked. It was safe to say that she had definitely not thought before speaking. Those were the exact words that had popped into her head. She'd shoved them out of the door that verbalized her mental thoughts without even putting a hat and coat on them to make them all warm and fuzzy. Nope, they were just cold. Casey's and Paris's ways really was starting to rub off on her.

"As a matter of fact, I am crazy," Terrance said proudly. "I'm crazy about you, Sasha."

Sasha could see the genuine excitement in Terrance's eyes. No other agenda seemed to be hidden behind them. His sincerity truly did melt Sasha's heart. And if she'd ever had a wall up to protect her heart and mind, it must have been made out of chocolate, because the warmth Terrance was giving off was melting it, too.

"Terrance, I . . ." Sasha's words trailed off. What could she say to all this? She'd only known Terrance three months and already he was talking about the two of them moving in together. Sure, she'd spent hours talking to him on the phone and they'd FaceTimed, but still, moving in together? She had to get into his head just a bit more. "Terrance, you honestly don't think we are moving too fast?"

"I'm not trying to be funny, but baby girl, we surpassed moving too fast when you let me hit it on day one."

That stung Sasha somewhat, and it showed on her face.

"I'm not saying that to make you feel some kind of way," Terrance said, grabbing her shoulders, "but when something is meant to be, it just happens. We let it happen on night one, so let's keep letting it happen," Terrance said. "Or was our first night together not special to you? Do you make it a habit of sleeping with someone you don't have feelings for, or don't feel that instant love at first sight for?"

"No, I don't just sleep with any ole body," Sasha said, sounding slightly offended because she was.

"And neither do I," Terrance was glad to say.

"Do you honestly want me to believe that an NBA star who has women throwing it at him twenty-four-seven hasn't had his share of one-night stands?" Sasha asked in total disbelief.

"No, I don't want you to believe that, because I have had my share of one-night stands, and they were just that, one-night stands. But you and I clearly are beyond just one night. What we have isn't a one-night stand kind of a relationship, but a we're-still-standing kind of relationship." Terrance took Sasha's hands into his. "I'm tired of chicks and dating women who just want to be an NBA trophy. I need a partner. Like how Eric and Casey are. Seeing them together made me realize that I want that, too. I'm not coveting another man's wife, but when I see how down Casey is for Eric, I want someone just like her by my side. You can ask my boy. Believe it or not, I've been talking about it with him. And I won't lie, I've even asked Eric to ask Casey if she would hook me up with one of her friends." He let out a chuckle.

"Desperate times call for desperate measures, huh?" Sasha said.

"I won't say all that. A brotha wasn't desperate." He looked Sasha in her eyes. "Just determined. And forgive me for sounding corny, but the fact is that I saw you even before I ever knew you were Casey's friend." He shook his head in disbelief. "You can't tell me we weren't meant to be."

Sasha blushed, eating up Terrance's words just as quickly as he could serve them.

"When I met you, it was a sign from God that it was time for me to stop messing around and give up the life of just random women with no one woman to call my own. A man can have all the women out there in the world, but there is something about having that one to come home to. And I don't just want a chick to come home to, I need someone who is about something. I'm not asking you to marry me. Do I feel in my spirit that you are going to be my wife? Yes. But I figured if I showed up with an engagement ring instead of a leather couch, you'd really think I was nuts. But please don't think I'm some sicko when I say this. I know you're my wife, the mother of my children. I know it a little sooner than you. I just need you to know that. But don't worry, I'm sure you'll catch up with me eventually."

Sasha couldn't remember the last time she'd felt this sentimental. Her eyes were becoming moist. She blinked her tears away. She could not let this man think she was putty in his hands. "So you really expect me to just give up my place, give up everything, and come stay with you so that the minute you decide to move on to the next chick, I'm left out in the cold?"

"I'd never do you like that," Terrance said, heartfelt. "We can even keep this place. Keep all your stuff here. You moving in with me can be like on a trial basis. It could be like you're spending the night . . . a lot." He chuckled.

Sasha shook her head. "Terrance, I don't know. This isn't what I came to Atlanta for." Sasha got up off the couch. "I came here to start a new life, to start my own business, to live out my dreams, to—"

"Isn't finding love part of your dreams?" Terrance asked. "Isn't that part of everybody's dreams?" He didn't wait for Sasha to answer. "So let me at least make that part of your dream come true." He stood up and pulled Sasha to him. "Let me make all your dreams come true." He kissed Sasha on the lips. "They say the things that happen that you don't plan are the best things in life. I didn't plan on meeting you and falling this hard for you, but yet it feels like the best thing that has ever happened in my life."

Sasha melted in his arms pretty much just like she always did whenever he touched her, whenever he looked at her.

"Just think about it," Terrance said after pulling away. "For now, though, at least happily and without reservations accept the furniture as a gift. Okay?"

Sasha could do that much. She nodded. "Okay."

Terrance kissed her on the forehead. "I'm going to head on home. I got training early in the morning."

Sasha nodded. She was drowning in her emotions. She didn't know whether to be happy, scared, confused, or flattered. If she didn't know any better, she would say was experiencing all of those emotions at once. The boys she went to school with back home and dated just didn't do things like this. They weren't even certain if they wanted to put on new underwear each day, let alone spend the rest of their days with someone. But maybe that was the difference between them and Terrance; they were boys and Terrance was a man. Perhaps Sasha shouldn't see this as strange at all, but as how a real man with class and coins handles his business.

Why should Sasha look at his actions as weird or too soon? Like her, Terrance knew what he wanted and had a plan, and it wasn't a five-year plan like the average person's. Geesh, it wasn't even a one-year plan like hers. Could it be that Sasha had met a man who could keep up with her, if not surpass her? Not one she'd have to wait around on to make up his mind? It truly was time that Sasha looked at the glass as half full.

"Let me at least make you something to eat before you go," Sasha said to Terrance.

"I ate right before I got here." He rubbed his stomach. "But thank you anyway."

Terrance kissed Sasha good-bye and then left. Once he was gone, Sasha looked at her beautiful new furniture. It was all hers, free and clear. She raced over and plopped down on the couch, looking up at the ceiling with a huge grin on her face. But then her grin soon faded as she thought about something someone had once told her.

"Nothing in life is ever free. There's always someone else who has paid the price or someone who will eventually pay the price."

Chapter 16

"Thank you for meeting with me today," Sasha said once Paris was seated nice and comfortably in her chair at the outdoor patio of the restaurant.

This time it was Paris who had arrived last. This time it was Sasha who had, via text, invited Paris to join her for brunch. And this time Casey was present as well. And even though Casey was there to run interference just in case anything did jump off, Sasha had settled on dining outside versus indoors. She'd rather they tussle outside on the ground than tear up the inside of the restaurant and owe the owner repair costs. But Sasha definitely didn't expect any such ghetto nonsense to go down. Even if Paris wasn't, she herself was mature enough to communicate using her mouth and not her fists, although that was kinda sorta what caused things to somewhat escalate the last go-round: her mouth. But life was going *wayyyyy* too well for Sasha to be risking a case. Besides, she was on cloud nine and she'd be damned if she'd let Paris's size eleven shoe kick her off of it. In addition to that, maybe two weeks ago her catching a case and landing an Instagram mugshot might have gone unnoticed, but she wasn't so sure that would be the case now with folks starting to link her with NBA star Terrance McKinley.

"So you said you wanted to talk," Paris said stubbornly, already in defense mode. "Then talk." She was staring straight ahead at Sasha. She hadn't even looked at Casey since arriving and giving her their standard initial hug, once-over, and compliment.

Needless to say, Sasha did not receive that same greeting. She didn't even get a "Hey." But that was okay. If things went Sasha's way, all would end well between her and Paris soon enough. They could still kick it with Casey and be cordial around each other, or they would go their separate ways with no hard feelings. Either way Sasha was good. She had far too many other things of importance going on that had transpired in the last two weeks.

Sasha wasn't too keen on being given orders by anyone other than her boss at work, but once again, putting all things aside and trying to stay positive and upbeat, she obliged Paris's request.

"I'm really sorry about how things went down between us," Sasha started before the tension could thicken and things could get worse before they got better. "I was wrong to put your child in it. If you and I have something going on between us, then that's where it should stay. Children are off limits."

Paris began shaking the foot of her crossed leg. "See, that's the thing, *Sasha*, I didn't even know there was something between us. I liked you. I thought you were real. Thought you were cool peo-

ple. The time before last when we were together,
we were shopping in the mall, hee-hee and hee-
hawing it up over smoothies. Next thing I know, my
girl"—she pointed to Casey—"telling me you said
this and you said that about me being a mother."

Sasha looked over to Casey, who in turn was staring straight at Paris as if refusing to acknowledge
her stare. Watching how Casey was trying to play it
off and avoid her part in starting all this mess in
the first place hit a nerve with Sasha, but she stayed
focused on the situation at hand. She was not
going to move backward, so she allowed Paris to
continue without addressing Casey at all.

"How hard would it have been for you to say,
'Girl, what? I've never seen you with him, heard
you say a word about him,'" Paris said. "Then we
could have taken it from there. But no, you go saying it behind my back to Casey. So maybe you didn't
say it the way I took it and felt. But can you blame
me? I'm thinking you could have just as easily said
it to me, so the fact that you didn't had my mind
conjuring all kinds of stuff up. You see what I'm
saying, *Sasha*?" Paris said, leaning in.

The way Paris was saying her name made Sasha
feel as though she was being spoken to like a child.
It made her feel as though she was being talked
down to and belittled. But the same way she wanted
Paris to come up out of her feelings, she wasn't
about to go into hers, so she brushed it off, straightened her shoulders, and pulled her big-girl panties
up. After all, that's what she'd seen Casey and Paris
do many times. Perhaps Sasha was learning the
ATL way of communicating—or not communicating—more quickly than she thought she could be
taught. Even if it was shade (be it intentional or

unintentional) coming out of a person's mouth, put on a sweater to get rid of the chill, or go find your own shine in the sun.

Sasha crossed her arms over her chest. "Yes, I see exactly what you're saying, *Paris*," Sasha said, exaggerating Paris's name the same way Paris had exaggerated hers. Okay, so sometimes it was even okay to pop up a parasol and create some shade of her own. "Next time, in order to eliminate any misunderstandings or confusions, I won't suppress any thoughts." She looked to Casey. "With either of you."

"Good," Paris said, "'Cause you best believe I won't suppress mine. Open communication is the only way. That way can't nobody go back and say anything you've said to somebody else because they would have already heard it and therefore nobody will get upset."

Casey and Sasha looked to Paris with tilted heads and question marks in their eyes.

"Girl, what the hell did you just say?" Casey said, then she and Sasha burst out laughing.

"Forget y'all," Paris said, shooing the girls before joining in on the laughter. "Anyway, y'all know what the hell I was trying to say."

"I don't know, girl," Sasha said, shaking her head. "On second thought, maybe you might not want to say everything that comes to your mind. That might make things worse!"

The women chuckled as the waiter came over and took their food orders. As soon as the waiter left, Casey dived right into the conversation she'd actually been wanting to have with Sasha.

"So, now that we are all back on good terms, let's do some girlfriend talk." She looked to Sasha.

Paris followed Casey's lead and looked to Sasha as well.

Sasha was taking a sip from her Coke. Back home she'd been a die-hard Pepsi fan, but one soon learns that you can't move to Atlanta and not become a Coke fanatic; not with the Coca Cola factory being one of the most popular tourist attractions in the city.

"What? Why y'all looking at me?" Sasha asked after pushing her Coke to the side.

Paris shrugged. "I don't know. Casey was just looking at you like she got some tea, so I'm looking to you to spill it."

"Well, I have some Coke," Sasha said, pulling her glass back to her, "but no tea today, ladies." She fluttered her eyelids as she took another sip of her soda. "Sorry."

"Well, sorry," Casey mocked, taking a sip from her vodka and cranberry with a splash of Sprite. "But I heard otherwise," she sang as she took another sip of her drink and allowed her eyeballs to dart this way and that.

Sasha sat back and crossed her legs. "And just exactly what did you hear?"

Casey took her time sipping her drink, wiped her mouth, pushed her drink to the side and then looked to Sasha. "That you've been spending quite a bit of time with Terrance."

"Oh, yeah," Paris said, rolling her eyes as if she was expecting a much juicier piece of fruit. "I think I did read on a blog that Atlanta's golden boy has got a boo." She didn't sound impressed.

"Not just that," Casey clarified, her tone the complete opposite of Paris's. She sounded excited and ready to get in Sasha's business. "But I hear there's more. That she's been laying her head quite a few nights at Terrance's place." She shrugged. "It's like you've practically moved in." She sipped her drink again.

Sasha tried her best to control her facial expressions as both Casey and Paris tried their best to read her facial expressions. She didn't want to give away the truth one way or the other. Not yet. She wanted to do a little reading of her own first.

"First of all, just who are you getting your information from?" Sasha asked Casey.

"The streets are talking," Casey said.

"Bullshit," Paris jumped in. "Them niggas is talking, that's whose talking. Men are worse than women. All they do is run their mouths." Paris looked to Casey. "Wasn't we having a similar conversation not too long ago in the mall where Terrance was telling Eric stuff and then Eric was coming back to you and then you were telling Sasha?" Paris sucked her teeth. "Talk about some he-said, she-said." Paris looked to Sasha. "So just put it together. Your boy is putting your business in the streets."

If Sasha had been allergic to bees, that sting would have done her in. Now her facial expression, the aftermath of being stung, she couldn't manage to hide.

Casey jumped in to pull the stinger out and rub a little alcohol on it. "He's not putting your business on the streets. He's just rapping with his bestie is all."

"Yeah, yeah, yeah," Paris said, rolling her eyes. "Then maybe Eric is spreading some things around. Or at least he be spreading something around." Paris raised an eyebrow at Casey.

"Seriously," Casey said to Sasha before giving Paris *the look*, telling her to chill out. "The same way I'm sure you and Terrance have pillow talk, so do Eric and I. We are husband and wife. We are one. My boo tells me everything."

"Well, hell, does that make him Terrance's boo, too, since Terrance is telling his ass everything?" Paris said.

Sasha sat there and watched the back-and-forth game of Ping-Pong between Casey and Paris until the waiter brought their food. After so long, Sasha jumped in. "Look, ladies, never mind about those insignificant details about who is telling who what." She looked to Casey. "What I want to know is exactly what was said."

Sasha would have liked to have been the one to tell her girlfriends about her almost moving in with Terrance. Yes, most of her clothing and personal belongings were now at Terrance's home, but per his suggestion, she had not given up her place.

"Well, you know I'm just a temp at a law firm," Sasha had said to Terrance when she'd finally decided to move in with him, two days after he'd proposed it. "I can't afford to pay my rent at my place and chip in at yours." She did not want to come across as some bum bitch just laying up at Terrance's place.

Terrance had laughed so hard that tears formed in his eyes. Once his laughter subsided, he said, "Woman, I wish I might have you chipping in on the roof I keep over my head. What kind of man do you take me for? I'm old school. I'm a provider. Even though my mother has her own business, my pops still pays all the bills. That's how his pops taught him things were supposed to be done in the home. He passed it on to me, and I'll pass it on to my son as well if I ever have one. If not, I'll pass it on to my daughter that she better not think about getting with a man who makes her pay for the roof over his head."

Sasha both respected and appreciated Terrance's way of thinking. So it was decided she would stay at Terrance's place rent-free and continue paying out her lease agreement on her own apartment. But just yesterday when Sasha went to her rental office to pay this month's rent, she was informed that her lease had been paid up. As if that alone hadn't been a shocker, when Sasha asked the manager when it had been paid up, she was even more shocked to learn that it had just happened to have been the same day her new leather furniture was delivered. Not only had Terrance paid the manager a thousand dollars to let him into her place, but he'd paid off the remaining months of her lease agreement. Terrance was definitely a man with a plan, but perhaps Sasha shouldn't be so quick to assume that his plan lined up with hers.

"Whether you moved into my place or not," Terrance had said to Sasha when she confronted him about her findings, "I still wanted to pay your rent for you."

When Sasha was torn about how to feel about Terrance doing something so drastic for her, he had to remind her that she wasn't dealing with some okey-doke dude. She was dealing with a man who had been raised to treat women like the queens they were, so she'd have to get used to it.

Sasha made up her mind that she'd get used to

it all right. And not only that, but she deserved it. Why let the next chick get blessings that were meant for her? But even though Sasha had reasoned and justified everything in her mind, that didn't necessarily mean the rest of the world would see things the same way. The rest of the world, being Casey and Paris, of course, might look at things totally different.

"Not too much was said," Casey told Sasha. "Eric just said that every time he's talked to Terrance this past week, you were there. Not to mention that anytime I call or text you, you're *'not home right now.'*" Casey used her fingers to make quotation marks, because those had been Sasha's exact words to Casey every time she asked her where she was.

Paris squinted her eyes. "Why you acting all funny?" Paris used her long acrylic nail to point at Sasha. "It's like you trying to get everything out of Casey about what she knows in order to see if you need to tell her something she doesn't know."

Both Sasha and Casey shot Paris a puzzled look.

"Girl, will you stop talking in riddles?" Casey said to Paris, then turned back to Sasha. "But she's right, you know. I think."

"Oh, I know I'm right," Paris shot. "She holding out on us, Casey. Trying to keep all the tea to herself while we sit over here thirsty. I see how you are, Sasha. You like to drink up other people's stuff but then leave us in a drought."

Sasha laughed. She wholeheartedly loved Paris's sayings. "You and your comparisons, girl!" She shook her head. Being around Paris did keep her laughing, when they weren't pulling out each other's hair that is. When they were good, they were good, but when they were bad . . .

"But she's right," Casey said. "And you have no idea how hard it is for me to try to untwist the riddles she's talking in, make sense out of them, and then admit that I agree with them. So please, just come out and say whatever is going on before everything she says starts making sense out the gate!" Casey threw her hands up, exasperated. "Hell, I need another drink. And not no damn tea."

"Although it would be nice if you just went on and spilled it," Paris said, not letting up. She could tell Sasha had something to hide. Paris took a bite of her food.

Sasha thought for a moment, then, not able to keep it in any longer herself, she blurted out, "Terrance bought me this bomb leather furniture set, but then when it all wouldn't fit into my house, he suggested that I get a house that it all could fit in . . . his house. So I moved in with Terrance. There." Sasha said it all in one breath and then began eating her food without making eye contact with the ladies. She sucked up that Coke like she'd been dying of thirst. She used the straw to maneuver around the ice cubes to get every last drop.

"You do know they have free refills, don't you?" Paris said.

"Yeah," Casey concurred. "Free refills, free furniture, hell, you get all kinds of stuff for free these days."

Both Paris and Casey chuckled.

"You two stop it," Sasha said. "That's why I didn't want to say anything. I knew you two were going to try to clown me. I practically just arrived in Atlanta yesterday and now today I've already moved in with someone." Sasha let out an "Ugh," and then said, "My mother is going to kill me."

"For what?" Paris said. "Casey's momma didn't kill her and I think she'd met and married Eric within that same time frame as you met and moved in with Terrance."

Casey picked a crumb of bread off the sandwich she'd been eating and threw it at Paris. "Did not."

"Go on and lie to yourself while I tell Sasha the truth," Paris said. "But anyway," she said to Sasha, "you ain't got nothing to feel bad about. I'd be shouting it at the rooftop. Bitches would be hating me." Paris's tone dampened. "If only I'd played my cards right. That could be—" Paris's words faded, but Casey had cut them off, anyway.

"I can't believe you didn't tell me," Casey said, pouting.

"Duh, I didn't even tell my own mother," Sasha said. "And I tell her everything."

"I don't see why you're being all secretive about it." Paris shrugged. "You have nothing to be ashamed about."

"What would your mother say if after all these years she raised you to be a strong, independent woman, you move out on your own and then shacked up with the first thing smoking?" Sasha said to Paris.

"I wouldn't know," Paris said, kind of sadly, "my mother didn't raise me." She cast her eyes down.

Sasha, feeling like she'd touched a sore spot, looked to Casey.

Casey did a quick shake of her head, signaling Sasha not to go there with Paris.

Once again Sasha felt like Paris and Casey had so many things between them. They wanted to be all up in Sasha's business, but seemed to keep the most intimate details about their own lives under lock and key, and they'd made copies only for each other. For the first time ever, a tinge of jealously poked at Sasha. But then she quickly had to reason with herself that Casey and Paris had been friends longer than she'd been friends with either of them. In time she'd no longer feel like an outsider. Perhaps eventually they'd all make copies of their keys for each other.

Paris cleared her throat. "But my grandmother, the woman who did raise me," she said, brushing off her emotions and putting on her tough act again, "would have said, 'Granny ain't raise no fool.' "

Casey laughed. Sasha only laughed in hopes of keeping the spirits up.

"She's right, though," Casey said to Sasha while nodding toward Paris. "You don't have anything to be ashamed about. You can't let what other people will think and what other people will say affect or define your relationship with Terrance. I told you about me and Eric hooking up. Just imagine if I'd let the rest of the world and what they thought get to me. I'd still be pumping pom-poms."

"Or like you so eloquently put it before," Paris said, "dancing at a strip club."

Aha, Sasha thought. So way back when Casey had made that comment, Paris had, too, thought it was shady.

Casey acted as if she hadn't even heard Paris's comment. She floated right on over it. "I personally am happy for you." Casey put her hands on top of Sasha's. "Our dudes are besties," Casey squealed. "So you know what that means . . . lots of double dates."

Sasha smiled and then exhaled. "God, it feels good to get that out. I felt like a teenager sneaking over her boyfriend's house." Sasha and Casey laughed.

"Well, you just better hurry up and change the title from boyfriend to husband," Paris said. "Hoes in Atlanta move fast." She sipped her drink. "Hell, looks like even the hoes from Ohio move fast, too."

Sasha turned her head sharply toward Paris.

Paris looked up from her straw and saw the look Sasha was giving her. She sucked her teeth and put on a happy face. "Girl, I was just playing." She started chuckling.

Casey started chuckling, too, a little louder and more exaggerated than she should have. Sasha, just like she had a few moments ago, chuckled as well, just to keep the spirits up. But something told her that this little threesome she was trying so hard to fit into might take its toll on her own spirit.

Chapter 17

The next couple of months went by like a montage for Sasha. Her life was truly like scene after scene of the greatest romance movie there ever was, and she was the leading lady. Her life with Terrance was nonstop excitement. One minute Sasha and Terrance would be on a tropical beach sipping drinks out of pineapples. The next minute they'd be like two crazy teens, adrenaline pumping as they conquered roller coaster rides at Six Flags. Sasha walked around the theme park with stuffed animals Terrance had won her shooting basketball, of course.

What Sasha really enjoyed was attending Terrance's games. Casey had taken her shopping, of course, to show her how she needed to dress for the games. On game day, Casey made sure Sasha was at her house three hours before tipoff for hair and makeup.

"Honey, now that you are dating a baller, the game has changed," Casey had told her. "And I don't want to hear none of that shit about this all being foreign to you. You better learn to speak the language and learn the customs is all I can say."

"This is just too much," Sasha had said one day while having her makeup professionally done at Casey's house. "I can't remember the last time I've attended a seminar, gone to the library to do some research, or even sketched at home." Spending time with Terrance was taking away from Sasha's regular schedule, and those three hours of preparation getting ready to attend one of his games didn't allow her any free time after work. Whether Sasha wanted to admit it or not, the love train had come full speed down the tracks. It had hit her, thrown her several thousand feet in the air, with her landing way off course.

"You think this is too much?" Casey said to Sasha, letting out a harrumph. "Then don't even think about marrying that man. Dating a baller is one thing, but being the wife of a baller is a whole other animal. Trust me."

"How so?" Sasha asked.

Casey looked Sasha up and down. "Ummm, let's see if you make the team first, then we'll talk."

There was no need in Casey wasting her time and breath if Sasha couldn't even handle hair and makeup. Casey sent her shoe stylist away and said, "You give up a lot of things if you decide on this lifestyle, but you gain a lot of Manolo Blahniks."

In spite of how much time being with Terrance was taking from Sasha's schedule, she was loving it. One day she would be at one of Terrance's games, and the next she'd be in a restaurant he'd had shut down for the night just to entertain her. Then there were the evenings of mad, passionate love, and mornings, and afternoons as well.

And just as Casey had mentioned, there were the double dates. On a Monday Sasha and Casey would be at the mall on a shopping spree to pick out clothes for a weekend get-away with their men. Sasha was surrounded by Valentino and Armani clothes and she couldn't be happier about it. Her thrift store dress was thrust to the back of her closet so she could make room for her new Balmain pants.

By the Friday after their latest shopping spree, they were in another country altogether. Just when Sasha thought things couldn't get any better, she and Terrance now found themselves on a private jet to Europe, compliments of Eric and Casey. Sasha thought Terrance did things big; well, Eric did them bigger. Not only had Eric flipped the tab for their transportation to France, but he'd paid for their hotel stay as well.

Terrance and Sasha arrived to a beautiful room that was twice the size of her old apartment. Sasha was certain it was one of the best rooms in Le Royal Monceau until the next evening when Eric and Casey invited them to their suite for evening cocktails.

"You've got to be kidding me," Sasha said when she entered the two-story suite. This would be their second night in Paris, but their first time see-ing Casey's and Eric's living quarters. "Your hotel room has a spiral staircase leading to a second floor? This is sick." Sasha, without being offered a tour, took it upon herself to take a few steps and enter the living area of the suite.

Casey followed on her heels, ready to take on the role as tour guide . . . in more ways than one. Sasha had never seen Casey in anything so slinky and low cut. Although the girl was always happy to show off her assets, Sasha was sure that her underwear had more fabric than the jumpsuit that Casey was rocking.

Eric had a proud look on his face when he said, "Only the best for my lady." He finished up the alcoholic beverage he had in his hand. "They had another one available that I tried to get your boy to stay in," Eric said to Sasha as he and Terrance followed behind Casey. "But he wouldn't accept."

"What?" Sasha said and spun around. "You mean to tell me we could have been staying in a room like this?" She raised her arms and allowed them to drop to her sides. Although Sasha still had frugal streaks, suddenly being around so much money made her realize exactly what money could buy. And she wasn't about to ignore the finer things.

Terrance sucked his teeth. "Man, I'm not going to ask anybody to spend money on something I wouldn't spend it on," Terrance said. "It's nice and all, but I'm not giving them people, or having someone else do it on my behalf, that much damn money to lay my head somewhere for a night. It's robbery, and I won't be an accomplice."

"It's not robbery," Eric said. "It's living, so stop being frugal and live a little."

"I do live," Terrance countered, "and quite well. But I ain't one to just throw my money away."

"But it was Eric's money you would have been throwing away," Sasha said, just as serious as ever.

Eric laughed. "Yeah, but your boy was being all humble and shit."

Eric and Terrance might have been best friends, they both played for the NBA on the same team and enjoyed some of the same things, but when it came to money, they were very different. Eric was a

bit more—okay, a lot more—flashy than Terrance.
He wanted the world to know he had money at his
disposal, even if it meant he was on some Floyd
Mayweather ish and simply burned it just to show
that he literally had money to burn. Sasha noticed
that Casey would be right there smiling beside him
whenever she saw things on the Internet about the
couple on one of their extravagant evenings out.
Eric and Casey always seemed to have an entourage, mainly women, trailing them. Eric was an attention getter. What better way to get attention
than not only to be in the company of his beautiful
trophy wife, but in addition to that, have five to
eight more beautiful women surrounding him?
Why he didn't want folks to know he was a partner
in that sex circus was beyond Sasha, especially
when he walked around looking like a pimp anyway.

At first Sasha did find the fact that his entourage was female instead of male just a tad unusual.
But leave it to this couple to switch things up. And
it worked for them. Definitely kept them in the
limelight enough to make them local celebrities.
Casey always looked completely fine with her gag-
gle of scantily clad followers. She was always smiling for the cameras.

Sasha was glad that Terrance didn't feel the
need to roll like that. Having a bunch of men always around them period would aggravate her, but
having beautiful women around would make her
feel a certain type of way. But Casey's concept was
always the more, the merrier. To Sasha it appeared
as if, for Casey, having just a couple good friends in
her life wouldn't suffice. She wanted to be surrounded by lots of people who, at least to the world,

looked like they were friends even if they really weren't. After all, Sasha had never met any of Casey and Eric's party groupies. So it didn't seem like Casey was all that close to them. It was always about what things looked like from the outside looking in with Eric and Casey. But in a few moments, Sasha would get a clear vision of the view from the inside looking in.

"Man, I paid two thousand a month for Sasha's rent at her apartment," Terrance declared, "I wish the hell I would spend that kind of money per night for one hotel room. I'd rather spend that money shopping for my girl where I can see my money."

"Four thousand a night," Eric bragged.

"And you weren't spending it," Sasha said. "He was." She nodded to Eric. "And aren't you the one who said something about not blocking blessings, not accepting them, or something like that?"

"Yeah, but this is different," Terrance said. He looked around at the huge open living area with snow-white furniture and a killer view over Paris. "This is just overboard. And besides,"—he took Sasha into his arms—"if my lady ever stays in a place like this, it will be on my dime and not another man's." He gave Eric the side-eye. "'Cause I know how this nigga rolls."

"If I pay, you gotta play." Eric winked, then grabbed Casey and pulled her into his arms. Her back was against his chest while she nestled in his arms. He kissed her on the back of the head.

Sasha looked to see if Casey was maybe feeling some kind of way about Terrance's comment and Eric's reaction to it. How did Eric roll? Pay to play? What was that comment supposed to mean? Did

Eric expect something from Terrance for paying for the trip? Did he expect something from Sasha?

When Sasha saw that Casey was all smiles, looking quite secure in her man's arms, she figured if Casey wasn't bothered, then why should she be? It was probably just another case of Sasha, once again, looking more into things than she needed to. There was no reason for Sasha to have taken Terrance's comment as anything other than silly guy talk. After all, that was the motto of Eric's strip club: pay to play.

"Come on, let's head into the den." Casey pointed, exiting her husband's arms.

"Den? This joint has a living area and a den?" Sasha said, stomping off to where Casey had pointed.

"Don't be mad at us," Casey said as she followed behind Sasha. "Be mad at ya man, because y'all could have been right next door."

"Yep, adjoining rooms," Eric added with a hint of seduction behind his tone as the women entered the den area without him and Terrance.

"Which is another reason why I ain't want this cat putting us up in no pimped-out penthouse suite like this," Terrance said. "Might think I owe his ass something." He headed toward the den.

"Oh, there wouldn't have been no might about it," Eric joked. "You know I'm into barter and trade." He laughed as he, too, headed into the den.

"Will you two stop being silly?" Casey turned to face her husband. "And nasty, and just come on." Casey, who was leading the way, disappeared into the den area. Soon after, the men entered behind her.

Sasha had long ago entered the den, missing
out on the little conversation that was taking place
between the other three. She stood in the den
area trying her best to maintain her composure.
She figured she'd drooled enough over the adjoining couple's vacation space. She didn't want to
make it seem like she and Terrance were bum-
ming it. Their room was lovely, too, but Casey and
Eric's room was like comparing Sasha's apartment
to Terrance's house.

The couples sat down to a spread of appetizers
and fancy hors d'oeuvres Casey had ordered up to
the suite from room service. There was a fully
stocked bar in which Eric played bartender until
everyone was settled in with their favorite cocktail.
The couples were having a lovely time joking and
talking when Eric cleared his throat and looked to
Casey.

Casey straightened up and then grabbed her
drink. "I have an idea," Casey said. "Let's play Truth
or Dare."

"Truth or Dare?" Sasha snickered. "How old are
we?" She laughed and then took a drink of her
wine.

"Oh, come on, don't be a ruddy poo," Eric said.
He looked to Terrance. "You're game, aren't you,
man?"

"Uhhh, I don't know." Terrance shook his head.
He'd just taken a sip from his drink. "I've heard
grown-up games have ruined many a relationship,
especially the game of Truth or Dare." He sat his
drink down on the glass table that separated one
couple from the other.

"But you don't have anything to hide, do you,
Terrance?" Casey shot Terrance a knowing look.

Sasha turned to see what Terrance's reaction would be. Terrance simply picked up his glass and began drinking. It was almost as if he was giving himself a reason not to be able to talk.

Now all of a sudden Truth or Dare didn't sound so bad to Sasha. She and Terrance had talked about everything under the sun, so she couldn't imagine what he could have possibly left out that could play a part in the demise of their relationship. But if there was anything, Sasha wanted to find out. So if acting like she was some teenager back in high school was the way to do it, then so be it.

"You're right," Sasha said to Eric before Terrance could talk them out of the game. "I don't want to be the Debbie Downer, the party pooper. Y'all want to play Truth or Dare? Let's play." Sasha took another sip of her drink and then slammed the glass down like she was ready to go. A few drops splattered out and, surprisingly, it didn't break . . . the glass or the table.

"Awww, snaps," Casey said, "Miss Serious is going to come outside with the rest of the neighborhood kids and play. That's what I'm talking about." Casey stood and made her way to the bar. "And everybody knows that a game of Truth or Dare calls for tequila."

"I'll help you, hun," Eric said as he eagerly stood up and joined Casey at the bar.

"Tequila?" Sasha shot under her breath. Sure, she drank more since moving to Atlanta than she ever had. And sure she'd tried a few drinks outside of her usual wine. Norman had even talked her into a zombie. But tequila!

Eric gathered shot glasses for the couples while

Casey grabbed a bottle of tequila. The two raced back over ready to play like two kids who had been denied recess their entire lives up until now.

"It's time to separate the boys from the men and the girls from the women," Eric said as he placed a shot glass in front of everyone.

"You have no idea what you've gotten yourself into with these two, do you?" Terrance asked Sasha, shaking his head.

"No, but I'm starting to wish I'd just kept my mouth shut," Sasha said, looking at Casey and Eric's eagerness. "Y'all two look like lions about to devour their prey. I'm scared." Sasha poked out her lips. "Can I renege?"

"No, no, my sistah," Eric said. "Part of separating yourself from the girls is being a woman of your word. So here are the rules." He leaned back while Casey began to fill the shot glasses. "You either do the dare or you drink. You either tell the truth or you drink. Now if we were at home in Atlanta, getting drunk and spending the next twenty-four to forty-eight hours puking and crapping in the toilet might not be so bad. But we're in fucking Paris. Do you really want to spend your time in this beautiful city sick in your hotel room, especially when it's not the penthouse suite?"

Sasha looked to Terrance. The expression on her face screamed, "Save me!"

"Oh, no, Miss I Want to Play Truth or Dare," Terrance said. "Here goes."

"Don't be skeered," Eric said to Sasha and winked. "We'll let you go last just so you can see how it's done." He looked to his wife. "Honey, you go first. Truth or Dare?"

"Ummm . . ." Casey thought for a minute. "I don't

have enough liquor in me yet for a dare. So let's go with truth."

"Terrance, you're a guest in our temporary *casa*," Eric said. "You have the pleasure."

Terrance thought for a minute, then looked to Casey. "Casey, truth. Is it true you joined the Hawks cheerleading team just so you could get with my boy here?" He nodded to Eric.

Casey sucked her teeth. "Do you realize you ask me that every time we play? What? You trying to catch me in a lie or something? You've asked me sober and you've asked me drunk and my answer is always the same."

"And that answer is . . ." Terrance said, teasingly cupping his hand around his ear.

"Hell no!" Casey said. "The truth is Eric joined the Hawks just so he could get at me."

"That's right! You tell 'em, girl," Sasha said, giving Casey a high-five.

It had gone right over Sasha's head that Casey mentioned Terrance asked her the same question every time they played the game. That meant this was far from Terrance's first time at the rodeo. Was it possible he was more like his best friend than Sasha knew?

The two women laughed but Sasha was beginning to feel uneasy.

"Oh, so I see how this is going to go down," Terrance said. "Y'all two ladies gon' try to stick together and tag-team us men."

"Well, you know a brotha like myself don't mind a little tag-team." Eric laughed. He went to give Terrance a high-five, but Terrance didn't return the gesture. He just shook his head while letting out a snort.

"What? Oh, you gon' leave me hanging?" He put his hand down. "Don't act like we ain't tag-teamed before, you know what I'm saying?" Eric laughed and Casey let out a nervous chuckle.

Terrance's eyes pleaded with Eric to chill out. His lips were a little bit too loose right now.

Casey interceded. "Come on, babe, let's just play the game," Casey said, looking at Sasha with a smile that begged for Sasha to return one of her own.

Sasha cracked a little smile, but there was something about Eric's comment that didn't sit well with Sasha. Still, she decided to—for now—chalk Eric's rude sense of humor up to the fact that he'd already been doing a little drinking before she and Terrance had even arrived. But there was always that saying that when a person was drunk, they spoke the truth. But even if Terrance and Eric had participated in a tag team, more than likely a sexual tag team, she didn't know if she was ready for that kind of truth . . . liquored up or not.

Sasha immediately looked to a jittery Casey. Another thought entered her mind just as she'd swept the last ones under the rug. Her heart nearly stopped beating just thinking there was a chance Eric and Terrance had both . . .

No, her mind wouldn't allow her to think it. No way would Casey be all up in her face being her friend knowing she'd slept with her . . .

Again, Sasha couldn't complete her thoughts. She hadn't even taken a shot of tequila yet and already her mind was fuzzy.

"My turn!" Casey said. "Terrance, truth or dare?"

"Umm, what the hell? Dare," Terrance said.

"Oh, yeah." Casey rubbed her hands together like she was about to eat a meal. "Terrance, I dare you to kiss Sasha on the lips."

Sasha would have to thank Casey later for going easy on her.

"My pleasure," Terrance said as he leaned over and kissed Sasha on her mouth.

"Wait, you didn't let me finish," Casey said. "I meant for you to kiss her on her other lips." Casey raised her eyebrows up and down.

"Are you serious?" Sasha said. Now she no longer wanted to thank Casey, she wanted to throw her drink at her.

"I'm dead serious," Casey said. "What? You didn't think I was going to take it easy on you just because it's your first time, did you?" Casey asked.

Oh, the test was beginning indeed, but would Sasha pass, or refuse to take it altogether?

"Well," Sasha said, "actually, I did."

"Well, you thought like Nellie." Casey laughed.

Eric joined her in laughing but then stopped. "You know, I've always wondered just what it was that Nellie thought."

"She thought she had to shit but she only farted." Casey burst out laughing and Eric joined in with her.

"Well, it's Terrance's dare," Sasha said, not finding a thing funny. At least not that damn funny. "Nothing happens to me if I don't let him do the dare on me, does it?"

Terrance snapped his neck to look at Sasha. "You'd really throw me under the bus like that? You'd let me take the fall for your non-cooperation?"

"That doesn't sound like a ride-or-die chick," Eric interjected. "Sounds like a bye-bye chick." He waved his hand and started laughing at Terrance like he was clowning on him. "Me, I got a ride-or-die."

"You know it, baby," Casey said. "And I'll drink to that and it ain't even my turn." Casey threw her shot of tequila down her throat like a champ, then poured another one, ready to play; ready to win.

Sasha refused to be one-upped by Casey. Eric was sitting over there looking all smug as if to say to Terrance, "My girl is better than yours." Well, Sasha was not about to let that happen.

"So do you two have to watch as proof?" Sasha said, puffing out her chest like it wasn't nothing but a thing.

"Babe, you don't have to—" Terrance started before Sasha cut him off.

"But I want to," Sasha said with a raised eyebrow to Eric, letting him know she was about to shut his ass up. Sasha finished off the glass of wine she'd been drinking. If she had her way, that tequila was going to sit in that shot glass all night. She was bound and determined to win this game, as stupid as she thought it was.

All eyes were on Sasha as she turned her body toward Terrance. She was wearing some soft pink skinny jeans that were made out of material that allowed her to be somewhat mobile. She kicked her shoes off and then placed one leg up on the couch.

"Word?" Terrance asked, just to confirm that Sasha really was down.

Sasha bit her bottom lip. "You heard the girl. Kiss it."

Terrance rolled his tongue on the inside of his

mouth and then stared into Sasha's eyes. The two had a silent conversation as Terrance leaned his face in between her legs slowly.

Eric and Casey looked with great anticipation.

Terrance rubbed his hands on the inside of Sasha's thighs, spreading them just a tad more, before he planted his lips right between her legs and made a huge kissing sound.

"Aww, man!" Eric said, throwing his hands up with disappointment. "You cheated."

This time it was Sasha and Terrance laughing as they high-fived each other.

"He kissed it," Sasha said. "You didn't say it had to be bare." She pointed to Casey. "Gotcha. Looks like I'm going to beat you at your own game, literally."

"Yeah, by cheating," Casey said.

"I didn't cheat," Sasha was quick to say.

"Man, since when did you get all soft and reserved?" Eric said to Terrance.

"What?" Terrance said feigning ignorance.

"*What?*" Eric mocked. He looked to Casey. "Come on, babe. Let's show them how it's done."

Casey stared at her husband for a moment and then bit her bottom lip. "Sure, babe, anything for you."

Casey might not have told Sasha some of the hoops a basketball wife had to jump through or some of the games she had to play as a basketball wife, but she was about to show her. Casey pulled up the little sequined miniskirt she was wearing so that it settled at her waist.

Eric got on the ground in front of Casey as she spread her legs wide for him. Eric looked over his shoulder at Sasha and Terrance, licked his lips, and then dove in to lick Casey's lips, her bottom set.

Casey immediately threw her head back as she massaged the back of Eric's head.

"Okay, okay, we get it," Sasha said. "Y'all can stop now."

The couple paid Sasha no attention as Casey began moaning.

"Come on, you two, it's like eating pizza in front of someone who is hungry." Terrance laughed.

Sasha turned to face him. "Oh, you're hungry?" she asked, trying to hide her attitude, but just enough of it creeped out and revealed itself to Terrance.

"Uh, no, well, uh." He stammered as if not wanting to make Sasha feel bad for taking the punk route out.

It's not like he hadn't played the game with the couple before. But he would have to play by different rules with Sasha. Sasha was different. Sasha was one of those women who had to be shaped and molded into something they never saw themselves being. All it took was just the right man to do it. It took a man with skills both on and off the court. Sasha had to be lured out of her comfort zone. If not, perhaps Sasha and Terrance's relationship up to this point would be in vain.

Underneath that goal oriented, go-getter, good girl image Sasha portrayed, was there a bad girl dying to come out and play? After all, on the first night she and Terrance had met, another side of Sasha had definitely come out to play. Sasha's actions had spoken for themselves.

Sasha took a deep breath. She was no fool.

There was no way Terrance had been friends with Eric this long and not have some of his same traits. Clearly if Eric was comfortable enough to eat his wife out in front of Terrance, the two had shared some crazy experiences. That was in the past, though, and Sasha would not hold it against Terrance. But what did matter to her was the present. If Terrance was going to engage in some old freaky shit, then it would be with her. She recalled how adamant Paris had been about another chick being quick to move in on her man and try to take her place.

Sasha looked to the couple who, as far as they were concerned, were the only ones in the room. Clearly Casey knew how to keep her man. She then looked to Terrance, who was practically drooling over the act before him the same way Sasha had been drooling over the penthouse. If her man was that hungry, then damn it, she was going to feed him before any other woman had the chance to.

Sasha unsnapped her jeans. Just the sound alone of her pants unsnapping got Terrance excited. She closed her eyes as her heart began to beat faster. She then looked to the table at her glass of tequila. Although she'd planned on never drinking it, it was probably the only thing that was going to allow her to go through with this. She'd thrown caution in the wind the first night she'd met Terrance and allowed him to go down on her, but this was different. Witnesses were now involved.

"Oh, God, Eric, yes, baby, yes!"

Casey's cries shook Sasha from her thoughts. And it also reminded her that the last thing on the couple's mind was what Terrance and Sasha were over there doing, so without further delay, Sasha picked up that glass of hard liquor and threw it down her throat. She squinted her eyes tightly until the burning sensation went away.

When she opened her eyes she couldn't help but notice that Terrance's anticipation had put a bulge in his pants. As the alcohol quickly kicked in, in no time at all Sasha found herself in the same position Casey was in. Her head was thrown back on the couch as she called out Terrance's name, who was between her legs, diligently going to town on her clit.

Sasha was so into her experience with Terrance that she didn't even notice that Eric's full attention was on the couple while Casey used her hand to stroke him into pleasure. By the time the night was over, both couples, in the same room, had managed to please their mate in more ways than one. When all was said and done, they'd all had their share of shots of tequila by the time Terrance and Sasha made their way to the door to head back to their suite.

"I must say this night turned out to be much more exciting than I ever imagined it could be," Eric said as he stood at the door holding it open for Sasha and Terrance to exit.

"All right then, my man," Terrance said, giving Eric some dap. "We'll see you guys in the morning for breakfast."

"Bye, Sash," Casey said mischievously, waving as Sasha exited their suite.

Sasha looked back over her shoulder, barely able to make eye contact with Casey.

"Oh, don't worry," Casey said to her. "You didn't do anything I didn't do, so don't look so embarrassed."

Casey had a point, so Sasha smiled, looked Casey

dead in the eyes, and nodded. As she and Terrance headed back to their room and before Eric closed the door Casey called out one last thing that gave Sasha some comfort that all of Atlanta might not find out she was an undercover freak.

"Besides," Casey said, "what goes on in Europe stays in Europe."

The door closed, but a can of worms had already been opened.

Chapter 18

"I can't believe they fired me. I . . . I've never been fired from a job in my life. Especially not no temp job." Sasha bit into the pretzel bite she was eating as she and Casey walked the mall.

After Sasha had informed Casey of her termination from the law firm, Casey suggested a little retail therapy. Sasha concurred.

"Well, it was just that . . . temporary. So don't sweat it," Casey said.

"Easy for you to say. You still have your job."

"Ehhh, true," Casey said, grabbing the remaining pretzel bite out of Sasha's hand and popping it into her mouth.

Sasha rolled her eyes at her, not because she'd eaten her food, but because she still had a job to call her own. "Speaking of which." Sasha stopped walking. "Why the hell do you work anyway?"

Casey stopped next to Sasha and shot her a surprised look. "What's with all the cussing, potty mouth?"

Sasha wasn't one to just cuss to be cussing in conversation. She frowned at the revelation. "I know. It's just that, damn it, life in Atlanta is not turning out like I planned it."

"Okay, and what's so bad about that? Think about it. You live in a big ole house with a man who spoils you rotten." She let out a harrumph before she started walking again. "If you ask me, sounds like things are turning out better than you'd planned."

Sasha started walking next to Casey as she took in her friend's words.

"It wasn't your dream job anyway," Casey continued, "and it's not like you're strapped for cash. I mean you don't have rent to pay. Your Honda is paid for. You've got clothes on your back, you're in the mall right now buying new ones." Casey looked down at her own three shopping bags compared to the zero shopping bags Sasha was carrying. "Well, you're supposed to be buying new clothes anyway. But even still, hell, you know how to make your own clothes if push comes to shove. So come on. You needed that job again for what?"

Sasha thought for a minute. The scenario she was currently living wasn't bad at all. It just wasn't the one she'd outlined. Even though Terrance was taking good care of Sasha, her job had given her a sense of security. It allowed her to have her own money in her pocket. It didn't make her feel so kept. "I guess you're right to some degree," Sasha said.

"Of course I am," she said with certainty.

"I suppose all of my life I've been so focused on making a living that I haven't even lived." She smiled at thoughts of Terrance. "And Terrance does make me feel like I'm living. Like I'm alive." Sasha exhaled and continued smiling.

"Exactly. The hell with living a little, girl, live a lot. A whole lot. And if being a working woman is that dang serious for you," Casey said, "then just get another job." She dug into the cup of pretzel bites Sasha was holding and popped another pretzel into her mouth. "But if I were you, I wouldn't worry about it. You've got it made."

Sasha twisted her lips. "I suppose you're right," she agreed. "We both do. You even more so than me because you're married to your boo. So that takes me back to my original question to you. Why do you work at the firm? It's only part-time. Half days for just three days out of the week. I'm not throwing shade, but I can't imagine your weekly paycheck puts any kind of dent in y'all's mortgage."

Casey shrugged. "Unlike you, I knew better than to commit myself to a full-time job. I knew Eric would be taking me on surprise outings and last minute get-aways, wanting me to spend the afternoon with him just because it was Tuesday. Working only part-time gave me more freedom to do those things." She nodded to Sasha.

"Well, why didn't you share all this with me beforehand?"

"Don't you even try to go there with me," Casey said. "For one, you were already working the job when I met you, which was before you met Terrance. Two, I didn't know you were going to go back to the boy's house and put it on him the first night you met him and then move in with him on the second night." Casey laughed.

Sasha had to laugh at that one herself.

"Besides, you were the one who was calling in to work at least once a week. That doesn't have anything to do with me." She shook her head. "Did you seriously think that was going to fly with the position you are in at the firm? Those silver spoon bastards you work for don't even know how to use a landline to answer their own goddamn office phones."

"Was in," Sasha corrected Casey sadly.

"Huh?"

"The position I *was* in at the firm."

"Oh, yeah, sorry," Casey apologized.

"That's okay," Sasha said. "But you still didn't answer my question."

Sasha was going to get her answer if it was the last thing she did. Sasha had been curious for some time as to why Casey worked at the firm. She had concluded on her own that maybe Casey just liked having something to do and having something to call her own.

Sasha understood that now more than ever. Even though Terrance never allowed her to spend her money on him, or even on herself if he was around, she liked the feeling of independence having her own gave her. Even though she was taking less and less action these days toward reaching the goals that had brought her to Atlanta in the first place, Sasha had been storing her coins in the business account she'd started. At one of the seminars she'd gone to, the instructor had suggested registering a company so that they could at least file self-employment "doing business as." This would begin to age the company; show the company has been in business for some time. So that's just what Sasha did.

Initially, she'd only registered the name, She By Sasha, but then decided to go ahead and incorporate the company. While the name Norman had offered, Wellington Vogue Boutiques, had a nice ring to it, she'd decided to stick with her original business name. Registering her company allowed her to set up a business bank account, also per the instructor's advice. Sasha was not going to have to get ready, she was going to *be* ready.

Working at the firm had at least made Sasha feel as though to some degree she was still working toward her ultimate fashion goals, even though fashion had been the furthest thing from her mind thanks to her whirlwind romance with Terrance. But back to Casey: Eric had put a ring on it. What more security did Casey need, for Christ's sake?

"And why didn't they fire you, too?" Sasha asked on second thought. "Most of the time if I was out of the office in Europe or something, you were right alongside me."

A haughty look glowed across Casey's face. "Let's just say I'm a true *ass*et to the company." Casey giggled like she had the biggest secret in the world that she was just dying to tell.

Well, lucky for her, Sasha wanted to hear it. "Naw, bitch, enough of this. Ever since I've known you and Paris, y'all two act like there is some secret, elite world you all live in. Like there is some golden ticket one has to have in order to enter it." Sasha leaned in close to Casey's ear. "I let my man eat me out in front of you. Hell, I watched your man eat you out. That's got to get me at least a one-day pass."

"Shhh." Casey put her index finger on her lips and looked around the mall to make sure they hadn't caught anybody's attention. "I thought what happens in Europe stays in Europe. Isn't that what you wanted?"

That had been what Sasha wanted. And she'd appreciated the fact that Casey hadn't mentioned that night at the Concourse penthouse suite. Eric hadn't mentioned it, either, not even in one of his drunken states. In the moment of pleasure the couples each shared with their mates, it had been exciting to Sasha. She never thought for once she'd be the type of girl to participate in voyeuristic sex. But she had to admit that it had been exhilarating. Granted, once the climax had been reached and the liquor had worn off, there was a shadow of embarrassment. She and Casey now shared a connection, a bond of some sort. That had to count for something. That had to get her at least a sneak peek of what was going on inside that secluded little world of Casey's.

"It is what I wanted," Sasha said. "And I appreciate your discretion about that night, but I'm tired of feeling like the outsider, like everybody thinks I'm some stuck-up goody two-shoes who doesn't know how to live life."

"Well, Sasha, you kinda have to admit that's exactly who you were about six months ago." Casey laughed.

"It's not funny and I'm not joking," Sasha said. "I'm going crazy here. I don't even know who I am anymore sometimes." Sasha's eyes watered. She was so frustrated with the turn her life was taking. She didn't feel like she was in control of her destiny anymore.

"Just calm down," Casey said. "Come sit down." Casey led Sasha to the nearest bench and the two sat. She took Sasha's hands into hers. "I can trust you, can't I, Sasha?"

Sasha looked into Casey's eyes. "Are you really asking me that? For God's sake, I'm the same girl who back in France—"

"That doesn't mean anything to me," Casey said, cutting Sasha off. "Do you know how many other girls, couples, Eric and I have done that same thing with? And trust me, sweetheart, it's gone to much higher levels than what we experienced. But that doesn't mean I trust them hoes. Hell, some of them have not only watched Eric eat my pussy, but they've done it, too. Then they try to take my man behind my back, so do you think sex or sharing a sexual experience in any form or fashion equals trust?"

Sasha just sat there not knowing whether to feel shocked, surprised, disgusted, or what. Sasha had seen some subtle signs and had speculations about how Casey and Eric got down, but she never allowed herself to fully realize it in her mind. Thinking things in her head was one thing, but actually hearing the truth come out of the horse's mouth was a different animal, so to speak, altogether.

"Do you?" Casey asked, squeezing Sasha's hands. "Do you think that all equals trust? It's not trust just because someone keeps a secret, especially if somehow a couple truths about themselves will be revealed as well."

Sasha looked down at their joined hands as Casey's began to tremble. She looked up at Casey, who was clearly on the verge of crying.

"Why? Why do you do it, Casey?" Sasha asked.

"Because it's what Eric likes. It works for us, for our marriage. I mean. Sasha, our men are going to cheat, so if I get the power to pick out who he cheats with, then it's almost like not cheating at all, since I know about it."

"Casey, that is so twisted that I don't even think you believe it," Sasha said. She turned away.

"There are many things you start to believe as a basketball wife . . . if you want to stay one, that is."

Sasha didn't reply to Casey's statement. Casey was speaking for herself on that one. Sasha refused to believe that any woman would subject herself to that lifestyle or treatment just to maintain a certain standard of living. Sasha had met other basketball wives. Some of them were businesswomen running multimillion-dollar corporations. She was certain they would beg to differ. Sasha chalked Casey's statement up as just another case of misery loves company. She refused to entertain the comment.

"So, the job at the firm?" Sasha, once again, went back to the question that had started it all.

"My job at the firm?" Casey said. "Let's just say it's a win-win for all three of us."

"Three?" Casey was losing Sasha.

"The company, Eric's club, and of course Eric's and my marriage."

Wheels were just a-turning in Sasha's head, so much so that she was starting to get dizzy. Casey decided to make it a little easier on Sasha by clarifying it all for her.

"For show, business deals are made on the golf course. Power closes the deal. Real business deals are made with sex. Money closes the deal. For Eric and me, when it comes to the club, it's all about business. The firm, its partners, its clientele, is good for the club's business. The club is good for the firm's business. When it comes to my marriage, let's just say the firm is a nice feeding ground. So Eric and I definitely kill two birds with one stone, both business and pleasure."

Sasha processed what Casey was saying. "So the firm is kind of like a playground for the games you and Eric play?"

"We like to play on the swings, Sasha. We're swingers," Casey came right out and said. "Most of our playmates I find at the firm." Casey looked to Sasha. "Now you know why my boss really won't fire me." She winked.

"Casey, I'm so sorry," Sasha said, putting her hand on Casey's shoulder.

"Sorry? For what?"

"That you feel you have to do this kind of thing just to keep—"

"Whoa, hold up. I don't have to do this. I want to."

"Do you really?" Sasha asked sincerely.

Casey twisted her body around so that she was turned directly toward Sasha. "Back in Europe, did I look like I was being forced to do anything I didn't want to do?"

Sasha allowed moments of that evening to skip about her mind. Casey had appeared to be enjoying every moment of that evening. It had been like she'd been on a stage performing. "No, but that night some other woman wasn't screwing your man. I don't care what you say, it can't be easy to sit back and watch your husband get intimate with another woman."

"It is when he has to watch you get intimate with another man."

This was too much for a Midwest girl like Sasha. "I can't." Sasha shook her head and put her hand up.

"Then you shouldn't have asked," Casey said. "Not that you hadn't already put two and two together in the first place." She let out a "psst."

"What?" Sasha said. "I had no idea . . ." Sasha allowed her own words to trail off before she could finish the lie. "Okay, so maybe there were signs, but I—"

"Just swept it up under the rug because you couldn't fathom that a girl like me would be involved in such a lifestyle."

"Well, yeah, I guess," Sasha admitted. "Maybe Paris, but not you." Realizing the words that had fallen out of her mouth, Sasha looked up to face Casey. "Wait, I didn't mean it like that."

Casey put her hand up to silence Sasha. "No worries, I'm not going to go back and tell Paris that you think she's some kind of horny freak," Casey said. "Even though she is." Casey and Sasha both burst out laughing. Casey pointed at Sasha. "Now don't you go running back telling her I said that."

Sasha shooed her hand. "Oh, girl, please. You know I don't get down like that."

"Yeah, I know," Casey said. "That's why I trust you."

"You trust Paris, too, so does that mean she knows about, you know, you and Eric's lifestyle?"

Casey nodded. "Oh, she knows all right."

"Oh, Lord," Sasha said. "I won't even delve into that by asking any questions."

Casey looked at Sasha seriously. "And you'd be smart not to." Realizing she'd just changed the mood with such seriousness, Casey jumped up off the bench. "Come on, we have some shopping to do. Come pick out something nice." Casey pulled Sasha up by the arm. "And it's on me, considering you don't have a job and all."

"Screw you," Sasha said playfully, rolling her eyes as she stood.

"I'm just joking," Casey said. "Besides, consider it my payback for making sure Eric didn't drink and drive last night."

"Huh?" Sasha asked, confused.

"Oh, yeah, Eric told me that you insisted he stay at you and Terrance's last night after he and your boy had one too many."

Sasha opened her mouth, but no words came out. She had to think for a minute. Last night she'd definitely seen Eric over at the house, but she'd also seen him leave their house. And from what she could tell, he was pretty sober. Sasha had insisted he stay for dinner, but he declined, stating the he had dinner plans. Obviously those plans had not been with Casey. Now here Sasha stood between a rock and a hard place.

If the tables were turned, Sasha would have definitely wanted Casey to tell her the truth of the matter. But then again, Casey and Eric had a *wayyyy* different kind of relationship than Sasha and Terrance's. Usually when a man lied to a woman regarding his whereabouts, he was cheating. But Eric and Casey were swingers. Could swingers technically cheat on each other?

"What's the matter? You okay?" Casey asked Sasha, realizing she seemed a bit out of it.

"Yeah, I'm good," Sasha said, deciding just to keep it all to herself.

"Good, then let's go. Anything you want, it's on me."

With Casey standing there all cheerful and happy, Sasha just couldn't take out a pin and pop her happy balloon. But neither could she allow Casey to walk around clueless, either. Casey had just expressed how much she trusted Sasha. Within not even five minutes passing, could Sasha really let her down like that?

"Casey, hold up a minute," Sasha said, somberly and hesitantly.

"What it is?" Casey asked, concerned.

"Eric, didn't, uh, stay at our place last night," Sasha said, then braced herself for whatever type of emotion Casey was going to let loose. It was a known fact among females that there were two things that could happen if one friend told the other friend she thought her mate was cheating on her. One thing was that the woman got pissed off at the man, told him the information she had on him and whom she'd gotten it from. More than likely she'd end up staying with him anyway, causing pure awkwardness when all three were all around one another. And of course from that point on the cheating mate would accuse the ratting best friend of trying to break them up.

The second thing that could happen was that the girlfriend who had the cheating mate could go into denial and end up getting mad at the friend who spilled the beans. What made this situation all the more challenging for Sasha was that Eric and Terrance were best friends. Anything Sasha said or did in this moment could affect the two men's relationship . . . and careers, seeing they had to have a relationship on and off the court. The world saw firsthand how that worked out for Shaq and Kobe.

All of a sudden Sasha was full of regret. She wished she could take her words back, but they'd already escaped her lips and made their way to Casey's ears. Well, perhaps not the latter.

"What did you say?" Casey asked, having stopped walking and turned to face Sasha.

This was the moment of second chances for Sasha. She could continue on with the truth, or lie by omission.

"I, uhh . . ." Sasha was still undecided.

"Come on. Someone could be snatching up the last perfect dress for you in your size," Casey said.

The two friends stood there staring at each other. Their eyes had a silent conversation. Casey's eyes pleaded with Sasha not to repeat her words. They were better left unspoken. The truth might have been way more painful than a lie. Casey's eyes begged Sasha to allow her to live in the fairy tale she'd convinced herself she was living in.

Sasha, being the friend she was, obliged Casey. "Yeah, we wouldn't want that to happen, now would we? Let's go get that perfect dress."

Sasha smiled. Casey smiled. Casey quickly turned and headed into a store, her smile fading quicker than she's painted it on. Sasha's smile faded just as quickly after Casey had turned away.

It looked like both women had something more in common after all. They both were great pretenders. But for Sasha, whether she liked it or not, things were about to get real.

Chapter 19

"Dear, you should go to bed now."

Sasha jerked her head up at the sound of Miss Hart's voice. She looked around the room, becoming familiar with her surroundings. "Huh, what?" She wiped the sides of her mouth, realizing she was in the great room on the couch.

"I said, you should go on up to bed. It's late. That couch can't be comfortable."

Sasha sat up on the couch and gathered her bearings. "What time is it?"

With a look of pity, Miss Hart replied, "Late. Go on to bed now."

Sasha read between the lines of the house-keeper's words. She looked over at the clock hanging on the wall. Miss Hart's unspoken words penetrated Sasha's heart. It was late, or early, however one looked at it. She should just go up to bed, because waiting on that couch clearly wasn't bringing Terrance home.

The last she'd seen him was early in the morning the day before. She'd been half asleep, but she remembered him kissing her on the forehead, informing her that he'd left his credit card on the nightstand. He wanted her to enjoy a spa day to rejuvenate herself and get her mind right before going on a job hunt. That was exactly what Sasha had done. She'd spent her entire morning at the full-service spa and salon. She'd not only gotten a full body massage, but she enjoyed a facial, spent time in the steam room, the sauna, and the pool. She got a mani plus a pedicure that included a hot towel wrap and sea salt rub. Lastly, she got her hair done while she sipped on mimosas, followed by having her makeup applied. By the time she'd finished all that, it was too late in the day to go on a job hunt.

The old Sasha would have never put pleasure and pampering before business, but the new Sasha that was emerging from within was enjoying the treatment she was now privy to at the drop of a dime . . . Terrance's dime. She had to refocus, but right now Terrance had her vision blurred.

Sasha wiped the blurriness from her eyes and looked at the clock again. It was four in the morning. Four in the morning. The last Sasha recalled, the clock had read midnight. All evening she forced herself not to call Terrance to check on his whereabouts. She'd never done it before and she wasn't going to start doing it. Then again, Terrance had never given her reason to. He'd always come home. Sure, she understood that on occasion he and the team would go hang out, celebrate a win or mourn a loss. He'd come home late, but he came home nonetheless. Sometimes promoters would even pay Terrance to make an appearance at a venue. Sasha had even attended some of those events with him. Again, Terrance always came home. So Sasha wasn't so much worried that Terrance was out and up to no good. She feared that maybe something bad had happened. The emotion she'd experienced all night was fear, not insecurity or jealousy.

That was until she saw the look in Miss Hart's eyes; the tone in her voice and the words she didn't speak out loud. Sasha didn't sense worry in Miss Hart's heart for her boss, just empathy for her boss's lady friend. If Sasha wasn't mistaken, it was actually that same look Miss Hart had given her the first night she'd met Terrance and he'd brought her home. It was as if Miss Hart had expected what Sasha found to be the unexpected. It just so happened that Sasha didn't end up being another one of Terrance's side-chicks who bites the dust. She was wifey. But that didn't mean there wasn't a side-chick out there engraving her name on Terrance's penis with her tongue.

That's when jealousy and insecurity began to creep up on Sasha.

"Have you talked to Terrance, Miss Hart? I hope he's okay." Now Sasha was fishing. She wanted to know why Miss Hart wasn't the least bit worried. *Is this something Terrance has done before?* Sasha asked herself, truly wanting to ask Miss Hart. But of course this was something Terrance had done before. Up until just a few months ago he'd been a single man. A grown-ass, single man. He didn't have to come home if he didn't want to. But that was a few months ago. Now Terrance was a grown-ass man with a woman. Hopefully he hadn't just slipped and bumped his head, but slipped back into an old habit.

"You know what, never mind," Sasha said to Miss Hart. She was not about to sit there and try to pick her man's employee for information on him. She wasn't going to be that chick. She thought back to Kels, her overly possessive and jealous neighbor from her old apartment. She refused to be that chick. Casey, who had good reason to be that chick, wasn't even that chick. She'd heard with her own two ears Casey brush off Eric's not coming home . . . and those two were married. Granted, Sasha and Terrance were exclusive, but not married. No commitment had been made under the eyes of God. No contract to love, honor, and not stray had been signed. No promises, legal or otherwise, had been made, therefore none had been broken. That was the reasoning and justification Sasha would use to keep her heart together . . . to keep it from breaking apart.

"You're right, Miss Hart. I should go to bed." Sasha got up from the couch and an hour later she was lying in bed—her bed back at her old apartment. The same theory Sasha had used to justify why she shouldn't feel some kind of way about Terrance not coming home was the same justification she used as to why she shouldn't be laying up in Terrance's bed waiting for him to come home. That was his bed, not their marital bed.

Terrance always made comments about how Sasha didn't play, yet he didn't mind playing house with her. What made her any different than some groupie camping out outside of his hotel room waiting for him? Nothing, with the exception that the king-size bed was a lot more comfortable than the hotel hallway floor.

"I knew I'd find you here."

Sasha looked from the bedroom ceiling she'd been staring at while in thought to the doorway where Terrance stood.

Sasha had given him the spare key to her apartment after she'd agreed to move into his place. He'd had movers pack up her clothing and personal items and take them to his place. Besides, she had a key to his big ole castle; of course it made sense for him to have a key to her little ole apartment.

Sasha looked away, back to the ceiling.

Terrance looked up at the ceiling then back at her. He was trying to be playful, as if to ask what it was about the ceiling that had Sasha's attention. But Sasha wasn't paying him any mind at all. She simply continued staring upward.

Eventually Terrance made his way over to Sasha's bed, lay down next to her, and stared up at the ceiling. After a few seconds, Sasha turned to look at him.

"What are you doing?" Sasha asked.

He shrugged. "I don't know. Doing whatever you're doing, I guess." He turned and looked at her.

After a few seconds of staring into his eyes, Sasha had to look away. The same way she'd been entrapped by his eyes that first night they met was about to be a repeat if she didn't look away.

They were both, once again, staring up at ceiling.

Terrance finally broke the silence. "I'm sorry."

"For what?" Sasha asked. A man could say he was sorry a million times just to appease or keep a woman quiet, but it meant nothing unless he knew what he was apologizing for.

"Come on, Sasha. We're grown. Let's not play games. I fucked up. I stayed out all night and I didn't call. I should have called. It's just that I had one drink too many and passed out."

"Well, maybe you shouldn't drink so much when you're out," Sasha suggested, and it seemed like easy enough advice to follow. After all, he never drank himself to a drunken stupor around Sasha. She couldn't understand why he couldn't control his drinking when she wasn't around. She'd never seen Terrance drunk to the point where he was going to pass out. She didn't even want to imagine how he acted in such a state.

"Once I woke up and realized what time it was," Terrance continued, "I knew I was already in the dog house. I knew you were going to kill me, so I figured why try to drive inebriated and end up killing myself, taking that honor away from you? I mean, if anybody deserved to kill me, it was you. I couldn't rob you of that privilege, could I?"

Sasha twisted up her lips and shot Terrance a look. "Oh, so you want to be Chris Rock right now. You're a real funny dude."

He smiled.

Sasha turned her face away from him. She was not going to smile. Not yet. Not so soon. He had to suffer a little more the same way she'd suffered while waiting on his ass to come home last night.

Terrance turned his body toward Sasha. He turned her head so that she faced him. "It will never happen again, I promise," Terrance said. "I have to remember that I have someone waiting for me at home that I have to give courtesy to. If I'm going to be late or something happens where I'm not going to make it home, I won't be a bitch about it, and I'll at least call you and tell you what's up. You deserve it."

"Yes, I do, and don't you forget it." She turned her attention back to the ceiling.

"So we good?"

Sasha sighed and thought for a minute. The Band-Aid. No commitment. But at least now there was a promise.

"You do believe me, don't you?" Terrance scooted in closer to Sasha and began to kiss her all over her neck.

Sasha moaned at the softness of Terrance's lips pressing against her neck. She didn't even care if they were lying lips or not. She loved him. She'd altered her entire life. She had to believe it wasn't all for nothing.

"Yes, I believe you," Sasha said as she closed her eyes and allowed her neck to roll, assuring that Terrance didn't miss a spot. Out of nowhere, words that Casey had once spoken suddenly filled her head.

"There are many things you start to believe as a basketball wife."

Sasha finally opened her eyes. But was it too late?

Chapter 20

Sasha stared down at the pink plus sign on the stick she'd just urinated on. Tears filled her eyes. Were they tears of joy? Were they tears of fear? What was there to be afraid of? Then again, she could also ask herself what there was to be happy about.

It was only last week when she'd finally gotten up the courage to tell her mother she'd vacated her apartment and moved in with Terrance. Actually, her mother hadn't taken the news as badly as Sasha had thought she would.

"Well, at least he isn't some broke jive turkey who just looks good," her mother had said. It made Sasha wonder if her mother was somehow related to Paris's grandmother. But then her mother added, "And he loves you, right? Because you must love him to go to such extremes as to give up your dreams to want to be up under him all like that."

"Ma, I'm not giving up my dreams," Sasha had quickly shot back.

"Oh?" her mother had said with kind of a question mark behind her tone. Not like she was questioning Sasha, but more like asking Sasha to question herself. "But what I need to know is that this man loves my baby girl and is going to treat her right," her mother had said.

Sasha eased her mother's mind by sharing with her how well Terrance had been treating her. She told her about the impromptu dates, outings, and vacations. She told her how well he'd been providing for her.

"Sounds like you're living an even better life than you envisioned when you moved to Atlanta," her mother had told her, now sounding just like Casey. "As long as you're happy is all that matters. That's all I've ever wanted. I didn't make sure you had a happy childhood just so you could grow up for some man to make you miserable. You are happy, aren't you, Sasha?"

Since Sasha had emphatically told her mother that she was happy, wouldn't that make her a liar if she wasn't happy now? Even if Sasha wasn't happy on the inside, she could at least try to fake it on the outside. She tried to curve the corners of her lips up into a smile, but it was a no go. She wasn't happy, nor could she fake being happy, which meant she wasn't about to call her mother up anytime soon to share this news with her. She'd wait until maybe she was . . . happy . . . if that ever happened.

"Well, one thing's for certain, we all know it ain't mine."

Sasha looked up at him from the edge of the Jacuzzi tub she was sitting on. He'd stood there by her side the entire time waiting for the results to appear on the pregnancy test. His comment was not the support she'd expected of him, a man who had said he'd loved her. A man who called himself her friend. A hurt look was visible on her face.

"What?" he said matter-of-factly. "It ain't mine."

"This is not the time for your humor, Norman," Sasha said, looking down at the stick again. "A real friend would know better than to make light of something this serious."

"I'm sorry," Norman said. "Just trying to cheer you up because you look all pitiful and suicidal. You should see your face. Shit, let me go hide all the damn razors." Norman headed in the direction of the medicine cabinet.

"Norman, seriously, stop it." Sasha shook her head. "Not now!" Usually Norman's off-the-wall comic relief had a way of making Sasha feel better, but it was only upsetting her even more right now.

Norman exhaled and walked back over and stood in front of his friend. "I'm sorry, I guess. Or should I be congratulating you? Hell, I don't know." He threw his hands up in surrender. "One second it looked like you were going to smile, and now it looks like you're going to cry. I don't know what to do with your bipolar ass."

Sasha shook her head. "I don't know what to do with myself either. A baby," Sasha mumbled under her breath.

Norman looked at how genuinely torn Sasha was. "I can tell you really aren't from here, are you?"

"Why do you say that?" Sasha asked.

"Because do you know how many women, instead of sitting on the edge of the tub looking like their life just came to an end, would be jumping up and down ecstatic right about now? You sitting here whining about 'a baby,' " he mocked, "while they asses would be running around talking about 'a check.' " Norman put his hands on his hips. "Do you know this baby guarantees you a lifestyle of the rich and famous for the rest of your life, or at least for the next eighteen years?"

"But you know that's not what I'm about," Sasha said. "I love Terrance. He is a great man. Does he mess up sometimes? Sure, but trust me, there are women out there who have it far worse." Sasha didn't know who she was trying to convince more at this point, her or Norman. "We have a wonderful time together, but a baby changes everything. How can I start up and run my own business with a baby on my hip?"

"Heifer, women do that shit all the time. A baby on they hip, a baby on they titty, while another one is holding their hand."

Sasha instantly thought back to the day she arrived in Atlanta. She recalled watching the mother at her apartment complex struggle with all of her babies. "I don't want to struggle."

Norman looked around. "Have you seen where the hell you live? Does this look like a damn struggle to you?"

Sasha admired the huge marble sand-tone bathroom. It had a Jacuzzi and a walk-in shower that could fit at least six people at one time. It had his-and-hers sinks and a separate area for the commode. Some people's entire living spaces weren't as large as this bathroom. Norman was right. Sasha had been so blinded and swept up by Terrance that she paid no attention even to where she'd landed.

"You're right," Sasha said, sounding a little more

chipper and hopeful. "Not that I want any other woman raising my baby, but it's not like Terrance can't afford a nanny. And I can go back to work just as soon as I bounce back from having the baby. Terrance pays all the bills so any money I save up I can put it all right into my boutique." The more she spoke, the more motivated she felt. She stood up with a sudden burst of energy. "It won't be just about me anymore. I'd have to make it for the sake of my child. I have to leave a legacy for this baby." She held her stomach. "A baby." This time Sasha said it with a sense of pride. Perhaps a baby was all the motivation Sasha needed to get back on track and handle her business.

Norman just sat there watching Sasha, looking confused as all get-out. "So do you want me to go diaper shopping with you, or do you need me to go to the clinic with you and hold your hand during the procedure, because, bitch, I'm confused."

Sasha ignored Norman as she stared off and continued to think things through. There were pros of being pregnant, and there were definitely cons. She wouldn't be honest with herself if she denied being worried about her baby's future. The hell with even telling Terrance about the pregnancy at all. But if she did, maybe he would be for an abortion, since he was at the height of his career. How could they be in Atlanta one minute and then Paris the next with a newborn in their lives? How could they even get to know each other better if they were trying to get to know and learn how to take care of a little person?

"Jesus, take the wheel!" Sasha cried out.

"Well, I ain't Jesus, but I know Dirty Knife Donna who lives over in Bankhead. Then there's her cousin,

Five Finger Discount Freda who can get diapers and Similac for a steal, literally," Norman said. "You just pick your poison and I'm there for you. Just know that either decision you make is going to alter your life forever."

Norman's words left a lot for Sasha to consider. But she couldn't think on them for too long. Even though time had been moving pretty fast for her and Terrance's relationship, she knew that time was no longer on her side. A decision had to be made, and the clock was ticking.

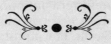

"I do," Sasha said, repeating after the minister.

She stood across from Terrance at the altar at Baptist Generation Church of the Saints. It was a church Norman had suggested. The first lady was one of his clients and was happy to host the last-minute wedding of Atlanta's basketball stars—for a nice offering, of course.

It was a beautiful church with breathtakingly beautiful stained glass windows. The sunlight beamed through it and hit just the right spot at the altar. It was the spot where Sasha and Terrance stood being joined together in holy matrimony.

She could feel the butterflies fluttering through her stomach. Or perhaps it was the seven-week-old fetus. Maybe it was even both. As she stood at the altar, exchanging vows with the man who had entered her life and swept her off her feet, taking her off course from her life plans, she was scared to death. Everything was happening so abruptly.

The feeling in Sasha's belly stole her thoughts. She pictured the child inside her belly chasing the

butterflies through their beautiful backyard. His—
or her—tiny hands, tiny bare feet, all part of a creation made by her and Terrance. Her eyes filled
with tears. That was love. Be it just plain ole love or
in love, it was enough. It was enough for her to—
just in case anyone missed it the first time—say "I
do" again. The few people in attendance chuckled
when Sasha did just that.

"Terrance Clark McKinley," the minister said as
he stood there with Bible in hand. "Do you take
Sasha Renea Wellington to be your lawfully wed-
ded wife?" The minister continued on, asking the
same things of Terrance regarding the marriage
that he'd asked Sasha. The minister stood between
the beautiful couple looking pretty dapper for
merely officiating the ceremony. He'd brought out
his good robe. It was a deep royal purple, which
happened to be one of the three wedding colors:
silver, black and purple. As good as the minister
looked, it didn't take away the shine of the bride
and groom.

"I do," Terrance said with a huge smile.

Sasha wore a matching smile. She had never felt
more beautiful in her life. Time hadn't allowed for
Sasha to get a gown specially made, but Norman
had worked his magic. He'd gotten Sasha a one-of-
a-kind original recently created by one of the top-
of-the-line designers for the stars in Atlanta. After
a little taking in and out of the seams here and
there, it was a perfect fit.

But could Sasha say the same about herself and
Terrance?

Not even a full year ago had she arrived in Atlanta, single and on a mission, and now she was
married and in love. Or did she just love Ter-

rance? How could one really describe being "in love" if it's something they'd never experienced before?

"Then I now pronounce you both man and wife," the minister said. "Terrance." He looked to Terrance, who stood across from Sasha all smiles in his white tuxedo.

Terrance wore a black cummerbund and bow-tie. Norman had tried his best to get the athlete to wear the purple accessories. Terrance said he felt like the late, great Prince and opted to wear only a purple boutonniere.

"You may kiss your bride," the minister announced.

There was no veil for Terrance to lift off his new bride's face. Sasha had settled for a crystal crown-like tiara that made her look like the queen she felt like at that moment.

Terrance gently pulled Sasha in by the face and planted the biggest, juiciest kiss ever on her. It looked like love. The guests laughed again.

Terrance pulled away and looked Sasha in her eyes. "I love you, wifey." He looked down at her stomach then back into her eyes. "I know it seems like we just met yesterday and everything moved fast, but we have to remind ourselves that life is not on our time." He looked upward. "It's on His."

Sasha looked up at the stained glass windows as well. The two just stood there together, holding hands, looking to the heavens. A warmth flowed through their beings. It felt like love.

This was the first time she and Terrance had stepped foot in a church together. In her mind she'd planned on them finding a church home to-gether and standing in the house of the Lord side by side someday getting their praise on, but it was clear that God had simply been laughing at her plans all along. It only made sense that Sasha finally accepted that now.

"I love you too, husband," Sasha said. It sounded like love.

Terrance kissed his new bride again; this time they devoured each other's tongues. It tasted like love.

Sasha inhaled the cologne that wafted from Terrance's neck into her nostrils. It was a bottle he'd had flown from Spain when he couldn't find it anywhere in the States. Hell, it even smelled like love.

Terrance looked down at the broom that lay on the ground. "Before we jump this thing, we have to agree to one thing," Terrance said.

"What's that?" Sasha asked.

"That for the sake of our child, divorce is never an option."

Terrance was wasting his breath on that one right there. Sasha had grown into a whole different woman since moving to Atlanta. But one thing that was not going to change about her was the fact of who she'd end up being. Never mind who she was now, but being a single momma donning the title of baby momma was not in the cards for her.

When she'd told Terrance she was pregnant, he displayed no mixed emotions at all. He jumped up with excitement and immediately began deciding which guest room would soon become the nursery. He looked more like a football player than a basketball player as he did the touchdown dance. The same you-are-not-the-father-dance Sasha had seen men do on talk shows was the one Terrance was doing upon finding out he *was* the father. He'd looked as though he'd been playing the lotto for years and finally hit. Once he was able to calm himself down, he looked to Sasha.

"You know what this means, don't you?" he'd asked Sasha. "It means I have to make an honest woman out of you." Terrance had then told her to hold on, that he'd be right back.

He zipped off and out of that house but was back in an hour. He raced up to Sasha with sweat on his forehead as he got down on one knee. "Sasha Wellington, the mother of my child, will you marry me? Will you be more than just my friend, more than just my confidante and way, way, much more than just my baby momma?" He chuckled while Sasha stood there in pure awe.

"Will you be the woman who I take care of for the rest of my life? Will you be the woman of my dreams and let me help to make all your dreams come true?"

In that moment Sasha was reminded that she had dreams. Just like she'd told Norman, she wasn't giving them up. But she was putting them on hold while life, love, and family happened.

Terrance opened the ring box he'd had balled in his hand. Staring at Sasha was not only Terrance, but a flawless seven-carat diamond ring. "Will you? Will you marry me, Sasha?" He put his other hand on her belly. "And will you marry me, too, little one?"

Either way it went, how could Sasha say no to that . . . How could she say no to him? She didn't say no, and now just a week and a half later they were married. Sasha was now a wife.

So the blueprint, at least the one Sasha had spent her entire life planning out, had been crumpled up and tossed into the wind. It had been blown away the same way Terrance had blown Sasha away. Right now, finding another job didn't matter, finding a space for a boutique didn't matter. The only thing that mattered, as Sasha's mother had said, was the fact that Sasha was happy. And in this moment she could honestly, one hundred percent say that she was happy.

Guests threw rice at the newlyweds and cheered as the couple made their way down the church aisle toward the doors.

"Well, I guess she's off to live her happily ever after," Paris said to Casey. "And just to think, that could have been me once upon a time had I let the fairy tale play out."

"Shhh." Casey was quick to elbow Paris and look around to make sure the handful of people hadn't heard her. "That's all water under the bridge now. This isn't about Terrance's past with you, but his future with Sasha. Now just stand there, clap, and be happy for her."

Paris rolled her eyes up in her head as she began to clap.

"Good girl," Casey said to her. "Besides, don't get too jealous. What looks like happily ever after is only part-time bliss. There's a lot of work that goes into being a baller's wife." Casey looked on as the couple made their way over the threshold. "And unless Sasha can get with the rules of the game quick, fast, and in a hurry, Terrance will be a free agent again before you know it. And who knows, maybe you'll get a second shot."

Paris took in Casey's words as a mischievous grin spread across her lips. "Humph, then I guess I better work on my free throws, huh?"

The two women laughed.

Terrance and Sasha disappeared from the doorway, headed to the waiting limousine to start their life together. Hopefully, prayerfully, as Sasha had cried out, Jesus would take the wheel, because unbeknownst to her, she and Terrance were headed in two different directions, which was going to make for one hell of a ride.

Epilogue

"Answer the damn phone, Terrance!" Sasha screamed at her cell phone. Sasha had been trying to get in touch with him all night. First she feared something bad had happened to him, because who tells their new wife that they have to go run and pick up something and then doesn't come back? When her call went to Terrance's voice mail, Sasha hit the end button and slammed the phone down next to her on the bed. At least the logical side of her thought to slam the phone down on the bed instead of throwing it across the room. Hearing the crashing sound and then looking up at the bedroom flat-screen television was a sign that the illogical, out-of-control side of Sasha had won out. Sasha had blacked out and could not account for the past two seconds, which is about how long it would have taken for her to fling that remote toward the television. Sasha had never broken a nail, let alone broken something in her home, on purpose!

Terrance wasn't answering his phone, and that

seemed like the only thing that was going to calm Sasha down right now. She needed to hear his voice, to know that he was okay. Once she learned that he was okay, she needed to know why in the hell he would leave his pregnant wife alone on their wedding night. Taking a deep breath, Sasha decided she'd make sure he wasn't somewhere in the mansion, maybe passed out from all the Champagne he'd drunk to the continuous toasts Eric's drunk ass kept making. There was a slim chance, but it was possible, that Terrance had come home, that he just hadn't made it up to bed and was perhaps in one of the other rooms in the home.

Sasha shot up off the bed and began going from room to room. "Terrance? Terrance?" she called out with each and every door she opened and closed. The more empty rooms Sasha found, the angrier she got. Before she knew it, if that room had a television in it, it now matched the one in their bedroom. It now matched her soul: damaged. But there was still hope as Sasha decided to go to the room she had yet to check, the home theatre.

"Terrance, are you down here?" she asked as she walked down the set of carpeted steps. "Please be down here," she whispered to herself.

When Sasha made it to the bottom landing, there was no Terrance in sight. The room was just as clean and untouched as Miss Hart had left it the day before their wedding. She'd made sure the house was cleaned to perfection from top to bottom since the couple had given her the weekend off.

"Damn you, Terrance!" Sasha screamed. This time there was no blackout. She saw her hand go for the huge pottery bowl they'd sometimes eat popcorn out of while watching a movie. She pulled her hand behind her head then let the bowl rip. The home theatre screen even—trashed!

If Terrance wasn't watching his past games on television, he was watching other teams play. If he wasn't doing that, he was playing a game of Madden. Well, he wouldn't be doing any of the above any time soon. Lucky for Terrance that Sasha was taking out her frustration on the televisions and not on him.

Busting up the television might have given Sasha a second of gratification and revenge, but not for long. A broken Sasha dropped to her knees where she'd stood and cried out in pain. This could not truly be day one of the beginning of her life as one with Terrance. The feeling was so surreal to her. She shook her head as if she could shake the happenings away. This person, this woman full of an emotion she'd never experienced before, as such pain had never been inflicted on her heart before, was a stranger to Sasha. She wanted her out of her house, but the best thing she could do right now was to pick herself up and attempt to leave that broken woman on the floor.

Sasha gathered her composure and stood. She brushed herself off and made her way up the steps with her head held high.

Even though the couple had pulled the wedding together in record time, because of Terrance's games, they hadn't been able to go on their honeymoon. They planned on taking one just as soon as the season was over. Ironically, it looked as though the honeymoon was over before it ever even began.

This wasn't the first time ever in their entire relationship that Terrance had stayed out all night. It had happened twice before. There was the one time when Sasha had fallen asleep on the couch waiting up all night for Terrance. Then there was the time not too shortly after that when he'd sworn he'd told her he had an overnight appearance in a neighboring town. He'd had what seemed like legitimate excuses. But to stay out all night—on their wedding night, no less—felt like an abomination. Sasha didn't know how to act. She wasn't used to this kind of behavior, but she knew someone who was.

She went into the kitchen, picked up the phone, and dialed. "Hey, girl!" Sasha said, trying to sound joyful, like a blushing new bride should sound.

"Hey, what's up?" Casey said, sounding a little confused. "But clearly not too much if you're calling me a day after your wedding. Shouldn't you and your man be having breakfast in bed? Or at least be each other's breakfast?" Casey laughed.

A sound came from Sasha's mouth that at first Casey thought was laughter. But once Casey stopped laughing her own self, she realized that the sound erupting from Sasha's throat was anything but.

"Sash, what's going on?"

"He's gone. He's not here. He didn't come home last night." Sasha hadn't intended on sounding so pitiful. Sasha breathed deep breaths through the phone line and into Casey's ear. It sounded as if Sasha was hyperventilating.

"Calm down. Just calm down, Sasha, please. You're pregnant. This is too much stress on the baby, I'm sure. Do you want me to come over?"

Sasha nodded, tears caught in her throat, preventing her from speaking.

"I'm on my way." Casey didn't even wait for Sasha to reply.

Sasha figured that if anyone knew all too well what she was going through, it was Casey. Even though it felt like a long shot, Sasha hoped that Casey could help her get through this; the same way she had many a time.

In hindsight, Sasha realized that Casey was a living example of what it was like to be the wife of an NBA player. Now Sasha wished that Casey had been less diplomatic. But Sasha had turned a deaf ear, feeling as though she was no Casey and Terrance was no Eric.

Sasha's mother had a saying that sometimes you just have to let a person jump in the water to see how deep it is for themselves. Perhaps this was one of those moments for Sasha. Hopefully she wouldn't drown.

"Okay," Sasha managed to say before hanging up the phone. Knowing Casey was on her way, Sasha went to her bathroom and retrieved the Visine. She didn't want to look as distraught as she felt.

Just as she put the last drop in her eye, she heard something. It sounded like the chiming sound the front door made whenever it opened. Sasha hurried down to the foyer, where she saw a staggering Terrance making his way into the great room.

It was when Terrance flopped down on the couch that he finally noticed Sasha. "Oh, hey," he said.

Even though Sasha could have burst a gasket, she tried to remain as cool, calm, and collected as she possibly could. She'd watched reality shows before. She'd seen how the scorned, pissed-off women had been portrayed. She'd always questioned whether or not that was all for ratings. Well, she had no viewers to appease, so there was no need for her to act out of character and try to go ham.

Sasha took a deep breath and simply looked down at her watch.

Terrance followed suit and looked down at his. "Oh, shit. It's eleven o'clock."

"So you can tell time," Sasha said sarcastically.

"Yes, I can," Terrance confirmed. He let out a hiccup. He then looked over Sasha's shoulder at the daylight peeking through the drapes. "Then, damn, what's for breakfast?"

Sasha had to wait for it . . . wait for Terrance to say that he was just kidding. No way was this man serious.

He doesn't come home or answer his phone all night, and when he does finally return, the next freaking morning, all he can say is, "What's for breakfast?"

"You practically leave me at the altar and that's all you have to say?" Sasha said.

"I didn't leave you at no altar." Terrance stood up. It was a struggle, but he managed to stop wobbling and stand erect. Sure, they'd had several toasts at the wedding reception, but it was clear Terrance had chased the Cristal down with something a little bit stronger. The alcohol emanating from his pores proved such. "I made an honest woman out of you, which is more than I can say I did for the ones before you."

Sasha's heart nearly dropped out of her chest. Terrance had never, ever spoken to her so callously and uncaringly. So this is what Terrance looked like in a drunken state. This is what he sounded like. This is how he acted. Even if this was just the alcohol talking, no way would she have ever agreed to marry a man who she even thought had those tendencies. She wouldn't have cared if she was pregnant or not. Had he come home drunk and out of control that night she'd waited on the couch for him until she'd fallen asleep, she would have moved back into her apartment and lost his number.

It was like Terrance had done this massive 180. He'd spun so quickly that she never even saw him turn in the slightest. Maybe it was because he had been too busy sweeping her off of her feet and spinning her around, purposely getting her too dizzy so that she wouldn't be fully in tune with what was going on around her. She was smarter than that. She was stronger than that. Wasn't she?

Sasha had to stop and think for a minute. Had the signs been there all along? Had this been Terrance's plan the entire time? To woo her, sweep her off of her feet, stake a claim on her, and get her exactly where he wanted her? Maybe she wasn't the beard Norman had spoken of, but was there such thing as a mustache? That woman that just makes a man look like he's a good guy because he's settled down and married? Makes him feel like a good guy because even though he's out being a whore, he's got this beautiful family to come home to and make him feel like a man?

"You know what, coffee is for breakfast," Sasha said, "because we gotta get that alcohol out of you before we end up in divorce court . . . before the ink even dries on the marriage certificate."

Terrance let out a drunken laugh. "Stop playing, you know you ain't going nowhere but in that kitchen to make me some scrambled eggs." Terrance laughed. "And since it is our wedding day—"

"Yesterday was our wedding day," Sasha snapped.

"Yeah, yeah, but anyway,"—Terrance waved her off—"since we just got married and all, why don't you make them eggs butt-naked in some heels?"

If breakfast was what Terrance wanted, then he shouldn't have given Miss Hart and the other staff the weekend off. And he definitely shouldn't have given security off, because if he didn't pull himself together, he was for certain going to need it.

"This isn't funny, Terrance," Sasha said, on the verge of tears. "I don't know what's gotten into you and why you're acting like this, but if you don't stop, I'm going to—"

"Nothing, that's what," Terrance said. "You gon' do the same thing all these other basketball wives out here do, which is nothing. Yeah, you might cuss, fuss, and hold out on giving me some for a minute, but you ain't going nowhere. You gon' keep shopping and keep looking pretty. I've seen it a million times. I know exactly how it goes with you women once you're wifey. Why you think I didn't drag this thing out and waste time with that boyfriend and girlfriend shit? Who needs the drama and headache that comes with that phase of the program? I've learned from the fellas' mistakes to just jump straight to the 'I dos' and get it over with. I've already given you a taste of this lifestyle, baby. You're hooked." He walked over to Sasha and put his hand on her stomach. "Hook, line, and sinker. In other words,"—a big grin was plastered across his face—"got her!" He began laughing such a horrible, wicked laugh that Sasha completely blacked out on him.

"You bastard!" She began flailing her arms at Terrance. While she flung her arms she realized that her being pregnant had been like Terrance hitting the lotto. He hadn't been overjoyed with impeding fatherhood. Oh, no. Sasha realized he'd been celebrating a whole other type of victory.

Terrance, still laughing, was able to grab hold of Sasha's wrists. "What, you mad you wasn't the only person with a plan?"

Sasha stood there staring at Terrance with her bottom lip trembling.

"I knew from the moment I saw you that you were the one," Terrance said. "You were the woman who was going to have my baby. I planned to sweep you off your feet so fast you'd forget about everything: your apartment, your job. I ain't know you was gon' forget about taking the pill." Terrance chuckled. "But it's all good. We gon' make pretty babies."

Sasha was sick to her stomach. She was better than this. She was smarter than this. None of this was happening. It wasn't real. "You're drunk, Terrance," Sasha said. "You're talking crazy." She refused to believe the words that were coming out of her husband's mouth.

"I may be drunk, but I ain't crazy," Terrance said.

"Ughhh!" Sasha yelled out like a madwoman as she broke loose from Terrance's grip. This time Sasha didn't swing on Terrance. She knew that big man was no match for her, so she began to destroy everything in sight that she could get her hands on.

It angered Sasha even more that Terrance stood there laughing as he watched her go on her rampage while cussing him out, calling him every name in the book. Even though Sasha had never acted like this, he didn't appear surprised or shocked. This was probably nothing new to him, Sasha surmised. He'd probably witnessed many of his team players' wives resort to the same antics . . . in public, and therefore had imagined what could go down in private. Well, he no longer had to imagine it.

Once Sasha finally took a breather she was huffing and puffing like she'd just run around a football field twice.

Terrance stood there looking around at all the damage that had been done. The only things left untouched were his trophy cabinet and a couple vases. "Guess this means you won't be making me breakfast butt-ass naked, huh?"

Terrance's reaction to Sasha's pain knocked the wind out of her as she clutched her stomach. She hunched over in pain.

Terrance, unmoved and battling a hangover, shook his head and headed for the door. Maybe once he was in his right mind he'd be somewhat sympathetic to his wife, but for now, his groaning stomach and throbbing headache only had him thinking about himself. "You want me to bring you anything back?" He grabbed the doorknob and turned around to face Sasha. When she just stood there saying nothing, he said, "I take that as a no." Before walking out of the door, he looked over his shoulder and said to Sasha, "You're a basketball wife, so you're gonna have to learn to play the game." He then closed the door behind him.

Sasha, for the second time, fell to her knees and cried out. The tears were nonstop, as was the pain. In the midst of her crying, still on her knees, Sasha reached up and grabbed the glass vase from the end table and threw it at the door. Even though Terrance had walked out of the front door a whole five minutes ago, she could only hope he'd left remnants of his soul at the doorway that the glass could cut into a million little pieces.

Sasha put her head down and began crying again. When she felt arms comfort her, her instincts went back into fight mode.

"Sasha, it's me."

She hadn't even heard Casey enter. Sasha's crying had been louder than the door chime. Hearing Casey's voice brought Sasha back to reality. But her reality wasn't anyplace she wanted to be right now. Sasha was in a place of darkness she'd never been before. So much so that even though she'd called Casey over to comfort her, she and Casey ended up getting into it. They each exchanged hurtful words that could damage their friendship forever. But right now, Sasha had to shift her focus back to her and Terrance's relationship. Sasha's reality was that she'd married a man who was turning out not to be the man she thought he was. Yeah, she could blame his actions on liquor all she wanted if that was going to make her feel better; if that was going to justify her staying with him. But she'd leave that dumb and naïve role for Casey.

Casey, Sasha said to herself. All of a sudden she remembered something Terrance had said about Casey. It was something about him wanting someone just like Casey by his side. And then there was the fact that he'd even asked Casey to hook him up with one of her friends, who he probably thought would be someone just like Casey. *How could I have been so stupid?* Sasha asked herself. Terrance had dropped breadcrumbs along the trail of his deceit after all.

Sasha stood by the cologne- and oil-covered couch she'd destroyed earlier before sliding down to the floor. As the morning turned to afternoon, the afternoon to evening, and the evening to night, Sasha sat in complete darkness. She struggled with Terrance's actions. She struggled with some of the things Casey had said to her during their argument.

"Not every woman is cut out to be a baller's wife," Casey had said. *"Did you really think your man would be any different than all the others? Especially since you decided to bring a poor, innocent baby into this. Even I had more sense than to make that mistake."*

Tears flowed down Sasha's face. As painful as the bottle of jagged pills Casey had fed her were to swallow, Sasha needed to just woman up, find a tall glass of water, and swallow them down without choking.

But there was also something that both Casey and Terrance had said that stuck out in Sasha's mind.

"You're a basketball wife now, so you better learn to play the game."

Once upon a time Sasha had questioned why people seemed to get angry at the truth. Well, truth be told, both Casey and Terrance had told their truths. A lie could be manipulated, but the truth was untouchable. So now Sasha needed to decide if she was willing to live a lie or someone else's truth.

Deep inside Sasha definitely still felt hurt, confused, sad, and betrayed, but the emotion that was now dominating them all was anger. She was scarred emotionally, but above all, she was scorned, which now made her the most dangerous bitch Terrance had ever invited into his life.

In that moment of feeling such outrage, Sasha decided that she would not let Terrance take her for some young, dumb chick. But if playing dumb made Terrance think he'd outsmarted her, then perhaps that's something she actually would consider doing.

"He's not going to break me," Sasha said with authority. "I won't let a man, any man, break me!" Her declaration gave her a newfound strength. Terrance may have lied to her, but what she was no longer going to do was lie to herself.

Sasha got up off the couch and began cleaning up the mess she'd made. After about an hour or so she'd managed to clean up the living room. She then headed upstairs to her room to begin cleaning up the shattered television. Just as she made it to her bedroom, her cell phone began to ring.

Well at least that didn't break, she thought to herself as she walked over and answered it. "Hello."

"Hey, I'm on my way home. You want something to eat?"

Sasha stood there for a moment, taking in Terrance's words before she replied. She swallowed. She swallowed the lump in her throat. She swallowed her tears. She swallowed what felt like her pride. "No, that won't be necessary. I was about to cook dinner for you," Sasha said through the phone receiver.

Terrance paused, more than likely stunned by Sasha's hospitality. "Uh, well, okay. I'll be there shortly."

"Okay, see you when you get here," Sasha said just as nonchalantly while sweeping her hurt and pain under the rug.

Once again, Terrance paused. "Babe, I just want you to know that I'm sorry about—"

"No need to apologize," Sasha said, cutting him off. "It was your wedding night. Now that I've had time to think about it, I figured that while out on your errand you got caught up in a celebration of your own. You know, you and your boys. I'm sure you didn't mean for the night to end that way. Let's just move forward because I don't want to stay in the past." This was the beginning of Sasha making excuses for her husband so he wouldn't have to find one on his own; save them both the time. It could be worse; like Casey, she could have to find women for him. So she was okay with just excuses.

"Uh, yeah. Me either."

"Cool, then hurry home because you might just catch me making dinner in the kitchen . . . butt-naked."

Terrance chuckled. "All right then. See you soon."

Sasha ended the call with a huge smile on her face. She then exhaled. "You wanna play, Terrance? You want me to start learning to play the game?" Sasha said. "Then let the games begin."

This time it was Sasha who let out a mischievous grin as she got herself together to prepare a meal for her new husband. Whether or not it was to be the last supper would remain to be seen. All Sasha knew for sure was that she'd just swallowed a hard pill, her tears, and her pride, but she would never swallow her dreams. She would never allow him to

break her. She would get back on the road to her
dreams, even if it meant breaking Terrance in the
process. And by breaking him that meant one of
two things: he was either going to end up being a
good husband or a man that nobody wanted.
Hopefully, for the sake of their marriage and the
sake of their child, it wouldn't be the latter.

DON'T MISS

Collusion

by De'nesha Diamond

Framed for a high-profile murder, Abrianna
Parker finds herself hurtling down a conspiracy
rabbit hole in a desperate attempt to clear her
name. Her only way out is to go after the most
powerful man in the country. But the powers
that be play dirty. . . .

Enjoy the following excerpt from *Collusion*. . . .

Prologue

Hay-Adams Hotel, Washington D.C.
Eight days ago

In the posh presidential suite of the five–star hotel, min-utes from the White House, the new House speaker spent his celebration night in a luxurious den of debauchery. High off a potent designer street drug, Cotton Candy, he fulfilled a lifelong ménage à trois fantasy with an ex-lover and one of Madam Nevaeh's sexy escort girls.

When he woke, he was surprised to see his ex-mistress preparing to leave.

"Where are you going?"

"Home."

"What?" He struggled to detangle himself from the bed's soft linen. "No. Wait. Don't go."

"Why not? You still got company." Kitty referred to the gorgeous cocoa-brown woman lying in a cocaine high among a cloud of white sheets. "By the way, where did you find her? She's stunning."

"Yeah. What can I say?" Kenneth Reynolds boasted,

his eyes glassy and his nose swollen with pink dust under it. "I'm Mr. Lucky tonight. I'm going to talk to Madam Nevaeh about keeping Miss Abrianna here on an exclusive arrangement." *He brushed strands of hair from the despondent girl's face.*

"Madam?" *Kitty arched one brow while she tightened the belt on her trench coat.* "You're paying for pussy now? Hell. I thought she was some chick that you picked up from one of those sleazy clubs you like so much."

He laughed. "I don't mind paying for the best." *He met Kitty's gaze.* "Not that you're not."

"Fuck you, Kenny."

"Where are you going?"

"Home."

Reynolds stood from the bed and reached for her, but she dodged his touch. "Aw, now. Don't be like that. I thought we were putting our little spat behind us?"

"Behind us? How? Are you pretending not to know what happens to my nomination to the Supreme Court if you impeach the president?"

He groaned. "Politics, politics, politics. Can't we have one night that doesn't involve politics?"

Kitty stood still while Reynolds slithered his arms around her waist. "Tonight is supposed to be a celebration. You're looking at the third most powerful man in the country . . . and I'm gunning for the man at the top."

"And fuck me, right?" *she clarified, brows arched.*

"C'mon, Kitty. Why are you killing the mood? Hmm?" *Reynolds snuggled his head in the crook of her neck.* "Don't you feel how much I've missed you? What we had together?" *Kenny's dick hardened against her.* "Why don't you take off that coat and come back to bed? Hmm?" *He nibbled on her earlobe.*

"So you get what you want and fuck me. Is that it?"

Reynolds groaned. "Look. You're a good judge. You'll eventually get your seat on the court."

Kitty laughed. "Are you fucking kidding me? These are once-in-a-lifetime appointments. Lightning doesn't strike twice. If you remove the president, then it's bye-bye to my nomination."

"That's not true," Reynolds whined, backpedaling to the bed. "As soon as we remove that asshole from the Oval Office, the vice president will uphold your nomination. We can impeach him and then confirm you with no problem."

"Right." Kitty slid her hand into her coat pocket and wrapped it around a gun.

"Contrary to popular opinion, Congress can walk and chew gum at the same time."

"Bullshit—or it would have been done before."

Reynolds exhaled and leaned against the headboard. "I don't know what you want. The House doesn't confirm judges. That's the Senate's job."

"Majority Leader McCullough is following your lead on this."

Reynolds chuckled. "You're giving me way too much credit." He reached over and groped the unconscious woman lying beside him. "I'm still horny." He cast his gaze back toward Kitty, surprised to see a gun leveled at him. After a few seconds, laughter rumbled low in his chest. "Now what are you going to do with that?"

"I'm about to make sure that I end up on that court . . . by getting you out of the way." Kitty clicked off the safety.

Too high to realize how much danger he was in, Reynolds laughed more deeply. "C'mon, Kitty. It's only politics. It's not personal."

"Politics is always personal," she said and pulled the trigger.

PART TWO

Chaos and Disorder

1

In the rich suburbs of Alexandria, Virginia, drug lord and political insider Zeke "Teflon Don" Jeffreys had gathered his friends and valuable political D.C. clients at his lavish home to celebrate his thirtieth birthday.

While he mixed and mingled, a motley crew of party-crashers was kidnapping his business partner-slash-lover, Madam Nevaeh, right from under his nose.

"Hurry! Load her up." Draya, dressed as a server for La Plume's catering service, opened the back doors of the van.

"We are going as fast as we can." Abrianna Parker, disguised as a male server, complete with a mustache and padded chest, banged the madam's head on one of the doors.

"Easy," Kadir Kahlifa, in disguise as a man twice his age, whispered back.

Annoyed, Abrianna banged the madam's head again.

He frowned.

Abrianna shrugged. "I'm petty."

"Are you two for real?" Draya hissed.

Abrianna climbed up, still holding the front of Madam's body.

"Hey!"

Everyone froze.

"What are you guys doing over there?"

Abrianna, out of view, mouthed to Kadir, "Who is it?"

"Hey, I asked you guys a question!"

"Security," Kadir mouthed back.

Horrified, Abrianna glanced around for a weapon.

Draya spun. "Nothing. We're . . . grabbing supplies for the kitchen."

A large, lineman-shaped security guy waddled closer to the open van door.

Draya attempted to close one of the back doors to block his line of vision.

"But what the hell is that?" He gestured to the bag and leaned forward.

Panicked, Draya rammed the door into the nosy security guard's face, shocking him. However, she hadn't seen the drawn gun until it went off.

BANG!

Abrianna dropped Madam Nevaeh and screamed, "No!"

Instantly, the four-hundred-plus-pound man flew backward and slammed against the back of the house and then dropped like a stone.

Abrianna raced forward. "Draya, are you all right?" She gathered her friend into her arms. "Speak to me. Say something."

Draya lifted her shocked gaze. "How the fuck did you do that?"

Julian croaked, "Somebody tell me that I didn't see that."

Everyone stared at Abrianna, especially Kadir. "I, uh, uh—"

"It came from over there," a man shouted from the distance.

"Fuck. We gotta go," Kadir said, picking up Draya. "Get in the van," he ordered.

Everyone hauled ass.

Julian climbed behind Kadir and placed Draya in the back of the van along with Abrianna and Madam Nevaeh.

For a brief moment, Kadir's questioning gaze met Abrianna's, but then he slammed the doors shut—and raced to climb into the passenger seat. "Let's go!"

Julian jumped behind the wheel.

The van peeled off as an army of security goons rushed around the corner and found their unconscious colleague.

Rat-at-tat-tat-tat.

Bullets punctured the back of the van; a few ricocheted, forcing them to duck or dive for cover.

"What the hell?" Julian shouted, bringing everyone's attention to the police cars streaming onto the estate.

"Holy shit," Kadir said, incredulous.

Julian's foot lifted off the accelerator.

"Don't stop," Kadir shouted.

Julian hesitated on seeing the swarm of blue lights, but then slammed his foot back down on the gas.

The last two patrol cars swerved and blocked the van's exit.

"Don't you fucking stop," Kadir threatened again.

Julian tightened his grip on the steering wheel. When they blazed closer and made it clear that the van wasn't stopping, the cops scrambled to get out of the way.

It was too late.

"Hold on!" Julian cried, closing his eyes.

BAM!

Everyone and everything slammed forward.

The two police cars spun like pinwheels in the van's wake.

Draya groaned.

"You guys okay back there?" Kadir asked.

Abrianna, sprawled beneath pans and supplies, pushed herself up and crawled to Draya.

Draya rolled onto her back. "What the hell, Jules? Are you trying to kill me?"

"She's fine," Julian said. "If Draya is bitching, then she's okay."

"Are they following us?" Abrianna asked.

The guys checked their mirrors. "Not that I can tell," Julian said, relieved.

"Yeah. Well. We better get off this road just in case."

"How is our other passenger?" Kadir asked.

Abrianna turned and moved over to the insulated nylon bag and stopped short. "Uh, guys . . ."

"What?" everyone asked.

"There's blood," Abrianna announced.

"She was hit?" Kadir asked, coming out of his seat to climb into the back.

Abrianna pulled down the zipper down and opened the bag. "Damn."

Blood bloomed across the center of Madam's white dress, but Abrianna was certain that it was

the bullet lodged in the center of Madam's forehead that had killed her.

Draya shook her head. "Well, I guess she won't
be telling us shit."

Zeke Jeffreys hid his humiliation behind a stony
mask while former police lieutenant Gizella
Castillo gloated as they shoved his large frame into
the back of a squad car. Once he was tucked inside
and the door slammed shut, his black gaze zoomed
to hers and transmitted the message that this game
wasn't over by a long shot.

She knew that he was probably right.

His guests were equally humiliated but more
outraged at having to be loaded up in the back of
police vans. Many of them had no idea of Jeffreys's
double life. They had no idea that while they were
mixing and mingling, he was trafficking the designer street drug Cotton Candy. However, this
time he had done so with undercover cop Steven
O'Day.

Castillo had wanted to bring the drug lord
down for years but had never been able to scratch
the surface. Police Captain Dennis Holder, an ex-
lover and colleague, had clued her in about the
planned raid and permitted her to be here to
watch the whole thing go down. Other than a
strange shoot-out involving someone jacking a
caterer's van, the raid had gone down smoothly.

Now she wanted to see about putting the screws
to Madam Nevaeh, Zeke's business partner and ru-
mored lover, about Abrianna Parker. Castillo had

learned from Abrianna's best friend, Shawn White, that Parker had been working for the infamous madam the night of Speaker Reynolds's death. The first time Castillo confronted Nevaeh about this, she stonewalled her.

But Castillo had a bad habit of never giving up. Holder had often joked that she was like a bloodhound. She never deviated from a trail. Never. Plus, Castillo had a history with Abrianna Parker. Six years ago she'd led a team that had rescued Abrianna Parker, Tomi Lehane, and Shalisa Young from the basement of madman and serial killer Craig Avery. Back then, Parker was a tough but scarred teenage runaway, who didn't stick around long enough to answer questions about her abduction.

It surprised Castillo when Parker blipped on her radar while investigating the new House speaker for Tomi Lehane, who was now a *Washington Post* reporter. It *shocked* Castillo when she realized that Parker was actually running from a murder scene.

After a near forty minutes of threading through the handcuffed crowd, she couldn't find any trace of the madam when she was certain that she had been in attendance earlier. For a fleeting moment, Castillo wondered whether the madam had been the one who'd hijacked La Plume's catering van, but then dismissed it when she overheard someone say they saw that it was group of servers.

Suddenly a group of officers scrambled to their cars.

"What's going on?" she asked, rushing alongside Officer Donovan.

"They found the van," she told her.

"From the shoot-out?"

"Yeah. Apparently it crashed down an embankment. The driver is deceased."

"What about the others?"

Donovan frowned. "Others?"

"Wasn't it a group of servers?"

She shook her head. "Dispatch only mentioned the driver."

Castillo's hackles rose. "Male or female?"

"Female."

Connect with Us

Visit us online at
KensingtonBooks.com
to read more from your favorite authors, see books
by series, view reading group guides, and more.

Join us on social media

for sneak peeks, chances to win books and prize packs,
and to share your thoughts with other readers.

facebook.com/kensingtonpublishing
twitter.com/kensingtonbooks

Tell us what you think!

To share your thoughts, submit a review,
or sign up for our eNewsletters, please visit:
KensingtonBooks.com/TellUs.

JUL - - 2018